Death of a Political Plant

Other Gardening Mysteries
by Ann Ripley

MULCH

DEATH OF A GARDEN PEST

Death of a Political Plant

Ann Ripley

BANTAM BOOKS

New York Toronto London Sydney Auckland

DEATH OF A POLITICAL PLANT

A Bantam Book

Book design by Dana Leigh Treglia
Border design and illustrations by Joanna Roy

For information address: Bantam Books.

ISBN 0-553-10778-X

Bantam Books are published by Bantam Books, a division of Bantam Doubleday Dell Publishing Group, Inc. Its trademark, consisting of the words "Bantam Books" and the portrayal of a rooster, is Registered in U.S. Patent and Trademark Office and in other countries. Marca Registrada. Bantam Books, 1540 Broadway, New York, New York 10036.

PRINTED IN THE UNITED STATES OF AMERICA

TO VIRGINIA

Acknowledgments

Thanks to the many people who encouraged me and helped me in the writing of this book, notably, Kate Miciak, my editor, for her spirited ideas; and Jane Jordan Browne, my agent, for her counsel. Special expertise came from koi experts Jim Brunk, Joyce Conrad, and Bob Kennedy; Steve Still of the Perennial Plant Association; the National Gallery of Art; The Denver Botanic Gardens; the Fairfax County, Virginia, Medical Examiner; and Emeritus Professor Roger Knutson, who writes about roadkill, skunk cabbage, and other flora and fauna. My gratitude goes to those who patiently read, listened, and offered advice: Margaret Coel, Sybil Downing, Karen Gilleland, Connie and Tom Lynch, Beverly Carrigan, Ken and Phyllis Baker, Jim Mahoney, Bill Barnds, Keith Jackson, Irene Sinclair, Jessie Lew Mahoney, James K. Anderson, Mary Lou Butcher, and my husband, Tony. I also am indebted to the houseguests over the years who provided me with so much useful material.

Gardening Essays

by Ann Ripley

Chapter One

THE BRAT WAS HEADED straight for her prize stand of toad lilies.

Only a little surprised at her hostility toward her innocent cousin's child, Louise knew her irritation lay with the child's parents. Their lax supervision during a five-day visit with the Eldridges had resulted in golden-haired three-year-old Sally ravaging her gardens, one by one. Toddler feet stomping on plants that were babies themselves. Pudgy hands snapping off precious flowers like a plant ogre and stuffing them in her mouth. And the crowning blow: the pulling to bits of the five precious blooms of Louise's French tree peony—that otherwise would have bestowed its effulgent beauty upon the world for a week or more.

Now, she wasn't about to sacrifice her purple-spotted toad lilies to this toddler tornado, certainly not seconds before these houseguests went back to where they came from!

"Sally," cried Louise, "*not* in there." She paused for a half second to allow her cousin to control her own child. The mother wasn't paying attention. The child veered away from the toad lilies and took rapid baby steps across prostrate campanula and epimedium and hurled her little body toward a thicket of wickedly thorned mahonia—taller than she was, likely to tear skin or eyes.

Louise lunged forward, reached her in three steps, and scooped her up in her arms. Her cousin had finally noticed and yelped, "Oh, thank God you saw her!" Louise looked down at the blond, doll-like cherub in her arms. Happy to be saved? No way. Tears were forming in the combative blue eyes: Sally was building up for a good howl.

She stepped carefully out of her garden and handed the child over to the mother, just as the explosion of tears and rage gushed forth.

Having done his part packing the bags, the husband stood casually by with hands in the pockets of his chinos. He nodded toward the mahonia. "I can see why Sally wanted to touch them, Louise—those plants are beautiful, with those glossy leaves and bunches of big blue berries."

"Yes, but notice the vicious thorns," she said through tight lips. "It pays to train children to stay out of gardens. They can be deadly." The parents seemed to think that because Louise had gardens in a woods, they were fair game for stepping on and tasting. Besides, weren't they all *relatives* here?

Her cousin deposited the girl in the car without mussing her bandbox-fresh traveling outfit, then turned and smiled as she looked at a perspiring Louise in her many-pocketed shorts, boots, and grimy T-shirt. She elaborately embraced her, and for some reason Louise was reminded of *The Godfather*. "Louise, I love your house, and its little addition, and all the beautiful flowers. Especially now that you have become a TV garden lady, I know gardening comes first with you and always will."

Louise wiped sweat from her brow with the back of a hand. "Actually, my family comes first." Why would she argue with this least-favorite cousin? But why not? "My family definitely comes first, then gardens."

The two of them kissed insincerely, and her guests climbed into their car. Louise peeked into the backseat, where the strapped-in three-year-old was still whimpering from not getting her way. Seeing Louise, she turned her face away, scorning Louise's good-bye wave. Her cousin powered her car window down at the last moment and said, mysteriously, "And sorry about the mattress."

With a little pang of worry for Sally's future, Louise returned up the mossy flagstone path to her modern one-story house in the woods, the gray timbers of the pergola above the path and the glint of sun on the floor-to-ceiling glass windows giving her a sense she was entering a very special house.

Alone, and blissfully without company for the first time in eight weeks.

Inside and outside, it was time for damage control. It would take a while to erase signs of this particular visit.

With big plastic bag in hand, she swept up left-behind toys, toilet articles, and a couple of paperbacks. She put the bag on the shelf of a tiny hall closet that her husband Bill facetiously nicknamed "the morgue," because it had smelled so rotten from the stale air from under their slab house when they moved in. She'd blocked the smell out by covering cracks with duct tape; later, he plastered it up for her. She would send on her cousin's possessions when she had a spare moment.

Armed with her special carpet spotter and a spray bottle of vinegar solution, she scrubbed away spots and stains left in the wake of the three visitors. Next came stripping the beds and taking down the crib. Standing over the baby bed, she realized with distaste what her cousin meant: Sally's parents, optimists, apparently, hadn't bothered with night diapering on that last night. Giving a good sniff, she decided to pitch the crib mattress and get a new one. She heaved it out of the bed and carried it out to the garbage area, which was tucked discreetly behind a row of hollies. Then, she administered the coup de grâce, a squirting of air freshener through the entire house.

Her mouth set in a grim line as she next attacked the patio garden. Plants near the edge, delicate corydalis, lamium, miniature mat daisies, and a maidenhair fern, had taken a bad beating from little footsteps. Some were kaput for the season, while others looked as if they would recover.

Except for the tree peony. The loss of those translucent, six-inch-wide yellow repeat blossoms nearly made her cry. It was the second day of the visit, after Louise had made repeated discreet entreaties about keeping Sally out of the gardens. Her guard was down, as she prepared a special company lunch in the kitchen. When she came outside with laden tray, the child had picked the golden petals off, one by one. "Oh, so sorry," said the inattentive parents.

Not quite so destructive was the child's desperate leap into her neighbor Mary Mougey's fishpond, where Louise had taken the restless child as a late afternoon diversion. Sally had jumped instantly in with the prize Kohako koi, throwing the fish into a frenzy, and destroying a couple of water lily blossoms in the process. The child had surfaced like a little Venus out of the sea, spluttering but happy at wringing a little more excitement out of the boring world.

Louise went in the house, for she had more important things to do than sorrow over a picked bush, or destroyed water lilies. Slumping onto the couch, she tried to relax and clear her mind. She and Bill had been flooded with company all summer, including visits from both sets of parents. With her full-time job, the pressure was beginning to tell. It wasn't like the old days of just a year or so ago, when one of her main purposes in life as a foreign-service wife was to play the part of the gracious hostess. Now, she was wife, mom, *and* TV host. Where was she supposed to find time to nurture houseguests and handle toddler versions of Dennis the Menace?

Trying to find a cheery side, she realized she and Bill had a window of opportunity. For the next week, they would be alone. Then came the next onslaught of company. She frowned. *That* company was an unknown: they had invited themselves, and as usual, she had been too polite to say no. "Damn it, Louise," she reproached herself, "you could have wiggled out of that one."

And yet they might prove interesting: three vigorous women from the National Perennial Plant Society, whom she had met just once. They were coming to the Washington

Hilton for their yearly convention and were valuable contacts; while in town, they would be part of a gardening show for WTBA-TV, Louise's public broadcasting station sponsor.

Touchingly enough, the P.P.S. was adding to the luster of Louise's new career, which was very young and needed as much luster as it could gather. The Perennial Plant Society was making her its "Plant Person of the Year" for her series of environmentally sound garden shows.

But at least she could look forward to privacy during the coming week. She had a slow work schedule at Channel Five, and that meant time for her and Bill to be alone together, and to wallow in the news, specifically, national presidential election coverage.

She leaned back in the cushions and lifted up a long, bare leg: It had several dirt swipes, for she had worked in her sloppy bog garden while her company packed. She raised an arm and smelled her armpit. The "Plant Person of the Year" sorely needed a bath, for normal life, such as it was, resumed tonight. She and Bill were going to dress up for a fund-raiser in the East Building of the National Gallery. It was organized by Mary Mougey, her neighbor. At five hundred dollars a head, they would feast on shrimp and oysters, pâtés and roast beef, raising funds for starving, fly-ridden people in African countries torn by civil war.

She went into the master bathroom, flipping on the radio as she assembled shampoo, conditioner, glycerin soap, facial cleanser, and a fluffy ball of apricot-colored nylon netting—her "exfoliating sponge." She noted ruefully it was made out of the same material that household expert Heloise recommended for scrubbing pans clean.

She was just in time for some breaking news. The newscaster was about as excited as National Public Radio newscasters ever got. He reported that a spokesman for

President Fairchild's opponent, Congressman Lloyd Goodrich, had leveled still another charge at the sitting President: that not only had Fairchild participated in the assassination of President Ngo Dinh Diem of South Vietnam back in 1963, but that he was involved in the murder of an army clerk handling records in Saigon, this in an effort to keep Fairchild's complicity out of his army file.

Louise uttered an audible groan. The President, as checkered a person as he might be, was her supporter. After the murder at Louise's TV station and her subsequent exposure of the murderer, Fairchild had appointed her to the National Environmental Commission.

She flipped the bathwater on and the radio off. Fairchild was honest, while Goodrich's campaign was so far below the belt it made her sick. And yet it was working: Fairchild, who had been twenty points ahead, was now almost even in the polls. This latest disclosure had to be the most harmful. What could be worse than an accusation of murder? As she peeled off her sweaty clothes, she reflected that Goodrich's people had better have proof this time. That was the worry: The newscaster said the Goodrich campaign had the goods in "black and white," whatever that meant.

She stepped in and slid herself down into the relaxing hot water that slapped gently against her body. What was black and white anymore in this world? Except that gardens were wonderful, and she loved Bill and the girls? But in reverse order, of course.

Chapter Two

THE RED-AND-BLUE paddles on Calder's giant mobile swung slowly over the crowd. Louise, standing with her husband on the mezzanine of the East Building, felt as if she could reach over and almost touch one as it passed. The movement overhead gave her a mild sense of vertigo that substituted just fine for the fact that she declined to drink the champagne being served rapid-fire to glittering guests by tuxedoed waiters and waitresses.

They had just arrived, and immediately

took in the scene: upper-crust Washingtonians clustered around the hors d'oeuvres table, like vultures before roadkill, as fresh batches of lobster and shrimp were brought out. Once fortified with goodies on small plates, people hovered around in constellation groups, of which the "suns" were celebrities: congressmen, movers and shakers and, she noticed, the President's chief of staff, Tom Paschen. Not a big man, but handsome in a way, with a thin, brooding face. Paschen was a man whom she barely knew, but with whom Bill had once worked.

The vivacious hostess was in full swing. Blond and petite, Mary Mougey was elegant in a scarlet gown, and encircled by her own constellation of what Louise supposed were the biggest donors. The champagne and predinner snacks, which would precede a silent art auction of donated art items, would loosen purse strings and result in more big checks being pressed into Mary's hand. Big donors and small donors alike would be co-opted by her intrepid friend before the party was over.

Before Louise knew it, Mary had spotted her and broken away from her group and hurried over. "Bill. Louise. Hello," she said breathlessly; her eyes sparkled with party excitement. She put a hand on Louise's arm and in a low voice said, "My dear, you look absolutely ravishing," and gave her a broad wink. "I just have a moment: I *so* appreciate you babysitting our fish while we're gone to the Caribbean. Remember, they like carbohydrates *and* protein, so I'll bring you over a container of earthworms to feed them each afternoon." Her pretty blue eyes looked concerned, as if talking about children who would be in Louise's care: "Please don't forget to chop them up a little; our babies aren't big enough to eat them whole."

Louise's empty stomach gripped up in a knot.

"We leave first thing in the morning," Mary blithely continued, "and if you need more room for that constant stream of houseguests of yours, please do send someone over to our house—*mi casa es* su *casa!*" Then she dashed back to her donors.

While Louise was talking to Mary, their other neighbors, Roger and Laurie Kendricks, had joined Bill. They stood on the edge of the crowd and exchanged a little comfortable, down-home conversation before they parted to work the room.

"Long time no see," cracked Roger. He was tall, balding, slightly potbellied, and wearing thick glasses: not what Louise would call good-looking. Formal attire had transformed him: He could be anything from the night manager of a fine hotel to a foreign diplomat. In contrast, her own blond-haired husband, already handsome, in tux and cummerbund looked like a model from the pages of *Gentlemen's Quarterly.* Certainly not like a State Department employee who was in reality an undercover CIA agent.

"How debonair you look tonight, Roger," she replied, and then turned to Laurie, in a silky white gown that set off her upswept red hair, "and you, Laurie, so pretty."

"Sure did clean up good, didn't we?" drawled Roger. Apparently weary of being treated with deference by people because of his status at the *Washington Post,* he liked to toss in a country bumpkin phrase once in a while.

Both Roger and Laurie were giving Louise a discreet once-over, but she had realized the impact of her outfit from the moment she entered the museum: As she trod up the pink Tennessee marble stairs, she saw the raised eyebrows and delighted expressions on the faces of the men standing at the top. She had blushed redly and clutched Bill's arm tighter. Was the outfit a mistake? It was a Donna Karan pantsuit that she had found, like a hidden treasure from Egypt, in a Fairfax resale shop. Black, silk, and cut so low she could feel the pressure of the satin lapels on her half-naked breasts.

"Very nice suit *you're* wearing, Louise," said Roger.

Bill linked his arm in Louise's. "Wasn't sure I'd let her out in public like this, but decided since she's a gardening personality now, people expect her to look ravishing."

"How are the girls doing, Louise?" asked Laurie.

"Great. Both are out there helping to save the world."

Laurie raised an eyebrow. "Sounds like they've been talking to Mary Mougey."

"Mary's very persuasive. And your boys—is Michael breaking records at tennis camp?" Even though Louise was a strong player, Roger and Laurie's bright-eyed teenager could wipe her off the court in one set.

"A real champ," said Roger. "And our younger guy is showin' em how at computer camp."

"Meanwhile, we're alone at home," added Laurie, with a smile and sideways look at Roger. She leaned toward him provocatively. "I hate to admit it, but it's very nice to have the summer to ourselves. You seem to have company running in and out continually, while we have just been . . ."

"À deux?" said Louise, smiling. "I hear what you're saying, Laurie. We'll be alone for exactly one week, and then more company is coming and the girls return home."

Bill smiled sagely. "Ah, I think you ladies do protest too much. Look how our children progress, ever upward, ever away from us. Pretty soon they'll all be gone, and we'll be old folks whining for them to visit."

During this banter, they had paid little attention to the ebb and flow of the party, so they were surprised when Tom Paschen, entourage respectfully hanging behind, came up and joined them. The President's chief of staff was barely as tall as Louise in her spike-heeled Manolo mules, though he looked elegant in evening clothes that reeked of Savile Row. Unfortunately, it was spoiled by his expression of the harried rabbit out of *Alice in Wonderland.* Louise thought he would buttonhole Roger Kendricks. Roger had stepped down from his executive editor position to join other *Post* staffers in covering the presidential election. So she was surprised when Paschen came straight to her side.

Casting a quick look that took in her face, semirevealed bosom, and slim hips in black pants complete with satin stripe down the side, he extended a hand to the foursome and breezily summarized his mission: "Hi, Roger, and, Laurie Kendricks—isn't it? Bill, I've come over here to hit on your wife."

They laughed. Even then, Paschen didn't break a grin, and looked thoroughly distracted, all business. "Just for a minute." He put a firm hand under her elbow and steered her to the stone railing, beyond which Calder's artwork sailed soundlessly in the chatter-filled building, like a silent chaperon.

"Louise," he said in a confidential tone, "I've only got five minutes."

That was not surprising; the man probably had the busiest job in the country.

"Something about my program."

Paschen looked surprised. "Yes. Smart girl. You knew. You're aware of the scoundrels Congressman Goodrich has taken on board to try to damage the President: Rawlings and Upchurch, the terrible twosome, and Upchurch's reprehensible staff. They're spewing out the damndest lies." Still looking beyond her, casing the room as he spoke, he said, "Look at Franklin Rawlings. He's keeping his head above the cesspool: He just shoves Upchurch out front to be the impetuous bad boy, the new guy in the political game who may reach too far, but whom we're supposed to forgive because of his youth and zeal.''

She thought Tom sounded a little sour grapes. Rawlings was a tall, thin man in his fifties who did his magicianlike campaign strategizing for whoever would pay him his exorbitant fees, smiling all the way. And Goodrich had reached him first, or she was sure that the President would have been happy to hire him on.

''Yeah, I think Rawlings has put himself in a bind: His young compatriots have spun out of control, and in the end he's responsible.'' The chief of staff gave a curt nod at a man bunched over the nearby refreshments table. ''And you must recognize their campaign's *enfant terrible,* Willie Upchurch. There he is, with his fat little hands in the shrimp. That's his gang of three: the worst pissant lowlifes I've ever seen.'' His patrician nose elevated a bit. ''They're no better than thugs.'' Louise knew Paschen himself was renowned as a vicious political infighter, so why was he complaining about how the game was played? Then, as if reading her mind, he said, with asperity, ''There's politics and politics, and dirty politics has reached a new low in this election.''

Upchurch, a rosy-cheeked, baby-faced man, was shoveling in food as if he were one of the clients of the fundraiser rather than a benefactor. ''So that's the infamous Willie,'' she said, ''and he's only in his twenties: I guess that makes him a political prodigy.''

''Depends on how you define prodigy. That California senatorial campaign he ran for Rawlings wasn't genius—it was pure sleaze. But of course their guy won.'' He nodded his head at the group clustered near Upchurch. ''And you can easily pick out Ted French, Willie's number one man;

he's the tall muscular guy over there with the crewcut who looks like a leftover from the Hitler Youth. Only thing missing with him is an armband with a swastika, and a Sam Browne belt and shorts. And of course he's taken lessons from Miss Manners on smiling. I tell you, Louise, they are vipers, and the babies of the family are the worst. French can't be more than in his late twenties, and he's vicious—doesn't know the definition of 'going too far.' Collectively, they have become known as the most cutthroat political players Washington has ever seen: That, as you realize, takes one hell of a lot of doing. Of course, it wouldn't matter so much if we weren't in an era of yellow journalism: Not one damned paper, including the *Times,* the *Post,* the *L.A. Times,* is above printing their garbage. Up and down the media food chain, it's all the same bait. This was stuff that only the tabloids used to print.'' He glowered at his enemies. ''You might call it the twilight of the media. God knows if we'll ever recover.''

At that moment, the blond man looked over at Paschen, then at Louise, and his smile became a leer. In a few long strides, he had joined them. ''Well, Tom, I guess the news of the day hasn't made you happy.'' His voice was high and nasal. He was talking to Tom, but his eyes stayed on Louise; his hand reached out tentatively as if he wanted to touch her black jet hanging earrings. She instinctively drew away from him and looked at Tom.

Paschen practically barked at him. ''This Vietnam stuff is your lowest moment yet, French: it's all fabrications and lies, and don't think we won't prove it and throw it back into your face.'' Not even deigning to look at the younger man, he took Louise's elbow and propelled her away to a place farther along the balcony where they could talk.

French delivered a parting shot in his sneering voice. ''Remains to be seen, Tom. Just keep your eye on those dwindling poll numbers. I just called CNN: You're down another two points!''

Paschen and Louise were now wedged against the rail by the growing crowd, and she could see her companion was feeling claustrophobic and anxious to get his message across and bail out.

''See what I mean?'' he growled. ''It beats me how the public is willing to believe the worst kind of lies put out by people like him. We need damage control, and that's where you come in, Louise. We both know President Fairchild's environmental bill is the linchpin of his four years as president.''

At last he turned his eyes toward her, and she could see he was battling a tendency to look at her cleavage. ''Louise, you have a good program. It's earned you a lot of a good press—I mean the program, and those other escapades of yours.''

''You mean, finding a murderer.''

''Finding *two* murderers,'' he reminded her. ''And the President thinks very highly of your program content: That's why he named you to that environmental group. So, what I'd like you to do is feature the new law on one of your programs. I know you have a short lead time. Do it, maybe, in early October?''

Paschen's stormy gray eyes, not quite level with hers, now had a hard-driving, focused expression. He wanted a quid pro quo for her appointment to the National Environmental Commission, it was as simple as that. She realized then how desperate the man was. He would try everything, even a PBS Saturday morning garden show, to strengthen Jack Fairchild's chances for reelection.

And she had no doubt Paschen expected to get everything he asked for.

She stepped back and slid her hands against the stone railing to keep from stumbling awkwardly in her satin stiletto heels.

Quietly, she said, "I hope you realize I do not call the shots on program topics, Tom. That's up to Marty Corbin. I think the new environmental law is great, and I will do everything I can to persuade Marty."

Paschen smiled. It added a more attractive, vulnerable element to his thin face.

"But please," she said, "just because I like the idea, that doesn't mean it's a *fait accompli,* Tom. Public television is very chary about promoting things. It is *not* what we do. In fact, why don't I simply have Marty call you and you can settle it between the two of you?"

He gave her an unfathomable look. Louise had heard from Bill that this man was in the midst of a divorce from his powerful businesswoman wife, who had gone to New York to join a top firm at top salary. As her husband put it, "Tom has had to do some heavy couch time to get over the trauma of it, and even then it's left him with a jaundiced view of women."

Now he looked down at her speculatively, as if considering whether or not she was trustworthy. "I think I'd rather deal with you, Louise. Getting all clicked in with another source takes time. I already spend one hundred fifty percent of my time on this job."

She studied the chief of staff—the tired eyes, the cowlicked hair that wouldn't stay in place. Standing so close, she could detect a tic that was bothering his right eye. Compassion welled up from somewhere inside her and she thought of an idea to help this beleaguered public servant. "Tom, I bet you don't have much fun these days."

"You got that right," he said, hands in pockets now, and rocking back and forth on his expensive Italian patent leather dress shoes. "Boring embassy receptions and White House dinners are about all I have time for." He looked like a petulant overaged youth on whose life a curfew had been clamped.

Impulsively, she put out her hand and took his. "Just come with me for about four minutes. I want to show you something really great—that is, unless you've already *been* to the tower."

"A tower, in this building?"

"Come on," she said, tugging on his hand, and skirted past the glittering crowd across to the art galleries themselves. As they passed a display of Claes Oldenberg's pop art, Tom Paschen stared at the grossly distorted objects—a half-deflated toilet, an inflated pile of raisin toast, a giant lipstick—as if they had come from an alien planet. "We're not going to see more like *this,* are we?"

"Not to worry," she said. The marble-lined stairwell to the tower echoed hollowly as they hurried up the steps into the quiet tower room. Now they were in the world of Matisse cutouts. The pictures danced out from tall, stark walls: artworks in vibrant colors with delightful forms as simple as a child's paper cutouts, but with all the depth of the artist's imagination and humor.

Paschen stood with hands on hips, surveying it all. "Well, I have to admit, I've never been here, but it's interesting."

"I just thought a little change of pace would be nice for you. So, do you like them?" She strode around to give each a closer look, then circled back to Tom.

"Yeah, I guess I do. It's a nice interlude here, Louise, and it would probably do me good to just take some time in this place"—he jerked a thumb toward the west—"or better still, in the main gallery where they have the old masters."

She noticed his attention had refocused from the Matisse cutouts to her, and suddenly she realized how alone they were up in this tower. "Um, I suppose Bill will be wondering where I am. . . ."

Tom guided her toward the door, and they went back down the stairway. At the sound of their feet clattering on the pink marble steps, they looked at each other and laughed, like two children caught up in a new adventure.

On their way back to the party, Tom seemed measurably more relaxed. She reassured him. "I understand what you want, and I'll do my best for you with Marty."

"Good girl," he said, giving her a fond look and squeezing her upper arm in a gesture of approval. "I'll call you." Then he delivered her to Bill, gave her husband a mock half-salute, and strode quickly away.

What a strange throwback of a man, Louise thought. Good girl, indeed: She hadn't heard that since she had requested her father to stop saying it to her back in 1975. She tossed her long brown hair and slipped her arm through her husband's; Bill was standing in his own little crowd of people. "Darling," she said *sotto voce* in his ear, "now that I have my marching orders from your friend Paschen, it's time to chow down before the scavengers eat it all."

But it was not to be: Someone came up from the crowd behind her and rested his hand under her elbow. She turned and looked into the sallow, bony face of Franklin Rawlings. Black evening attire accentuated his cadaverous look. His thin hair was combed optimistically over his balding pate. His eyes were unusual, Louise thought, shining with an almost messianic intensity. His amiable smile that seemed to signal all was right with the world was firmly in place.

"Now, is it my turn to get to the gardening lady who loves the environment? You *are* Louise Eldridge, I believe?"

"Why, yes, Mr. Rawlings." She twisted away to give herself some space and extended her hand. As with royalty, Franklin Rawlings assumed she knew who he was. "This is my husband, Bill." The two men shook hands.

"I just saw Tom Paschen holding your attention," Rawlings said, "for an inordinate amount of time, considering it's Tom. Most likely he was promoting that pie-in-the-sky environmental bill that was passed in the waning moments of Congress."

"Are you telling me that it won't hold?"

He stepped closer to her to give his words an air of confidentiality. "Mrs. Eldridge, it's easy to draw the conclusion that Mr. Paschen wants you to do one of your excellent programs on the President's bill." He raised a finger, as if he were a teacher giving gentle instruction to a pupil. "But before you decide to do it, you should look at the poll figures: The sentiment in this country is rapidly shifting. People want *jobs* from the land, and they don't want huge tracts set aside for the use of a few effete hikers and bikers." She was taken aback by the contrast between his pleasant expression and his harsh words. "Congressman Goodrich has now pulled even with the incumbent, and the election is three months away. The odds for a Goodrich landslide are big, and that means a new congress and repeal of that give-away bill."

"You seem very confident."

Rawlings looked down at her like a fond uncle. "Very. But I don't want to press you too much on the issue. I'm certain that WTBA-TV has the wisdom to do the right thing.

And then sometime soon we'll have to talk about Congressman *Goodrich*'s plans for the environment.''

Still smiling, he moved away to join another group. Bill said to her, ''Still hungry?''

From another corner of the room she could see Tom Paschen scowling over at her. ''Not very,'' Louise replied.

Chapter Three

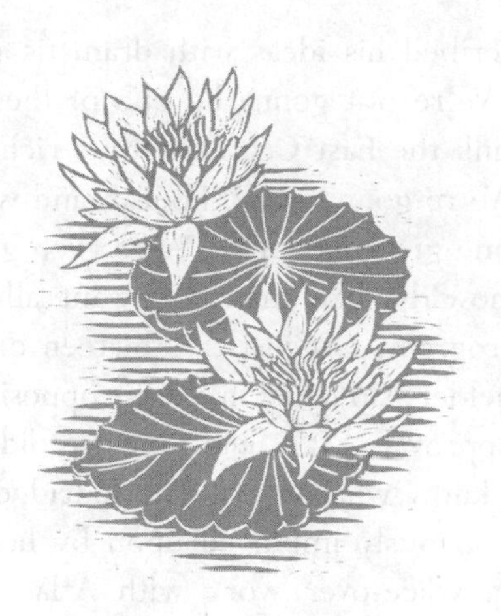

IT WAS AT THE end of a long day. They had been on location in Manassas, Virginia, doing a show on the restoration of an Early American garden near the Occoquan River. Their attire was an echo of colonial life: Louise in a flowing mauve skirt and lace-edged blouse; and John Batchelder, her cohost, in a loose-fitting poetic shirt that emphasized John's dashing looks. When they were finished there, Marty Corbin had insisted they return to the station to discuss program ideas for *Gardening with Nature.*

The producer was large, with dark, curly hair, shaggy eyebrows, and big brown eyes that most of the time were filled with life, fire, and kindliness. Sitting in Marty's office for one of his typical "powwows," he outlined to them an ambitious travel schedule that threw Louise into a profound silence.

Marty described his ideas with dramatic gestures of his big hands: "We're not gonna be one of these garden programs that think the East Coast, with its rich, acidic soil, is all there is. We're gonna *travel,* Louise, and we're not going to leave out one growing zone. We're even going to Hawaii and Alaska, how'dja like that? We want all fifty states to watch your program, not just the thirteen original."

John Batchelder, slouched in a chair opposite hers, smiled and nodded approval. "It's high time we did it, Marty."

She didn't know what to say. The Eldridge home life had already been seriously impinged upon by her full-time job and her extra voice-over work with Atlas Mowers. How much more away-time could her family handle?

Marty read her expression. "Think of it this way, Louise: at least it will discourage houseguests." He grinned at her, anxious to have her happy.

It seemed a propitious time to ask *him* a favor in return. She quickly laid out her proposal for a two-part program on the President's environmental bill, making it sound as if the idea came from her.

"You're kiddin'." His eyebrows skidded down over his skeptical eyes.

"Why would I be kidding? I am quite serious, Marty. The bill just got through Congress. It's timely, and the topic merits it."

He hooted. "Timely, all right: just in time for the November vote. Hey, I know you have a pipeline to the President. Don't tell me *this* show is going to save Fairchild's ass: That man's down the tubes, Louise; hate to tell you.''

She saw he was hungry and impatient, ready to go home to one of his wife Steffi's fabulous meals. ''Okay, but can we talk about it again?''

''Sure we can, when my stomach isn't protesting.'' They left Marty's office, and the staff drifted off.

When she gathered her things and walked to the lobby exit, a stranger was waiting, smiling at her. It took her a moment to recognize the man, and when she did, her heart began to pound. For an instant, she was swept back to her college days and a romantic interlude in Washington, D.C.

''It couldn't be. Not Jay McCormick.''

''Oh, yes, it could be,'' said the voice, a familiar, jesting baritone.

Tall and slightly stoop-shouldered, he approached her slowly. He came right up and took both her hands in his and gave her one of his crooked Irish smiles. He planted the faintest of kisses on her lips, and it made her tingle.

''Louise, you dear thing, you haven't changed at all.''

Standing before her was her former boyfriend from that brief summer more than two decades ago when they were both graduate students at Georgetown University. His face was unremarkable, with an anonymity that made you wonder, once he was out of your presence, what he really looked like. No high cheekbones or other defining features; sandy, nondescript hair that tended to fall in his face. Pale blue eyes: again, unremarkable. And yet, a man with an inner light, who could make her heart beat faster simply because he cared more about other human beings than he cared about himself.

That quality had nearly persuaded her to commit herself to Jay McCormick, to go forward into life like a team of missionaries and try to make the world better for suffering people. Then, through a fluke, along came Bill Eldridge from Harvard to the same campus to substitute for another lecturer at Georgetown's International Institute; she turned onto another path with a man who soon became a spy for his country.

"Outside of the glasses, you haven't changed, either, Jay." But even as she spoke, she saw the worry lines in his face: What kind of disappointments had he suffered during the past two decades? He looked to be on hard times: His dress shirt and pants were scruffy.

"Look a little closer, Louise. I'm having one hell of a hard time right now. I came here today because I sort of need a friend. You may not have heard of what I've been doing."

"Oh, I heard different things, that you were speech writing—or was it reporting—out in California."

"I've done both. I live in Sacramento. But I've been in Washington for a little while now, five months, actually. I've heard about your show and how well you're doing. I've even seen you on that TV ad promoting some mower."

"Yeah," she said sheepishly, "on-air spokesman for the Atlas mulching mower. It helps us make ends meet at the Eldridge house."

"And I also got wind of your detecting." There came that smile again. "Pretty cool of you, Louise, solving two crimes."

"All of a sudden, I have a career of my own, Jay. But what kind of a problem are you having? How can I help you?"

He looked around, as if to be sure no one was listening. No fear of that. Channel Five's crew had gone home. "Let's just say I'm in a bit of, uh, hot water, and I need a safe place to stay until I finish some writing. Do you know anywhere I can hole up? I'm trying to avoid hotels and motels. Checked out of one yesterday morning and ended up sleeping in my car.''

As always, she decided quickly. ''Come to our place. Bill and I live eight miles from here; it's just south of Alexandria. We have empty bedrooms, because both of our girls are away.''

''Where are your girls?''

''Martha goes to Northwestern, but this summer she's involved in a self-help project in Detroit. Janie, our sixteen-year-old, is in Mexico City for three weeks, helping build houses for people.''

Jay raised his eyebrows. ''You and Bill have done something right with those kids. As for your offer of a room, that would be perfect, Louise. I won't bother you. I'll eat out; if I could just stay for a week or so, it would be a lifesaver.''

A week! The warmth of this reunion suddenly evaporated, and cold reality set in. There went that window of opportunity, that interlude alone with Bill, without kids, without company, maybe making mad love on the living room floor. It dissolved instantly in the name of an old and once very torrid friendship.

Houseguests Are Like Gardens—Both Should Be Low-Maintenance

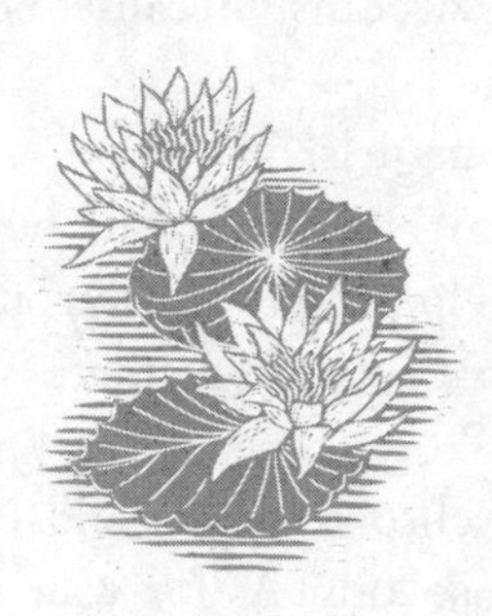

BIG BLUEGRASS LAWNS AND fussy flowers such as black-spot-prone tea roses are habits we can give up, just like smoking. They don't fit into the American gardening scene as they used to, for leisure is ephemeral. Few of us live the life of the Victorian lady who had the time to walk up and down the borders with a basket on her arm, dallying with the flowers and picking off diseased leaves by hand. Instead, we are a nation of frenetic, fast-moving people, balancing our time between jobs, shopping, errands, taking kids to game practice, plugging into the Internet, ministering to aging parents, and sneaking away occasionally for a couple of hours' relaxation at a movie.

And still we garden. To many of us, it is an oasis in the midst of our busy lives, a spiritual refreshment that we simply cannot do without. But when is there even the time for gardening? The way we do it is to garden smarter. Through sheer necessity, we are turning to low-maintenance methods that reduce garden labor to two hours or less a week.

There are two principles involved in low-maintenance gardening: plant selection and plant care. Of course, this entire subject may depress the person who has large expanses of bluegrass lawn and beds of perennials with the equivalent of PMS. This is a gardener who is chained to his or her garden, both financially and timewise, and who probably doesn't stint on chemical pest control and heavy fertilization.

The best advice to this gardener is to *change*. Do it little by little, but remember the rewards are great. Put the lawn in its place. Get rid of as much as possible, or replace it with turf that suits your climate. Lawns are water-gobbling, high-care prima donnas. Get your soil right: Make it rich, loose, friable. Make your motto, "Let no bare earth show its face to the sun." This means mulching heavily to avoid water loss and weed growth. Seriously consider replacing high-maintenance plants, no matter how beloved, with regional plants that are fully as

beautiful and don't need chemicals to stay healthy. Group them together according to their water needs.

These are basic tenets that define "xeriscape." Xeriscaping is the only smart way to garden, if we are to conserve America's precious water resources and to guard against the harm done by chemicals. Here are further tips from successful low-maintenance gardeners:

- Design lawn areas compactly for easy watering.

- Eliminate hand trimming by putting a barrier between earth and gardens: A row of submerged bricks is an easy, attractive solution.

- Plant thickly. This sounds arduous, but spacing plants so that they can grow together quickly reduces weeding and watering. Besides, it makes a wonderful picture. Some plants, of course, are takeover artists; though it is nice to have them filling in, we don't want them smothering their delicate neighbors. When planting, use polymers to aid in water retention and thus give plants a good start.

- When planting shrubs and trees, you could surround them with landscaping cloth,

but heavy mulching with organic materials is just as effective, and much cheaper. Keep the mulch away from tree trunks so they can breathe.

Select plants for your climate. Don't waste your time with plants that won't thrive there. Visit the best gardens in your area—they may be your friend's garden or the botanic or civic garden—and copy what you see. Talk to the person who made the plant selection and find out what works and what doesn't.

Even if you failed physics, get scientific about water use. Use a timer when watering. Establish simple drip systems in gardens and circular watering rings around individual trees. These cheap and easy practices can reduce your weekly workload by literally hours.

Know your yard as intimately as you know your spouse, its temperamental microclimates, the effect of wind on its well-being, its watering idiosyncrasies, how the movement of the sun affects the plant through the seasons. This will lead you to put plants and trees in just the right places for a handsome, carefree garden.

Chapter Four

THE ODORS OF FRYING onions and draft beer, soaked into the walls and wood floor of Joe's Raw Bar, went with college days. They awakened memories of the summer of 1975.

Jay had pleaded the need for a cup of coffee, and this nostalgic bar was on the way home. He slowly shook his head. ''We really had something going.''

''For a few weeks we did,'' amended Louise, stirring her cream soda with a straw.

''Six weeks.'' Jay looked straight into her eyes. ''Then came that son-of-a-gun Bill down from bloody Harvard.'' He grinned, to take the sting out of the words.

''It happens, Jay. I fell in love with Bill. I'm sorry, but remember, you liked Bill. You even came to our wedding. You'll like him when you meet him again.''

He reached a hand over to cover hers as a gesture of remorse. ''I don't know why I'm sounding like a vindictive spoilsport. But he sure grabbed you up in a hurry.'' The pain in his eyes was unmistakable. ''I turned my back one day, and you were gone.''

She realized how selfish it was to reminisce about those days. To her, it was romantic, but to Jay, it was painful. Back then, she had found him to be a man for all occasions: They went to foreign films and art events, explored Virginia waterfalls, and hiked the Shenandoah trail, Jay adroitly leading the way over rocks and ridges. She remembered best the simple walks along the C&O Canal at twilight and the canoe trips on the Potomac. Jay would beach the boat and hide their packed lunches so cleverly no animal could find them, while they skinny-dipped in the river.

Her face flushed at the memory. When she looked over at Jay, his pale eyes were shining with the same devotion that she had seen there twenty years ago. ''Louise, we would have been great together. Maybe I would have done better if only you'd been with me.''

''Jay, we both know this is useless. Let's just remember those lovely days, and not regret anything. You married, didn't you? I thought I heard that.'' She stopped, wishing she hadn't brought up his marriage. Who knows what happened to it?

His eyes changed, grew wary. ''I married a wonderful woman named Lannie Gordon; she was in law school at Georgetown. We settled in Sacramento after Lannie got a job out there. She was very successful—became the youngest partner in her law firm. Meantime, I got into investigative reporting at the *Sacramento Union.* Specialized in death row cases that were faulty and got a number of people freed, too. If anything in life was satisfying, that was."

"Was?"

"Lannie had a baby, and that meant getting a house, and Lannie wanted a pretty fancy house. I sure wasn't able to carry my part of the financial load on a reporter's salary, so I ended up joining a PR firm to make some bucks." He attempted a smile that was more of a grimace. "I became expert at writing speeches for candidates; I'd write speeches for anybody, as long as they were a paying client."

"So you felt like a sellout."

The faded eyes looked at her from underneath the unruly brows. "Yeah. I was no different from Lannie." Then he frowned down at the bar-finish table top. "Even with those concessions, I haven't made the marriage work; that left our daughter Melissa squarely in the middle."

"And Lannie . . ."

"She's a big-time lawyer now. She's here in D.C., a top litigator and lobbyist for the tobacco industry."

"I think I've seen her on television, speaking up for the tobacco companies. Shoulder-length red hair, very serious?"

"Yes, that's Lannie. We divorced five years ago, and a year after that, she moved to Washington for this new job and took Melissa with her. Like a dope, I went along with the idea, and that caused all the trouble. Melissa was nine then, thirteen now. She and I missed each other so much that I went to court to change things, and I succeeded beyond my wildest hopes. Lannie was upset, of course: She loves the girl just as much as I do. Melissa is wonderful and beautiful."

He strained for an image special enough for his daughter. "Just about as beautiful as that first day of spring. Loves to read and write, loves animals. She has a canny nature, and I like that because she reminds me of *me,* but maybe that comes from her mother, too."

"You were so idealistic. Was Lannie that way, too?"

He stared off into space, remembering. "Yes, like we all were in the seventies: idealistic, but with our old values undercut by the confusion of the sixties. She may still be idealistic way underneath; it was the job and the success that changed her. Maybe it's because she grew up on that pathetic little farm in southern Indiana, with so little in the way of material advantages, that she needs them so much now. Once her career got going out in California, it was as if we were two of the earth's plates that drifted apart."

He shook his head. "The funny thing is, I still love her, and if she ever asked me to come back, I'd do it. But she's heartbroken because of the judge's decision: He gave me custody for all of the school year. What really wrenched her was that our daughter got on the stand and told the judge she prefers to live with me."

"What a thing for a mother to hear!"

"I feel sorry for her, too, Louise, but what's going to happen is for the best. In a week, Melissa drives back with me to California, and then will stay with her mother in Great Falls at Christmas and for three months during the summer." His face clouded up again.

"Why are you concerned, Jay? It sounds like a great outcome for you."

"It's because my ex-wife's so darned disappointed, Louise. It's as if I've snatched her soul away. She firmly believes Melissa is better off with her: She gave her the best of everything and even took her to Europe a couple of times. I think the girl makes Lannie feel like a better *person*. So now, I'm hoping she doesn't do something desperate, like taking Melissa abroad to live. She has a house in Ireland, and God knows she has the money for the two of them to just emigrate."

He leaned forward, elbows on the table, intent on his story. "Right after the judge's decree in February, which takes effect next Friday, I flew here to D.C. to check things out. I was afraid Lannie might take off with our daughter then. I felt terrible spying on her, but I had to. Then, I came across a story that I first got wind of last fall in California. Got a deal going to stay in Washington, and I've been, well, working here ever since. And keeping an eye on Melissa, unbeknownst to my ex."

He shook his head, as if he had dwelled enough on the matter, and then looked at the clock on the greasy tan wall. "Louise, it's after six: Are you sure we aren't running overtime?"

She had called Bill from her office at Channel Five, telling him she was bringing Jay home. He sounded a little put out, but he remembered Jay. She told him they were going out to get coffee first. "We'd better go, so I can dream up something for supper."

Jay slid out of the booth, protesting. "Louise, I don't need care and feeding—just a room where I can stay out of sight."

"You're having dinner with us, don't be silly. Bill will be glad to see you again."

As they walked to the door, Jay looked around the bar. He said, "This place is just like our old college hangouts in Georgetown."

She smiled up at him. "That's why I brought you here."

He followed her the eight miles home on the crowded

highway in a dull-colored old Ford that looked like it wouldn't pass the emissions test. But Louise could figure it out: Her old flame was going incognito, and that included his car.

Of course, her seven-year-old Honda wagon, which smelled of all her garden acquisitions, from plants to peat to manure, wasn't much better.

Chapter Five

BILL ELDRIDGE RARELY HAD occasion to feel jealous regarding his wife. True, men always admired her. Even Tom Paschen, the other night, had expressed his appreciation of Louise, in his twisted, misogynist way. But this was usually a source of pride for him, to know he had such a willowy, attractive, and charming wife. But Jay McCormick was something else. Bill had hurried home from work and changed into his most youthful sports clothes when he heard Louise was bringing the guy home. For dinner, or maybe it was more than dinner: What did she say, *to stay awhile?*

Then they hadn't rolled in until after seven o'clock, reasonable in view of the heavy traffic across Fairfax County at that time. But they were laughing and chatting together in that damnably annoying, intimate way that they had been when he first met the two of them at Georgetown. And Louise, in the clothes she had worn on location, looked especially romantic: white frilly blouse and flowing lavender skirt, her long brown hair bundled up in an old-fashioned style with a ribbon, no less.

He smoothed back his barely thinning blond hair, and realized he didn't have the moxie he had back then. He had seen Louise that day twenty-one years ago in Washington and got carried away by a combination of lust and good judgment. He'd decided right then he would marry this luscious creature. And just by being his easy self, though a little more rooted than the mercurial Jay McCormick, and full of talk about his sexy new job with State, he had won the lady.

Louise had given their guest a tour of the house and he commented on how much he liked the antique furniture. He had smoothed the wood of the pine dining room table with knowledgeable, sensuous fingers and told Louise how he himself made furniture in his workshop. Louise was impressed. It figured: Bill himself hardly knew how to handle a handsaw.

Now, Jay sat across from him with a Scotch and water and looked, if anything, like a better bet than twenty years before. He had a lot going for him. He had a certain quiet poise. He also was five years younger than Bill, the same age as Louise. He was still good-humored and witty. And, most important, he had suffered: Louise liked to crawl right under the skin of suffering people in order to share their misery.

Jay had a track record for saving people. That always appealed to Louise, who liked nothing better than to save people herself. The two of them were like a couple of Don Quixotes.

But the man certainly was desultory-looking: For some reason, he had slept in his car last night. Despite this, he still had that careless Irish attractiveness and graceful way of handling his body.

Suddenly Bill became aware that he had been carefully watching Louise watch Jay while he ran his paranoid scenarios over in his mind. He took a large sip of his Wellers on the rocks and pulled himself together. Jealousy was profitless, he'd always read, and after a couple of moments indulging in it, he knew it was true. The fact was, he liked Jay McCormick.

Louise had been giving their guest a rundown on the Eldridge family's recent moves, and how they came to buy this, their first house.

"There's lots more I want to hear about," said Jay. "How's your job, Bill? Do you think you'll stay stateside, or are there more foreign assignments ahead?"

"That's still up in the air," he replied. "It's more complicated now, with Janie still to finish high school. And Louise, of course: Kind of hard to say to Louise, 'Give up your job.' So we have lots of decisions to make." That was enough to tell him about the family. He said, "Now, Jay, maybe I missed this: What are you doing in Washington?"

Their guest, who was slowly nursing his drink, put it down on a nearby table, careful to see it rested straight on its coaster. He folded his hands loosely across his chest. "Bill, I'm writing. But I've told Louise next to nothing about what I'm writing, and that's what I want to tell you, if I can prevail that much on your friendship."

"Sure, but what's this about being in some kind of hot water?"

Jay frowned and was silent, probably surprised that Louise had filled Bill in so thoroughly in the few minutes they had alone since the two had reached the house. Then the man appeared to make a conscious decision to relax, bringing a leg up and crossing it over the other, resting his arms against the sofa cushions. "I have a story to finish, Bill, and I want to do it here, out of sight of everybody, not back in Sacramento, because when it's finished, I can pick up my daughter and we'll return home together." He grinned at Louise. "It will be in a new car I plan to pick up here, by the way, not that junker I'm using right now."

Bill persisted. "Is someone giving you a hard time?"

The man gave him a tense look. Here he was, thought Bill, at age forty-three still clinging to the role of an adventurer. Christ, Bill had lived through scores of dangerous adventures during his twenty-year career with the Company, but he never dramatized them, even with colleagues who knew about his operations. Jay had been a well-known antiwar activist at Columbia during his undergraduate days, right there in the middle of things when the students closed down the Administration Building. This activist luster had carried over into grad school. Probably had been part of McCormick's attraction for Louise, who had done her share of work for the antiwar movement while at Northwestern. But by grad school, the world was changing. Bill remembered Jay frantically trying to switch gears and make a place for himself in mainstream American life, and finally choosing journalism. That idealism of his must have worn thin, for he apparently moved on to a more lucrative career in speech writing.

Right now the guy was clutching his secret around him as

tightly as Dracula clutched his cloak. What were all the dramatics about? Bill narrowed his eyes. He had the answer: Jay was back to his old pursuit of tilting at windmills. He was either breaking the law for justice's sake, or back to investigative reporting—or maybe both.

The guy looked at him with a dramatic expression in his washed-out blue eyes. "Let's just say I've been living a rather troublesome double life lately. I'd rather be invisible during this coming week and avoid any semblance of trouble."

Bill looked at Louise, who was looking at him. Jay was staying a whole week. That week they were to spend alone, shot. At least she had the good grace to look crestfallen. Then, he rose to the duties of gracious host: "You can be invisible here, Jay, that's for sure. Sylvan Valley is a backwater, not much traffic, just neighbors and their friends. We want you to feel welcome."

Bill wasn't a hundred percent sure of that. Maybe ninety percent.

"Thanks, Bill. And thanks to you both for keeping the lid on what I'm doing here, and not asking me too many questions—for both *your* sake, and mine. I've got a computer and clothes in the car. I won't bother you otherwise. I can eat out."

"You can eat with *us,*" insisted Louise. "What are friends for?"

He grinned at her, a strange kind of lopsided grin that, Bill thought, might have been the effect of Bell's palsy, or some other nerve problem. It had a warming effect on his wife, he could tell: her eyes were shining, and she was sitting forward attentively listening to his every word. The man was a bit of a magician, and he hoped Louise had her feet on the ground enough not to get emotionally confused.

To add to his concern was the fact that he had to take a brief and very sensitive trip to Vienna next week, a trip that involved a certain amount of danger at both ends of the journey, and required Louise's complete confidentiality. In fact, his responsibilities with the Company were all over the lot: He consulted on force protection of troops abroad, and at home studied the "off-normal occurrences" that kept dogging the transport of nuclear materials from one state to another. Worst-case analysis was that there was a tie-in to a worldwide nuclear smuggling ring. That was the subject of his imminent trip. It was like dealing with quicksilver, these international gangsters, who seemed not to realize the stakes were global destruction.

But on another level, there was danger at home, too: He wasn't at all sure he wanted to leave Louise in the house alone with this lonesome polecat, Jay McCormick.

"Uh, Louise," he said, stiffly, "hadn't you better change out of that costume, and then maybe I can help you with dinner. I bet Jay is hungry."

"No, please," said Jay, leaping up from his chair. "Let me help Louise—I'll feel better if you do. Less like a mooch."

"All right with me." Bill's tone was brisk. "But first let me help you carry your things in. By the way, we'll have to tell the neighbors in the cul-de-sac something."

Louise smiled broadly. "I'll just tell them the truth: We're entertaining one of my old boyfriends."

They were all standing now, ready to disperse, when Jay dramatically put his hands up to stop them. "Uh, there's one more thing you both need to know. As I said, Bill, I need to keep my presence at your home a secret. But I have an assistant, a kind of a leg man. He travels some and does research for me. He's the only one who should know I'm here.'' Their guest had that quirky smile on his face, so that Bill couldn't tell whether he was serious or not. ''The pity is, I'm not sure I even can trust him.''

''What's his name?'' said Louise.

''Charlie Hurd. He's a young fellow, fearfully ambitious: one of those small, quick men who are going to make it in this world, damn the torpedoes. I read his stories in *The Arlington Herald,* this twice-weekly paper in northern Virginia—you probably subscribe to it. I hired him to moonlight for me; it keeps him busy now, day and night, even weekends.'' Now the grin was for real. ''He's so ambitious that he wants me to call him 'Charles' now. His real name's Charles Hurd II.''

Bill chuckled. ''Sounds like a bit of a prick to me—sorry, Louise. What's the matter, is the guy realizing he's part of a big story?''

Jay looked at Bill admiringly. ''You hit it right on the nose. Mind you, while Charlie's found me a lot of good background stuff, I'm not at liberty to share the whole story with him by a long shot, and he doesn't like that one bit. But he figures the story's huge, that it's his ticket to the big time.'' Their guest suddenly sensed he had opened up too much, even if it was to old, trusted friends. ''I don't want to say more, just that Charlie may be phoning me.''

He turned to Louise. ''And don't mind him: he's kind of—rude.''

''Rude?''

''Apparently he comes from one of the old families of Virginia, but for some reason he has no manners at all. But he's a darned good researcher and writer.''

''Okay,'' said Bill, trying to mask his impatience, ''Charles Hurd's in the loop. Let's get those bags.''

As he and their new guest walked through the pergola on

the path to the street, Jay seemed oblivious to the pergola, the woods, and Louise's little garden areas, even the one near the path with those tall yellow-and-white flowers that looked so attractive right now. "Uh, Bill, I see your garage is full. Is there anywhere I could park my old heap that's out of sight of the street?"

"Well, sure, just drive it into the area alongside the addition, behind those hollies. I know it's not visible back there from the street, because that's where Louise hides the trash cans."

"Thanks. That will do it."

Bill could see the man striding next to him was even paler and more distracted than he had first thought. A pale, ravaged former lover of Louise. Or boyfriend, rather, according to what she told him. Well, it fit: she always did like to collect stray animals and people.

Louise had changed a lot in the last year. She had become less a foreign service wife and more of a personality unto herself. A healthful change, Bill thought, even though her language had gone straight downhill, and sometimes now she even shouted "Asshole!" at drivers, but in the privacy of their closed car. And she didn't suffer fools as gladly as she used to: She was the personification of gentility at one time, but now, instead of listening, she was apt to sound off with her own opinions, like one of those pugnacious pundits on TV. Was such a woman ready or willing to get involved again with her attractive former lover? He frowned, and rethought that: boyfriend, not lover, he was pretty sure.

"You're like a succubus, you know," Bill said.

They were cuddling before going off to sleep, with Louise molding her body to his, and resting a light hand on his waist. They wouldn't stay attached long, for the bedroom windows were open and the weather was a bit warm.

"What's a succubus?"

"An evil female spirit that sexually vanquishes men during their sleep."

"Oh. But I have no sexual designs on you tonight. Had too hard a day."

"Hard, isn't it, to bring an old flame back into your life? Takes a lot of energy."

That came out harsher than he had intended.

Louise let go of his waist and flopped like a giant fish to her side of the bed. Her voice was muffled but dangerous. "Bill, we went to that reception last night, and then I had to get up early and work my ass off all day, running from pillar to post, from Manassas to Fairfax."

"*Ass?*" he repeated sarcastically.

"Ass. Can't you handle the word? And then, at five, Jay arrives, and I entertain him over coffee for a while, bring him home, rush over to feed chopped worms to Mary's fish, make your dinner, and then do the dishes while the two of you discuss his favorite death row cases from his days as a reporter. Why wouldn't I be tired?"

"Said something like that, didn't I?"

Now they had both flopped on their backs, staring up through the skylight above their bed, at the view of a swaying sweetgum tree and a fingernail moon. Normally, this would have encouraged romance, but Bill was afraid he had poisoned the mood.

"Don't try to squirm out of it, Bill Eldridge: You were just being sarcastic and mean, making innuendos about Jay and me like that."

"Sorry." He reached out a tentative hand and put it on

top of hers, and after a few seconds she reluctantly turned hers over and entwined his fingers in hers.

After a moment, he said, "I know one thing about Jay."

"Yeah, what?" There were still icicles in her voice.

"This guy is only going to rate about a D with you, in your rankings of houseguests."

"How so?"

"Because I happened to go by his room once he'd unpacked, and I can tell already: he's a slob."

"He is?"

"Yeah. Clothes strewn around. Only thing neat is his desk, and he'll probably muck that up once he gets to writing."

"Oh." He knew she was tired of cleaning up after houseguests.

"Yep, Louise, you're going to have a whole bunch of left-behind items of Jay's—socks, shoes, papers—to put in the morgue."

She shoved him over on his side and cuddled close to him again. "I'll worry about that after he's gone. Now, be quiet and let's go to sleep."

But then her hand on his waist moved, slid over his relaxed abs and downward.

"I like that idea of the succubus," she said.

Chapter Six

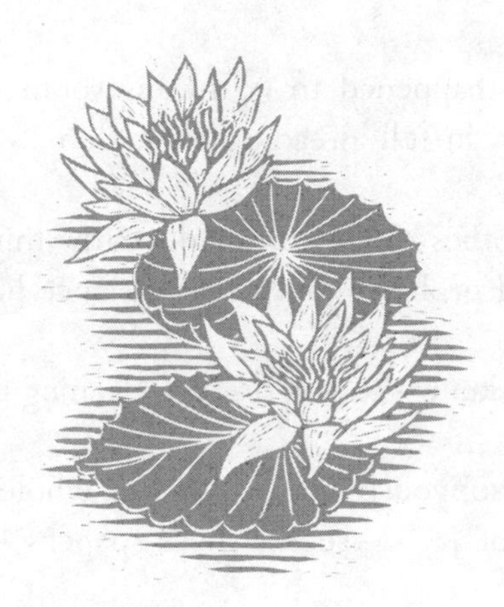

THE NEXT MORNING WHEN she woke, Louise grabbed her robe and went to the kitchen to find her husband gone and her houseguest ensconced in his bedroom. At her knock, Jay called out that he had shared bacon and eggs with Bill, and was coming along "just fine" with his work. She could hear the soft tap of his computer keys; they didn't stop even while he was talking to her through the closed door.

The obvious message was that he didn't want to be disturbed.

She pulled the belt to her robe tighter and walked resolutely back to the kitchen. It was hard to contain her disappointment; she had expected a quiet breakfast together on the patio, another sharing of reminiscences of the summer of '75.

But maybe she was being naive, and Jay knew better than she did that there was a limit to how far they could go with those reminiscences. Late last night, after making love, Bill had teased her and said that she still carried a torch for Jay. Nonsense, she had replied. But it was true that when she looked at her pale, rather tired former suitor, she still felt a strange pull. Whether it was attraction, or just a desire to help a lost soul, she didn't know.

Her feeling of being excluded was only exacerbated when Charlie Hurd phoned.

"Good *mor*ning, the Eldridges," said Louise in her usual pleasant way.

"Charles Hurd, here," snapped a haughty young voice. "Put Jay on the line."

Anger washed over her like a wave. She hung up the phone before she could even think about it. Then she stood there, breathing deeply to regain her good temper before the dratted instrument rang again. In seconds, it did.

"Good *mor*ning. The Eldridges."

"*All* right—*I* give. *Please* put Jay on the line." The youthful voice was larded with sarcasm.

Without responding, Louise set down the receiver and knocked on Jay's closed door. He hurried to the kitchen, declining her offer of the cordless phone. Holding the kitchen extension in one hand and notebook in the other, he sheepishly asked, "Louise, would you mind if I talked privately with Charles? I hate like the devil to inconvenience you—were you getting breakfast?"

"Oh, no, not at all. Actually, I was just going to get dressed." She waved her hand as if to reinforce the fact that the kitchen was his. "Go for it." And she strode down the hall back to her bedroom and closed the door like a dutiful hostess.

It took only two minutes for her to put on her many-pocketed shorts, a gardening shirt, and boots. Then she flicked on CNN news and did stretching exercises while she waited another fifteen minutes. When she opened the bedroom door she heard nothing. There was a hollow feeling inside her: Jay had not had the thoughtfulness to knock on her door to tell her when he was through occupying her kitchen.

It was clear Jay's life was to be no part of hers. She set her mouth tightly, and shook her head. Good thing she had a life of her own, and it was high time she was seeing to it. She went to the kitchen and resolutely examined the calendar. Almost immediately, she forgot her houseguest. This was Wednesday already. A broad black line was drawn through two days of next week, and overwritten with the initials P.P.S.: Perennial Plant Society. That meant two nights with three vivacious women as houseguests, who felt it their bounden duty to get acquainted with her and write her up in their newsletter before she became Plant Person of the Year. One of those days would be devoted to a long Channel Five shoot at the P.P.S. convention at the Washington Hilton. With a sudden sense of urgency, Louise looked out at her patio garden. Like the others in the yard, it had still not recovered from the incursions of little Sally.

Nose to the glass, she stared at the diminished garden and tried to fight the bothersome feelings of pride and vanity that swept over her. What would happen to her professional reputation if the P.P.S. people saw her beds in this state? These women were professional down to their toes. Then she tried to make light of it: After all, what could they do, rescind her honor of being named Plant Person of the Year? Nevertheless, she decided, she could do a little restoration work in the garden without making herself feel like a Mrs. Babbitt, who had to keep up appearances above all else. She got herself a bowl of shredded wheat and a cup of coffee and went out on the patio. As she ate, she noted spots in the garden that needed resuscitation.

With breakfast finished, she grabbed the cordless phone, and went out to the toolshed. Here, all was neatness and precision, just as she liked it. She took down the pruning shears and cultivator from their hooks, and placed them and the phone into separate pockets of the shorts. In another pocket she stuffed a large, folded trash bag. Bill always teased that she looked like an overequipped fisherman, but it worked. It wouldn't be easy to fix up the damage to the yard. It wasn't as if she had sun: she merely had little patch works of sun in the midst of dense shade. That meant she couldn't just plop in a blooming delphinium or daisy. She had to be more subtle.

Fortuntately, the rampaging little Sally had left a few daylilies unplucked, and they were providing accents of soft color in each of the garden areas, along with the burst of bright orange shady-hardy helenium and white echinacea that had been too rough for her tiny hands. Louise's garden of anemone, ligularia, and hosta also remained untouched, for it was far from the beaten path.

The phone rang, and she took it out of her shorts pocket. It was Janie from Mexico City, calling collect.

"Janie, honey, how are you?"

"Ma, I have big troubles," said the sorrowful, young voice.

"Troubles?" Her voice came out like a squawk and her heart sank with a thud. She went to a nearby stump in the woods and carefully sat down to hear the news. Her mind conjured up a picture of the slight, beautiful blond girl, who had become a woman in just the past few months: having "troubles" in that big, polluted, south-of-the-border city where Louise envisioned bandits on the highways. Anything could have happened to her. "Janie," she cried, "no one has hurt you, have they?"

"No, no, Ma, *hold* the hysteria. It's not like that." Louise could hear the teenaged impatience: Her mother had missed the point yet again. "It's much more basic. And simple. I have Montezuma's revenge, that's all."

Louise's shoulders sank as she gave an enormous sigh of relief. Fortunately, her motherly screech had been deadened by the surrounding woods and mulch-covered forest floor, and now she could speak without alarming the neighbors a block away. Her baby was all right. "Oh, honey, I'm so sorry. Diarrhea. How painful. But what about those pills you brought with you? Don't they work?"

"I'm taking them. It's not that easy to get rid of, they tell me." The girl's voice sounded wan. "I called you, because they made me stay home from work today to rest."

"And how is the work going?"

"It's great. I am a regular little carpenter now, though I have some sore fingers where the hammer didn't go where I thought it would. Maybe I'll take up carpentry as my career. But you know, just like Martha says, there're two worlds, the world of the rich and the poor." Another radicalized child, reflected Louise. "You should see the poor here, Ma. They live on the streets, under a stretched canvas, cooking there, sleeping there, making new babies there. Why, sometimes there're ten kids all huddled around one little home in the street.''

''It must be terrible. But you're helping, Janie. That's why you went there in the first place.''

''What we're doing is a drop in the bucket. You'll never know unless you come here. And I think you and Dad *should* come, to find out what poverty really means. Meantime, I hope you're all right?''

''Why, yes, I'm all right. Uh, we have a guest, my old friend from college, Jay McCormick.''

''Your old flame. The one that makes your eyes light up when you talk about him. How's Dad handling *that*?''

''Well, that's a bit of an exaggeration, but yes. Jay's had a hard time. He's sort of hiding out at our house.''

''Oh,'' said her daughter, and her voice changed from teasing to serious. ''Ma, you're either hiding out or you're not: there's no 'sort of' hiding out. Who, pray tell, is he hiding from?''

''Honey, we don't really know the particulars.''

''That doesn't sound good, and I'm not even there.'' It was as if the teenager believed she should be around constantly to monitor Louise's erratic comings and goings.

''Really, Janie, the situation is very simple. The man will be here just a few days. He's writing a story. I think it's something about the presidential election, or else about the courts. In a few days he will be out of here, and you can come home and have your room back.''

''I bet you aren't telling me everything, by a long shot. Try to stay out of trouble while I'm gone.''

''How are the other kids who are there with you? Do you like them as much as you did when we spoke last time?''

''Oh, more. They totally rule. Really bright. Very weird

musical tastes, though. None of them are very, oh, ordinary. They're all computer nerds, bookworms, that sort. They play all kinds of music, grunge, techno, rockabilly. Man, do we rock to rockabilly! They even like jazz. You'll really like them when you meet them."

"Meet them?"

Then she heard the girl gasp. "Oh, oh! I'd better go, if you know what I mean. I just called because I had nothing else to do, and I sort of miss you."

Louise got up from the stump and tucked the phone back in her pocket. How much she missed her youngest. As for Martha, nineteen, it was as if that child had left the nest long ago and ceased being a part of her life. She had turned instead into a brooding, egalitarian-minded feminist searching for answers in urban studies, her new major at Northwestern. Martha was in equal jeopardy, working in the core city of Detroit in a program run by a Catholic priest, helping people train for jobs and a future. Louise wished her older daughter would call, too, for phoning her room in Detroit was always fruitless, with only polite strangers taking careful messages that were never answered.

On her next circuit of the yard, she had pruning shears in hand and plastic bag unfurled and slung over one shoulder to hold the clippings. With the flourish of an artist, she fine-tuned bushes that had grown too exuberantly during the summer, snipping off unwanted growth and the occasional dead twig. With the cultivator she fluffed up mulch areas that had been compacted by the summer rains. After throwing the clippings in the compost heap, she went inside to clean up a bit to go to the gardening center over on Route One. These days, she was able to visit nurseries without guilt. It wasn't too long ago that she had been a garden binger, knocking the family budget out of kilter with her plant purchases. Bill would sit her down like a naughty schoolgirl and show her the disarrayed accounts.

It was great to be a working woman, able to spend money as she pleased.

She had just about completed her remedial gardening. In one of the only sunny spots she tucked in the satisfying chubby forms of three green santolina, with yellow button blooms waiting to burst open. A couple of hostas planted at its feet diverted attention from the damage done to the tree peony. Strategically placed clumps of fat-leafed bergenia filled in the foreground. Still, the garden looked wounded, but it was the best she could do.

Her phone rang again, and it was Marty Corbin with good news. ''Okay, Louise, you got it. We'll do a two-part program on the environmental bill. But we gotta act quick: I've lined up a couple of hunks already. We can trek over to the Shenandoah and illustrate the new commitment to acquiring wilderness areas. Actually, it's too bad we don't have time to travel west, because that's where the biggest federal land grabs will take place.''

''Marty, Marty,'' she rebuked.

''Hey, this bill really shows the President's chutzpah, taking that amount of acreage out of the hands of business and lumbering. Talk about wilderness regained!'' She could just imagine him grinning at his little jab. ''Just seeing if you were paying attention, Louise.''

''And don't forget,'' she said, ''we have to do something on those incentives in the bill for private landowners to restore habitat.''

''Then we gotta handle the part about those tougher pesticide controls. But no more bringing poisons into the studio.'' He chuckled, remembering the program where they had done just that, which led to the mysterious poisoning of Louise's rival at the studio. ''Research is getting an angle on dealing with the endangered species part of the bill. Something down at the Chesapeake Bay, maybe. It'd be a nice, easy run for us.''

''Great, Marty. I think our viewers will like it.''

''But just don't think this show is going to save President Fairchild from having his pants beat off by Goodrich.''

''Marty, I don't have a personal stake in the election. I only believe in the environment, and Fairchild stood up to a lot of people to get that bill passed. I admire him for it.''

Her producer chuckled on the other end of the phone line. ''I'm puttin' ya on, Louise. I prefer Fairchild, too, even though *I* can believe those stories about drinking and womanizing.''

She bet he did: Marty himself had been a boozer and a womanizer until he straightened himself out over the last year.

He went on: ''When I see you tomorrow, we'll work on some treatments, including that one for the perennial plant people; that's gonna be a challenge, a big convention like that. Meantime, I wanted to let you know you have what you want.''

''Thanks, Marty. I'm so glad this thing didn't get bogged down in Channel Five politics. I know the President will be grateful, too.''

Or, more specifically, she thought, Tom Paschen, that antsy chief of staff of the President's. She looked forward to telling him that she had succeeded in her small part in aiding the campaign.

And without compromising principle, of course.

Getting Bogged Down and Loving It: The Wonders of the Bog Garden

IT SEEMS AT FIRST glance that people with bog gardens* are just overgrown children who like to play in the mud. Actually, they are shrewd people. For ornamental bog gardens are the best of everything: They are

---

* Purists call them marsh gardens or damp gardens, for, strictly speaking, bog gardens are something else: very distinctive North American natural wetlands that lack mineral soils and have a deep substrata of sphagnum peat moss. They contain a high acidic content and minimal nutrition. Therefore, a limited number of plants grow there, but the ones that do are unique, and include certain orchids, the lady's slipper, bladderwort, Indian pipe, the calla lily, and the carnivorous pitcher plant, *Sarracenia*.

low-maintenance and enviromentally sound, cheaper than water gardens, and still they produce lush plants and flowers that cannot be found in terrestrial gardens.

The bog gardener can go wild, leaving the orbit of mere dry-land gardeners, and grow things in a soggy swamp that would be a struggle elsewhere: fine shows of iris in every shade and more than a dozen varieties, including the majestic Japanese iris *(Iris kaempferi);* big-leaved *Ligularia dentata;* the giant-leaved *Astilboides tabularis;* parrot feather *(Myriophyllum aquaticum);* marsh marigold *(Caltha palustris);* dwarf bamboo *(Dulichium areundinaceum);* double-flowering arrowhead, *Sagittaria japonica* ''Flore Pleno,'' with its distinctive leaves and fluffy double white blossoms; cattail *(Typha latifolia);* and rushes. People may balk at one rush, the handsome horsetail *(Equisetum hyemale),* because it is a garden invader. Those who have failed with the brilliant red *Lobelia cardinalis* in the perennial border will find it flourishes with its toes damp, as does its relative, *Lobelia siphilitica.* Tall, bold-flowered mallows; rosy joe-pye weeds *(Eupatorium purpureum);* goatsbeard *(Aruncus dioicus);* thalictrum; *Cimicifuga;* astilbe; yellow flag iris *(Iris pseudacorus);* blue flag iris *(Iris versicolor);* and the brilliant scarlet *Lychnis chalcedonica* not only grow, they prosper.

And then there are the tender plants, *Thalia geniculata;* the elegant bog lily, *Crinum*

americanum; and spider lily, *Hymenocallis liriosme;* and the lush-leaved, violet-stemmed taro, *Colocasia esculenta var. fontanesii;* and red-stemmed *Sagittaria lancifolia ruminoides* with its flaring leaves and bold, carmine stems. There is the incredibly handsome variegated-leaved canna, and the biblical bulrush from which the Dead Sea Scrolls were made, right there in your own backyard: *Cyperus papyrus,* or its smaller form, *Cyperus viviparus.* Treat the tender ones as annuals, although many can come inside for the winter provided you have a mansion with a big basement. That six-foot or taller biblical bulrush, in particular, doesn't fare well in the confines of the home.

Not only the garden itself, but its moist edges can become fertile propagating grounds for our favorite plants, including ferns, thalictrum, hostas, rhododendrons, and azaleas.

Less trouble than a water garden, a bog garden can be prepared easily by excavating the area twelve to eighteen inches deep and installing waterproof material to cover the excavation. People debate as to whether it should be watertight, or perforated here and there to allow some water to escape. Since the bog could dry up in periods of low rainfall, a simple access to water should be provided, such as burying a soaker hose in the garden during construction. Before earth is put back in the hole, sturdy stepping-stone

paths should be installed so the gardener doesn't have to step into the bog. Cinder blocks topped with decorative flagstones are effective. The removed soil is enriched with organic matter to provide both nutrition and increased water retention. Then, it is shoveled back in the hole in a dry state, so you can step around and plant without getting mucky feet.

Plants should be placed in this new environment with their pots on, so you have plenty of chance to move things around until you find the arrangement you like. Once you're satisfied, remove the pots, plant your specimens, and then flood the area with water. Since this is a great place for weeds to grow, the garden should be mulched heavily. A lovely smelling plant, sweet flag *(Acorus calamus),* makes a weed-deterring ground cover for a bog garden. It has bold cream-and-yellow spiky leaves.

Once established, this marshy space is easy to care for, and rewards us with all manner of robust plant growth. Just like a water garden, it will become a mecca for butterflies, dragonflies, damselflies, toads, and frogs.

There is a much more grandiose use for the bog garden: as a purifier of water for an adjacent larger water garden with fish. Certain bog plants perform the vital functions of settling sediment and encouraging positive bacterial growth. These include yellow flag

iris *(Iris pseudacorus),* dwarf cattail *(Typha minima);* and, according to some studies, the umbrella palm, *Cyperus alternifolius.* A pump brings water from the big pool to the higher elevation bog garden, and a waterfall often is used to tumble it back into the fishpond below.

Ornamental bog gardens are moist, alive places to try new things. An example is the skunk cabbage, a unique member of the aroid family that has its own ecosystem. It provides centrally heated housing for small creatures seeking refuge from the cold. Its magnificent spathe, which is a leaflike bract that protects the flowers, is used by top flower arrangers in bouquets.

Skunk cabbage is discounted by many because when its leaves are crushed, a rotten smell results. However, this odor is interpreted differently by different people: some even like it, since it reminds them of their happy childhood days slogging through wet marshes. The experimental rewards of growing skunk cabbage from seed are great for children: in a few years, there will be a big, speckled-leaved plant that has its own temperature system and live-in pets. As it grows and produces its flower, the skunk cabbage generates enough heat to pop right out of the

snow in springtime; amazingly, it keeps its temperature far above freezing—around seventy-two degrees—for weeks on end. This makes it a natural home for nearby little animals such as spiders and bees. One member of the aroid family houses "arum" frogs, which find plenty of fellow resident insects on which to dine. Naturally, the attraction of insects to these plants increases their chances for effective pollination.

There is both an eastern *(Symplocarpus foetidus)* and a western *(Lysichitum americanum)* skunk cabbage, and they are quite different, the western variety growing much larger and reflecting the plant's tropical origins. It gives forth gorgeous chartreuse and golden spathes. These protect the spadix, a long array of tightly packed fleshy flowers. Flower arrangers cut the leaves of the plant and plunge them immediately into warm water: This removes the skunky odor.

While some are holding their noses as they read this, remember the solution to the odor problem is simple; as you would with any smelly object—for instance, an alcoholic uncle—just be sure to place it downwind of the patio on which you entertain guests.

Chapter Seven

THE YOUNG MAN HAD arranged his six-foot frame comfortably over her recliner chair in the recreation room. With the fingers of one hand, he raked the hair out of his eyes, a signal to Louise that he was about to tell her something. "So, did you know I talked to Janie today, Mrs. Eldridge? She's doing better, with her, uh, condition." Chris Radebaugh, an able student who tossed math and science terms around with abandon, found the word "diarrhea" simply too mortifying to say out loud.

Chris, eighteen, had dropped over tonight, obviously with nothing better to do on Saturday night than visit Janie's parents. He was their younger daughter's bosom buddy, or more, perhaps: Louise could no longer tell. He'd been acting like a lost puppy since Janie left for Mexico City, shooting desultory baskets by himself at the neighborhood backboard when he came home from his summer job, dropping in frequently to compare notes on news of the girl. The rangy youth had stayed for dinner, eagerly eating up the portion that she had prepared for her absent houseguest. Now, having helped with the dishes, he was staying to watch a political program coming up on Channel Five. As Louise saw his hair slide into his eyes again, she wondered if he would get it cut before leaving for Princeton in a few weeks to begin his freshman year. She knew his poet mother, Nora, would leave the issue to Chris. *The kid is a math whiz,* she reflected, *and look at Einstein's hair.*

"I'm glad to hear Janie's improving. All in all, I think she's having a great time, don't you, Chris?"

"Yeah," he said, lazily waving a hand in the air, "but I sure miss her, though I don't know if she misses me. She has a bunch of new friends. Maybe we'll even get to meet them."

"That sounds ominous," said Bill, raising his eyebrows in mock concern. "Does that mean they're coming *here?*"

Chris laughed. "I don't know, Mr. Eldridge. Maybe, knowing Janie."

Her husband was crouched on the sofa, spending the few minutes before the program started by busily flipping through the TV channels, the remote cocked at the TV set as if he were holding it at gunpoint. Bill had flashed a game on the sports channel and then rapidly moved to another channel. Chris sat forward with a jolt, barely controlling his torment, wanting to rip the wielder from his host's hand and go back to sports. Louise concealed a smile. This desire for control of the remote must be a gender thing.

Bill's nonchalance tonight must be a cover-up, she thought. Tomorrow he would leave for Vienna. He had made her jittery when he informed her about the trip: it required secrecy on both his part and hers. He was dealing with the theft of nuclear materials by eastern European Mafia types organized in a worldwide ring. Apparently he had some crucial information to communicate to the International Atomic Energy Association. That was all she was permitted to know: She was to avoid telling anyone where he had gone or when he would return, and to be suspicious of strangers. Living on the edge again, she reflected, wasn't much fun.

They heard the front door open and soon were joined by their elusive houseguest.

Louise was perplexed by Jay. He had made himself into a virtual hermit since he arrived on Tuesday, sticking to his room after breakfast, sometimes slipping out in the afternoon and not returning until late: behavior that bordered on the rude. He didn't even join them for a minute or two in the evening to talk; it made her wonder if he wasn't in worse trouble than he was telling her.

She sometimes caught snatches of his conversations with Charlie Hurd, the mannerless research assistant. In these overheard snippets, the strain in her friend's voice betrayed the high level of tension under which he was operating. Although she was only hearing one side of the conversation, it was clear that Jay was pleased with the information he got from the young reporter, but was having demands put on him by Charlie to reveal the full extent of the story. But what story?

And Jay was about to commit the mortal sin of houseguests: overstaying his welcome. Her next guests, the perennial plant people, were due Tuesday, and she had told him this. But when she saw him as he came and went from the house, he would mention leaving next *Friday:* He was oblivious not only to time, but also to her personal timetable. Was she about to have an embarrassing confrontation with her dear old friend?

What was most disconcerting to Louise were Jay's evening prowls, although Bill had urged her to ignore these nocturnal wanderings. They could hear him foraging around through the woods, bumping into bushes and trees. Once, Louise was convinced she heard him poking around in the toolshed, and Bill teased her that she was afraid he was putting her tools out of order. Probably he was just an insomniac. He drank coffee at a heavy rate, and brought home big containers of it from fast-food places.

But what hurt the most was the way he had cleverly barricaded his room, so that any attempts she might have made to snoop into his possessions or into his writing were thwarted. It was embarrassing to know he thought of her as a sneak: On the other side of his door, he had piled a heap of clothes, probably dirty ones, for he never requested the use of the washer or dryer, and she would have had to shove the whole bunch out of position to open the door. Even so, in the crack that was available to her, she could see discarded food wrappers and paper cups strewn on the desk alongside a slim black computer.

What a frustrating man! To think she might have married him!

"Hi, folks," he said now, looking sheepish. Hoping, Louise suspected, that the charming, Irish, crooked smile he sent her way would assuage her feelings. For try as she might to feel otherwise, she felt . . . neglected.

Louise introduced him to Chris. In an effort to explain his absences, Jay said, "I've been writing, as you know, and going off to spend all the time I can with Melissa. Trying to keep things on track."

"No need to explain to us, Jay," said Bill good-naturedly, then zeroed in on the program. It was hosted by Jack Lederle. Louise knew Lederle, because his independent PBS news show was produced in one of the studios at WTBA-TV. Though his news staff operated in a separate studio and a rarified and separate world, she and Lederle sometimes met in the halls, at which times he would quippishly ask her, "And how does your garden grow?" She would reply just as quippishly, "Great, with the aid of blood meal and green sand."

Tonight's program was an in-depth look at the two presidential campaigns. Lederle tagged the campaign as "one of the most scurrilous in the history of American politics." He profiled the principal players, including the President's campaign chief and Tom Paschen. Louise was bemused to hear about some of the chief of staff's more famous political stunts, which had become public lore.

"Bill," she whispered to her husband, "isn't it ironic that Tom Paschen used to be considered the *bête noire* of politics, and now these people are doing him one better."

He looked at her sagely. "The difference is, Tom has a line he won't step across; these characters don't."

The focus shifted to Franklin Rawlings and Willie Upchurch and Ted French. There was taped footage showing the three men clustered together like the proverbial insiders, in the confines of Goodrich's campaign office in Washington. Louise couldn't help thinking of the trio of Watergate figures, Ehrlichman, Haldeman, and Mitchell. Innuendos and charges against the President were touched on briefly, including a tabloid piece purporting to tell of the peccadillos of the popular Mrs. Fairchild.

Chris, sitting forward now in rapt attention, said, "They've even gone low enough to smear the President's wife: what creeps." Then came the mention of the most serious charge of all, Fairchild's alleged responsibility for the murder of a file clerk back in the early 1960s, to cover up his part in the assassination of the president of South Vietnam. The word *cover-up* electrified Louise, for she remembered the way Nixon was brought down for lying about the Watergate affair.

"Womanizing, maybe," murmured Bill. "Excessive drinking, probably. But that last one sounds like bullpucky to me. Well, Jay, what do you think of that story?" Jay stood at the door, leaning against the door frame, a bland expression on his face.

"It's pretty bad stuff, especially that charge about knocking off the army clerk." He looked at Bill warily. "Now, if you'll excuse me, I think I'll go in and do a little more work tonight." He waved at Chris. "Nice to meet a friend of Janie's."

Louise watched him disappear through the dining room. What a strange reaction for a man who had been as attracted to political events as a dog was to a bone. What had happened to him over the years? And what was he writing there in his room, anyway? She suspected that, in spite of his seeming indifference, it could be politics. Or maybe it was about the bitter argument currently splitting the U.S. Supreme Court about overturning prisoner rights: That would be right up his alley.

With Bill leaving Sunday, she would be left to say the unpleasant words to their difficult guest. She would have to inform him he was being kicked out of his digs in just three short days. How did one put that tactfully?

Chapter Eight

ONE THING ABOUT NORA Radebaugh, no matter how funny something was, she rarely laughed: If one could get a smile out of Nora, that was considered the maximum reward. The smoky woman with the handsome looks so attractive to men, and who had loved her share of them, according to stories, had become one of Louise's close friends.

When Louise came to call on this Tuesday morning, Nora, wearing striped bib overalls, was on both knees in her backyard herb garden. She was doing some serious weeding and pruning of the plants; an aromatic cloud of released herb oils surrounded her. More enchanting, Louise thought, than any perfume. Nora looked up and pulled the black earplugs out of her ears and let them fall down around her neck; they were attached to a tape player that made a lump in the breastbone pocket of her overalls. *"Buon giorno,"* she said, a playful light in her eyes as she sat back on her haunches.

"Sorry to bother you when you're working," said Louise.

"No bother. I'm refreshing my Italian while I weed my fretty chervil and rosemary. Ron and I leave tomorrow for our trip to Tuscany."

"I just have a little news. Wanted you to know I'm moving a houseguest over to the Mougeys'."

With glossy brown hair falling gracefully over her face, Nora looked up at Louise, her amusement just barely detectable in the faint smile around her mouth. *"Grazie,"* she said, in a low, throaty Italian accent. "I've been watching your friend come and go for a few days now and wanted to meet him. He's very attractive. *Un buon uomo.* Irish, perhaps?"

Louise laughed and crouched down beside her neighbor. "Irish as the Blarney stone: Jay McCormick. But let me warn you: he's not very sociable. Too busy with his, uh, writing and so forth. I've been feeding the koi while the Mougeys are gone, and Mary said to use the house if we needed it, and we do—we're overflowing with guests."

Nora stopped her work and slid to a sitting position on the ground, thoughtfully waving the weeder still clutched in her hand as if she might give Louise a good spanking with it.

Her admonishment was gentle: "My dear, is there no end to these houseguests?"

"But they insisted on staying with me."

Nora became more direct. "Maybe it's time you learn that you have a life of your own. You deserve some privacy. What are you doing with your life, Louise?"

"All the company were relatives—both sets of parents, cousins, second cousins. And as for Jay, he was a surprise. I haven't seen him in twenty years and certainly didn't expect him to drop in. And the people coming tomorrow, well, that's all business-related; it will do me a lot of good."

"It will?" Nora actually chuckled, in total disbelief. "I see you racing back and forth to work, then running out again to shop, coming back loaded down with groceries in your arms. Giving parents yard tours and taking them on excursions to the Capitol. Taking toddlers for walks in the neighborhood . . ." She pointed to Louise's lean arms, revealed by her brief T-shirt. "Look at you: You're even losing weight. Are you *really* Superwoman?"

Louise sank down on the grassy spot next to Nora. As usual, her perceptive poet neighbor had gotten right to the nub of things. "I've had a lifetime of experience with houseguests, Nora. It's just something you have to put up with if you're a foreign service officer's wife."

"Like bearing the stigmata, perhaps?" Again, those smile lines near Nora's mouth had deepened.

"Kind of," Louise agreed good-heartedly. "Now, London, that was positively the worst. Let me tell you about London." Then she reeled off what she could remember of those two hectic years living on North Row in Mayfair in an apartment larger than the Eldridges required. The youthful friends of friends of theirs, dirty, tired, and hungry, with backpacks strapped on their bodies, ringing the doorbell at midnight after having made their way from the continent or Scotland. American politicians. Friends and former friends and relatives who hadn't been heard from in years.

"You mean you let them all in?" Nora's dark eyebrows went up in astonishment. "Didn't they even phone to warn you they were coming? Why didn't you just tell them to go elsewhere?"

Louise airily waved a hand. "Oh, you don't do that in the foreign service. In the first place, you're getting free lodging. Anyway, that was *our* arrangement. Since the American taxpayer is footing your housing costs, you can't turn away any American from the door. Of course, we had foreigners, too."

"I can believe anything."

Louise remembered well some of the European figures, contacts of Bill in his undercover activities, some undoubtedly ex-criminals and enemies of one state or another, dropping in and holing up for a few days in the back bedroom. Like Jay was doing right now. "These were old friends or associates of Bill's, some of them people making a change to London, who didn't want to move into one of those little efficiency apartments they give to singles."

Nora was smiling now. "And I suppose you cooked for them all. Where did you shop, the food halls of Harrods?"

"That was hard," Louise admitted, her arms aching even as she remembered the bulging plastic carryalls she would manage in either hand after visiting Selfridge's or Marks & Spencer. "No American woman has the right arm and hand muscles to survive it," she added wryly. "Actually, only British women, and they train for years to do it. I finally broke down and hailed taxis."

"It must have been nice to live in London."

"Quite wonderful, really, but dangerous, because of the IRA bombs." She decided not to tell Nora that Bill had nearly been killed by a bomb planted under a car on his route to work. It was too unpleasant and personal a memory. "We had an enforced busy social life, of course, but the girls flourished. They went to British schools. I took a history class, and volunteered with the other wives to help needy children."

"And entertained houseguests."

"Yes." They lapsed into silence.

Finally, Nora said, "You've come so far with your career. You could take another big step: Complete your emancipation from your old life by learning how to say 'no' to prospective houseguests."

Louise laughed. "I don't know, Nora. That old life isn't even over, you know. But as for turning away unwanted visitors, I agree. I have to be more firm."

"I'll keep an eye out for your Jay McCormick, but of course I can't see much because of the woods. Is he a friend of yours, or friend of Bill's?"

"An old college chum of mine." A chum who had disappointed her, for after that first couple of sentiment-soaked hours in Joe's Raw Bar, they had exchanged no more private reminiscences, and at this rate, with him hopelessly distracted with writing and daughter Melissa, they never would. "He doesn't need attention. He very much wants to be left alone. I just didn't want you to think anyone had broken into Mary's house."

Nora stood up, voluptuous even in her grimy overalls. Her face had become solemn, almost drawn. "I hope you will be surrounded with people. Do be careful, won't you?"

There was something unsettling in the woman's eyes. "Nora, you're not having one of your premonitions of danger?"

Nora slowly nodded her head. "I'm afraid I am. What its focus is, I'm not sure. I only beg you to tell me that you'll take care."

Louise promised she would, and bid her good-bye. Her neighbor, with her mysterious powers of extrasensory perception, had warned her once before, and she had ignored that warning.

She wouldn't do that this time, she told herself.

She hurried back across the street; she had little time to finish some last-minute work in the garden. Popping in a few mature nicotiana plants was her very last project before the perennial people arrived. Later, she would have the unpleasant task of gently shoving Jay McCormick out of her house into his new quarters across the street. At the moment, however, he and his car were gone, and she had a little reprieve.

First, she needed to put out the trash containers for the weekly pickup this afternoon. Bill's job, normally. The holly-shrouded garbage area concealed two big cans residing on a rolling cart. She took the cart by the handle and gave it a good tug, and then screamed at what she uncovered.

Crouching behind the cans was a man.

"Oh, *God*!" she cried, and jumped back.

He rose slowly from a crouch, but kept his knees bent and held his hands out to either side, like a karate expert moving into position for an attack.

"What are you doing in my yard?" she snapped. "Are you snooping in our *trash*?"

Stocky, with black hair and olive skin, the man wore dark glasses, a dark turtleneck, and a sports jacket. Trendy for New York, maybe, but out of place in Sylvan Valley. And what she noticed next made her mouth fall agape: the large bulge in one side of his jacket. Had it not seemed ridiculous in the bright light of a day in the northern Virginia suburbs, she would have sworn he was carrying a pistol. In fact, she realized he was, and her nerves clanged to attention. Adrenaline rushed through her body, and she tightened her grip on the trash cart.

"Lady," he said in an oily tone, "you won't believe this, but I'm in real estate."

There was more than a touch of hysteria in her frightened laugh. "You're right, it's hard to believe you," she said, and eased the trash cart back a little, to familiarize herself with its weight, perhaps to use it as a shield in case he pulled the gun.

As if her worst fears were being realized, his right hand had moved over toward the bulge in the jacket. Not in her wildest dreams could she imagine anyone wanting to kill her, at least not lately. "Why don't you just get out of here," she demanded shakily.

He was inching toward her, smiling, still with his hand in a ready position. "Let's put it this way," he said. "Why don't we call it a draw?"

"Why don't we *not*!" she shouted, and rammed the cart right at him, and with one motion upended it. The tops flew off the two cans; a stream of papers, plastic peanuts, catalogues, and plump garbage bags cascaded over him. She didn't wait to see more, but heard him cry out in shock as she raced around the addition and into the house. With clumsy fingers she turned the lock and stood inside the door, trembling. All was quiet in the world outside.

It only took her a moment to realize she had blown it. She should have left him alone. But instead she had to use force. Now, she was too embarrassed to call 911. What if he was what he said he was: a realtor, who was snooping around where he didn't belong?

She had to find out. Quickly she reopened the door and went outside. Hearing an engine being started, she ran down the front path in time to see a low black car turning out of the cul-de-sac. He was gone as mysteriously as he had arrived.

Then she recalled the big gray foreign car wheeling around Dogwood Court on the day before. It had not seemed remarkable at the time, since it came and left so quickly. What the cars had in common, she now remembered, was that both had tinted windows so the driver could barely be seen. Jay McCormick had to be the reason: Someone was bent on tracking him down, and at least had found the house where he lived.

Perhaps it was just as well he was moving across the street.

Out of curiosity, she followed the path next to the addition that the stranger must have used to flee her yard. She stood there, arms akimbo, staring at the ruin. He had plowed through her finest woods garden, bruising prized hostas and knocking over tall golden spires of ligularia, thalictrum, and white anemone. Worse yet, his path took him straight through her front garden, where he had trampled her toad lilies, which were just coming into magnificent spotted bloom!

Her cousin's child, Sally, had been equally bumbling, but not nearly as big.

Then she turned and went into the house, swallowed her pride, and called 911. She would feel foolish if the police discovered the man was a realtor. But as far as she knew, realtors didn't carry weapons. After all, that was no way to sell a house.

Chapter Nine

TESSIE STRAHAN WOULDN'T TAKE no for an answer. When she phoned, Louise did not come right out and say, "I'm afraid you can't stay at my house," an action Nora would have applauded. Instead, she merely pointed out to this past president of the Perennial Plant Society that it would be more convenient for her and her two colleagues to stay at the Hilton in Washington, where their convention was being held.

"But Louise, we're writing that big article about you," said Tessie, in a voice that sounded like a nail gun. "That's going to take sitting down together. Besides, it will be restful to get away from those two hundred growers and designers at the convention for a couple of nights. We won't be any trouble. You don't know us. We're the kind who pitch in and help a body. And we all want to see your garden. We bet it's wonderful."

Garden: Louise quaked inwardly. These rising expectations scared her. The gardens had been dandied up, true, but were still like patched-up patients who had been in very bad car accidents. *Oh, little Sally,* she thought, *how you have marked the world.* And now the clumsy stranger had diminished yet another one of her prize beds; it was yet to be seen whether the flower stalks were broken or merely bent.

"Then if you're sure," said Louise resignedly, "I'll expect you later this afternoon—and in time for dinner, of course."

"With setting our exhibits up in the convention hall, we may not get there until right around six," said Tessie. "Don't worry about dinner."

"Oh, but I already have it planned."

"Barbara McNeil and Donna Moore are the others, you remember, and Barbara is a gourmet cook: She's bringing some special fixings for the meal. You'll no doubt have a few basics. She has morel mushrooms, special herbs, pasta from Pennsylvania, things like that."

Louise thought of her carefully prepared fast-fix meal. "Oh, well, that will be fun," she said, wondering if it would be at all. "See you later. It will be wonderful to get better acquainted."

She had the vegetables prepped by the time she heard the puttering of the motor of Jay's old car, as it gave a last little flutter of rebellion after the motor was turned off. When he walked in the kitchen, she could see the man was in worse shape than when he had arrived a week ago: his color poor, his clothes scruffier, and lines of worry carving his face. He smiled nonetheless, that familiar, crooked smile that used to get right inside her.

"So you're really kicking me out."

"Those women are definitely coming. I'll help you move your things across the street."

"No way, Louise. I don't want to cause you more trouble. I don't have that much to move."

She busied herself putting the extra vegetables back into their plastic bags. "I'm sorry we haven't had more chance to talk since you've been here, Jay."

He watched her work with a stare like a sleepwalker, and she could tell that even now his mind wasn't here—it was far away. "You have to forgive me for being rude. It's just that I've been so nervous about Melissa and whether she'll still be there when it's time for me to pick her up."

"This is the eve of departure for the two of you, then."

"Friday's the big day." He leaned back, crossed his arms on his chest, and looked as if he might actually relax and share some of his thoughts with her. "Three days is all I'll need to finish my work. I have it all scheduled with Lannie, who of course doesn't know I'm already here; she thinks I'm flying in from California. I pick up a new car Friday morning, then swing over and get Melissa and her things, and we start our road trip across the country back to Sacramento." He swayed a little, as if overwhelmed with fatigue.

In two strides she had reached him and steadied him from falling. "Good heavens, Jay, you're dead tired, I can tell. Why don't you sit down; I'll fix you some dinner."

"No, no." He pulled away from her and walked slowly into the dining room and took hold of the back of a Hitchcock chair for support. "All right, that's a good idea: I'll eat something, but not dinner. Just coffee and a roll, if you have one.'' He lowered himself shakily into the chair. ''You're right, Louise, I'm worn out. I feel like I'm about a hundred years old, but I'll go to your friend's house and hit the sack tonight and feel great tomorrow.''

She made a fresh pot of coffee, defrosted some sticky buns in the microwave, and chopped a couple of peaches into big hunks, then brought the food and sat down at the dining room table with him. He rapidly consumed two of the pastries and devoured the peach chunks. Seeming to feel better, he gave her one of his slow smiles. ''How can I ever say to you the things I want to say? One of these days—soon—you'll understand what this is all about.''

''Look, your life is private; we don't need to know everything. I'm only sorry Bill is gone and won't be home in time to say good-bye to you, and that you won't get a chance to meet Janie.''

''But I want our families to meet, and soon. My life is going to settle down, there's no doubt about it: just Melissa and me in our little house.'' He reached out a hand and put it on top of hers and gave it a squeeze, and they sat there companionably, as old friends should.

She hated to spoil the mood by bringing up the subject of the strange man who had intruded upon her yard that morning, and the fact that she had called the police to check him out. When she described him, Jay chuckled. ''Mafia, maybe? But seriously, Louise, it probably was what you suspected: a real estate broker. They're always poking around, and the way you treated him, I doubt he'll ever make a cold call in *this* cul-de-sac again. It certainly hasn't anything to do with me, I can tell you that. The people who would be looking for me are 'suits,' suits who would look mad as hell.''

She drew in her breath in surprise. If that menacing man

hadn't sought Jay, who was he after? She would have mentioned the gray car, but now it seemingly had nothing to do with Jay. No, more likely to do with her husband. Bill's trip to Vienna had plunged them right back into the nervous world of spying.

Later, Jay packed his clothes and computer and she helped load things in his car. She promised that Charlie Hurd would be the only one to know his whereabouts. She watched him drive far into Mary Mougey's driveway, out of sight of anyone entering Dogwood Court. He left nothing behind in the room, not the smallest scrap of paper.

Then she was left alone for an hour, sans children, sans husband, sans houseguest, free to worry about strangers in the neighborhood and the state of her garden and to clean up the guest bedroom. She was glad her house would be filled with company tonight. It was one thing to confront a pistol-packing stranger by daylight, and quite another to encounter him at night.

Chapter Ten

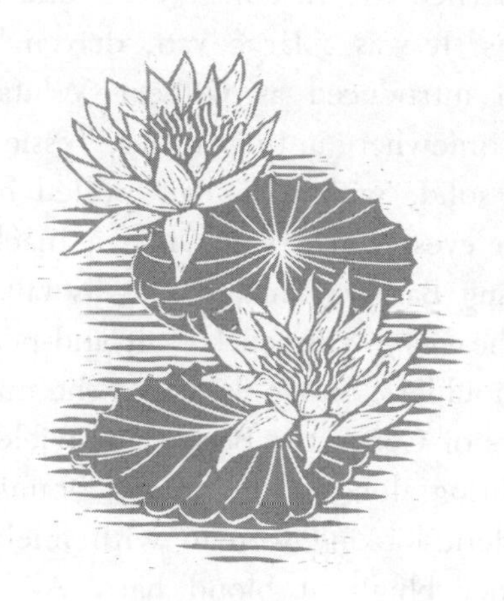

WHEN SHE HEARD THE car door slam out in the driveway, Louise went out to greet her guests. Looking straight through the woods, she was dismayed to see Jay McCormick's jalopy backing out of the driveway across the street. As she walked forward, she caught a glimpse of him. He wore a turtleneck, his hair was slicked straight back, and he had an anonymous expression on his hollow-eyed face. Altogether, this made him resemble no person she had ever seen before. It reminded her of how her own husband had altered his appearance when necessary. She felt a pang of guilt at having displaced Jay from her guest room. Maybe she should have made the P.P.S. guests double up. Now, instead of staying safely at the Mougeys, Jay was going to Great Falls again, to see that nothing went wrong with his plans.

Then she turned to greet her guests and help them unload their bags. It was a large van, driven by a man that Tessie Strahan introduced as Gilbert Whitson. All three women were somewhere in their fifties. Tessie was about five feet tall, and solid, with dark hair pulled back in a bun, intense brown eyes, and a voice like a machine gun. The throaty-sounding Barbara McNeil was as tall as Louise but fifty pounds heavier, with curly salt-and-pepper hair that reached her shoulders. She looked as if she might have come out of the days of Conan the Barbarian, wielding sword and shield and fighting alongside her man. Donna Moore was a muscular, athletic-looking woman with finely chiseled features under her blunt-cut blond hair. All of them were strong and competent, Louise realized, able to heave around fifty-pound flats of plants and run large nurseries.

All three felt at home with Louise before they ever set a step on her mossy path.

Gil, a garden designer, was different. He watched her warily as they stood in the path together. He was tall and graceful, his graying blond hair balding a little, and his unusual green eyes yellow near the pupils, like a cat's. His sunburned facial skin seemed excessively wrinkled, and she guessed it was from too much time in the sun. The four had ridden down from the New York/Philadelphia area and apparently were old friends; Gil teased the women constantly as he helped them gather food packages, luggage, and what would be unneeded coats in Washington's late July.

''Nice to be here, Mrs. Eldridge.''

"Please call me Louise."

"These gals intend to camp at your place indefinitely. Don't believe them when they say they're checking out in two days." He hefted a large suitcase that obviously weighed a lot. "Look at Tessie's suitcase: Just guess how long it will take you to get rid of her."

"Now, Gil," said Tessie in clipped tones, her brown eyes flashing merrily, "it's just the two nights. And who knows? Maybe some other folks will come out to see you tomorrow, Louise."

"That will be nice," she said automatically. She thought of Nora's warnings: She wasn't at all sure it would be nice to be deluged with strangers after she had spent all day in downtown Washington on a shoot that was already a "wild card," as Marty called it. This meant she, Marty, John, and crew would be winging it because it was impossible to script in advance. Nevertheless, she continued with her mild prevarications, the automatic impulse of twenty years of training as a foreign service wife: "Everybody's welcome."

It was gratifying when the guests exclaimed in delight over the front garden with its blue-berried mahonia and toad lilies, propped up after the stranger's destructive journey through it. They continued exclaiming as they walked the path through the woods. They were particularly impressed with the pergola.

"Except it's *bare,* my dear," said Tessie. "Why isn't it planted with vines?"

"I'd wanted grapes—"

"Too shady."

"Or clematis—"

"Also too shady."

Louise paused. "And then I was at a loss as to just what else I would like to grow there."

"Well, honey," said the tall Barbara, "I can give you several suggestions."

"But then my husband and I"—Louise threw in husband for further moral support as she noticed a certain ganging up—"decided we very much liked it bare."

As if the earth had just moved, Tessie stood stock-still under the midsection of the long pergola, and looked up. To Louise, those exposed cross-beams looming against the hugely tall woods were pure poetry. "*Like* it that way, does he? We'll have to talk to him about that."

"Unfortunately, he isn't going to be here."

"Oh, what a shame. Where is he?"

"Off on a business trip." She turned to Gil, who was helping to carry in the baggage before going to Washington to check into the convention. "Gil, what is your specialty?"

"I'm a koi doctor."

"Coy?" She grinned.

"No, koi, as in *fish*."

"Oh. You treat koi, the big carp?"

"Yes," he said, with a broad smile.

"Gil is not only a koi doctor, but a *marvelous* designer, and his gardens show it," effused Tessie.

"But playing doctor to fish is more fun, and it brings in a nice extra income."

Louise laughed. "I know what you mean about that."

A flash of recognition passed over his face. "Yes, I'm sure you do. You're the one who's the spokesman on those Atlas Mower ads, right?" He gave her a genuine smile that lit up his face, and it was as if she had passed some ambiguous test of trust.

"How do you care for koi?"

Gil waggled his head a little, a man used to expressing things with his hands, but whose hands at the moment were full. ''Very carefully, Louise.'' He gave her a conspiratorial smile. ''Mostly with over-the-counter drugs. Sometimes I shoot them up with antibiotics that I get from a vet. I don't want you to think I have a medical degree: I'm one of those entrepreneurs who have come into the field.''

''Hmmm,'' said Louise, ''are there many koi to doctor?''

''Loads of them. They're the rage of boomers who don't know what to do with their money.''

''You sound like the producer of *Gardening with Nature.* Marty Corbin always says baby boomers are responsible for the upsurge in gardening.''

He laughed. ''Aren't they responsible for the upsurge in *everything?* They're the ones who are going out and buying koi, and now there are koi clubs all over the country, did you know that?''

''I'll have to tell my neighbors. They worry so much about their fish that they could use a fish support group. They have a pond in the yard across the street and I'm currently the caretaker.'' An idea was forming: A segment on koi would be perfect for her cohost, John, to handle. ''I wish we could do something on this for the program we're taping tomorrow, but it's probably too late. We'd need a fishpond handy.''

He looked at her intently. ''That's *absolutely* doable: There's a koi pond in the courtyard at the Hilton; I'm sure we could persuade the hotel to cooperate. I could give you a nice interview on how to take care of the fish, what to do if they get sick, and when to consult a vet specialist, who can perform operations to fix lacerations and torn fins. We would need to arrange with the hotel to let me feed the fish. They're absolutely spectacular when they all concentrate in a little feeding frenzy.''

Louise thought quickly. After she pumped Whitson as

much as she could on the subject of koi, she had to get through to Marty Corbin so he in turn could alert John Batchelder. Somehow, she knew John would love the topic. "How many koi doctors are there, Gil?"

"That's the trouble," he said, his eyes shining with sincerity. "There are not enough koi experts for the number of koi around. Sort of like the shortage of physicians in America." He grinned good-naturedly, and she couldn't help smiling back at him.

They arranged a meeting time for the next day, and then Gil left. She was kind of sorry to see him go, because she had an inkling that this evening might prove difficult.

The Fishy Thing About a Water Garden

THE COUNTRY APPEARS TO be awash in water gardens. One reason is the serene attraction of flowers floating on water. Another is the good-natured, colorful fish, the *koi,* that have swum into the hearts of fish fanciers and weekend gardeners alike.

The intriguing nature of these aristocrats of the carp family, the most popular of which are patterned in red, white, and black, has led to a burgeoning of water gardens, to say nothing of koi clubs, koi competitions, and even a national koi convention. One koi fancier carts her fish about in a specially made "koimobile." These fish are long-lived: the grandpa of them is said to have died at the age of 215 years in Japan in the 1970s.

For the laid-back gardener, even a simple water garden may seem like more work, and it is: a big step up from the bog garden, for instance, in cleaning and maintenance. But there are many who are willing to make the trade-off. They will dig, line the hole with PVC or a formed pool liner, install filters, and spend large amounts of money buying magnificent water lilies, lotus, iris, and other support flowers to sprawl about on the watery surface.

Adding fish, and especially koi, expands the responsibilities many-fold, for suddenly we must take care of those exquisite swimming creatures, who engage us much like children. They clamor toward us in a stunning display of bright color at the sound of our whistle or the clap of our hands. They will look at us with beguiling eye movements. Then they will gently suck our fingers as we feed them at poolside, and who else will do that, except certain political consultants?

Since koi have no stomachs, they must be fed frequently, at least twice a day (except in winter), with pellets and live food, such as earthworms. And the pool itself requires daily maintenance and testing, for all is balance in the fishpond.

Water flower fanciers find that flowers must take second place to the koi. They are rooting fish, and like nothing better than to nose about in plant dirt. Some say that if

baby koi are put straight into a pool with plants, they will get used to their presence and leave them alone. Others recommend elaborate underground chimney netting systems to protect the plants. Fortunately, the water lily is one variety with which koi can live in peace. To avoid problems, some clever pool designers simply place a bog garden near the koi pond in order to have plants nearby but out of harm's way.

Clean water is essential to healthy koi, affecting not only the fish's health but also its color. Those brilliant swirls and spots of red and black on white can fade and lose their sheen unless given the best conditions. It helps to have the finest biological filtration system, and it doesn't hurt to be an engineer or a chemist. (An editor of *KOI USA*, the magazine of the Associated Koi Clubs of America, owner of two dozen koi, was teased about her real motives when it was learned she was marrying a water engineer.) The basic problem is to remove the voluminous wastes of these robust-sized fish without clogging the filter system. As far as the method chosen, one koi fancier declared it is a choice between paying capital costs at the outset or paying maintenance costs later on. Improvising can lead to problems. Hobbyists should be aware of simple basics such as the gallonage of their pool, for adding too much of anything to the water can endanger the fish's very existence.

Koi can cost big money, ranging from a few dollars for a small fish without a pedigree, to many thousands of dollars for a fine specimen from Japan. The winner of the all-Japan show will command six figures. The Japanese started this fish craze by breeding these carp back in the 1700s, but did not export them until after World War II. The fish have many names, with Kohako, Sanke, and Showa the most popular breeds. In Japan, koi competitions create a frenzy of interest, and it is no different in the U.S., and particularly California. Unfortunately, as in all competitions, contestants can bicker over the judging, proving koi owners are no different from Little League parents. As one hobbyist said, koi retailers and breeders aren't the best judges, because they have a natural bias: the best judge, in his opinion, is the hobbyist.

People who get involved in raising koi soon learn to become amateur vets, because these fish can succumb to a list of diseases that fills thirteen pages in an eight-point-type koi handbook. There is more literature coming out every day in veterinary medicine journals about operating on injured fins and lacerations in the fish's side. Many hobbyists learn to treat their own fish. Often, antibiotics are put in the water, but sometimes the fish is injected, and bigger fish undergo operations while anaesthetized. This is done by a vet or a trained koi "doctor," whose num-

bers are increasing, since all vets don't choose to toy with koi.

Breeding is another challenge. One seasoned hobbyist said, "Just don't do it." Fish sex is not fun for the female koi, as the males tend to bang her against the side of the pool to flog the eggs out of her body. (Could this be a payback because female koi invariably win at koi shows, being rounder and fuller?) One owner had his lovely lady koi jolted clear out of the pool. The 100,000 or more eggs laid, and the males' chemical reactions to them, create enormous changes in pool chemistry. That's why those who do breed koi often use separate holding pools. Next comes the job of culling the thousands of koi fry, mainly for color. This is done periodically until specimens with good color potential remain; however, those full, vibrant colors do not emerge for a while, some at six inches, some not until twenty inches, which is why koi can be so expensive.

And then there are the heron: they love to eat koi, and are a major threat. Keeping them out of pools is an engineering feat. Many a koi pond in California, especially, will be tented permanently with net, with multiple pools in one California yard making it look like the ingenious roof of Denver International Airport.

Once you read up on the responsibilities of raising this fish, your choice might be different: even a water garden with a twenty-

foot waterfall may look easier! And some pools are no trouble at all, not even requiring a filter if kept in proper balance with oxygenating plants and an appropriate number of fish. There are other splendid fish besides koi, such as the golden *orfe,* a pretty, smaller variety that always swims with its buddies in schools, likes to leap in the air for the sheer fun of it, and lives more sedately with water plants. They, too, will come when they're called and eat out of your hand.

This is, provided that you haven't already fallen in love with koi.

Chapter Eleven

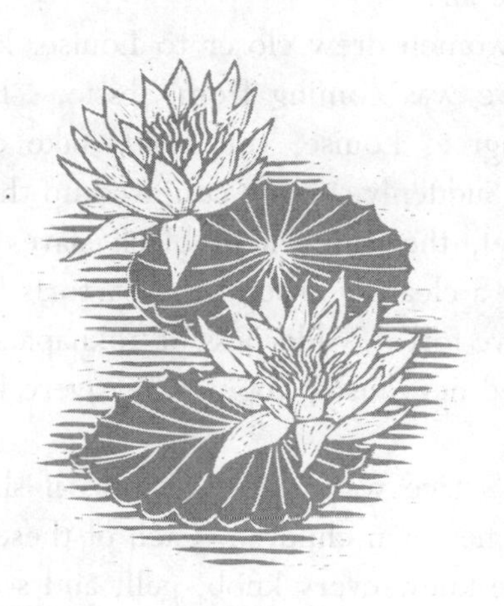

"BUT, DEAR, WE KNOW what it's like to have children tramping in gardens," said Tessie. She was absolving Louise as a priest would a sinner in the confessional for not having perfect gardens out back. "You have done quite well regardless. But—" She stopped in midsentence and looked around her at the trees, many of them twenty times her height.

Barbara took advantage of the pause. "I just love your bog garden, Louise. A nice commitment to skunk cabbages. *Magnificent,* in fact. Did you know Gil uses the western variety for arrangements? He also does fantastic flower arranging, in case you didn't know it.''

Louise was distracted from Barbara's commendation of her swamp plantings by Tessie's ominous ''but'' that was left hanging in the air.

All three women drew closer to Louise, knowing something definitive was coming from Tessie. ''But I think all three of us agree, Louise, you *should* take down some of these trees.'' Suddenly, Louise conjured up the scene from a Faulkner novel, the one where black slaves downed huge trees to make a clearing around the Sartoris family mansion in the primitive forest wilderness of Yoknapatawpha County.

She laughed nervously, hoping they were kidding. ''Take down trees?''

But Tessie's face was serious. It was if she were asking Louise to kill her own children. Each of these trees was her friend and she knew every knob, gall, and scald spot; why, these trees practically had names. ''And, just which trees would you have me take down?'' A huge swath, perhaps, down one side of the yard, from in back of the addition to the bog garden? Or maybe all around the house, to encircle it with open space to a radius of twenty feet or so? Her two mature prize yellowwoods, perhaps?

''There are lots of options, aren't there, girls?'' said Tess, and then described the very scenarios that already were running through Louise's head. There was no mention of touching the elegant yellowwoods: They were after those sweetgums and swamp oaks, Louise knew, just because they were the indigenous trees and probably not as precious in the eyes of these effete gardeners.

Donna, seeming to sense Louise's growing discomfort,

tried to smooth things out a bit. ''Maybe just a couple of trees nearer the house, to provide more sun for perennials.''

''Perennials aren't everything,'' Louise muttered under her breath.

''What did you say, Louise?'' asked Donna.

''Oh, nothing.''

Tessie, having paid no attention to any of this unimportant conversation, crossed her arms, her brown button eyes thoughtful. ''I'd go further than that, Barbara. More than a few trees must go. This yard is a veritable deep woods. It is almost impossible to support any decent amount of perennials.'' She shot a glance at Louise, to be sure she was taking all this in. ''It's nearer the house that she needs to do the work. I'd say, take two out of every three down, in a radius of thirty feet.'' Throwing out her hands in a magnanimous gesture, she said, ''Why, the Eldridges have over half an acre here. They would still have hundreds of trees.''

Louise was feeling shaky. Was it hunger, was it Jay McCormick's departure, or was it talk of tree felling that was getting to her?

She had to speak out and take control of this situation. ''Ladies, I appreciate your ideas. Bill and I will certainly think about them—''

''It is *such* a shame he isn't here,'' said Tessie.

''—but right now, let's go and start dinner. I don't know about you, but I'm famished.''

They went in the house, Tessie looking pointedly at the newly planted santolina, fat and sassy with bright, yellow blossoms. ''And just how long have those plants been here?'' she asked suspiciously.

''Just a week.''

''Not enough sun. They'll languish and die in a season.''

Louise sighed and opened the patio screen door and led the way into the house. In the kitchen, she flipped on the radio to *All Things Considered* on NPR. It being the turn of the half hour, she should hear any breaking political news. When she went to the refrigerator to take out the prepared dinner materials, she heard a click behind her. She turned.

Barbara, tall, gracious, and as intimidating as Wonder Woman, stood in front of the array of brown bags she had brought in earlier and put on the kitchen counter. She had her hand on the radio dial, having just switched it off. ''Sorry, Louise, can you go watch TV news in the other room? I can't work with the radio on.''

''Barbara,'' Louise said in a careful tone, ''I know you brought some things, but I have a dinner prepared. Tell me what you have, and we'll work this out.''

The woman put a hand on Louise's shoulder. ''No, you tell me what *you* have. Chicken breasts, did Tessie tell me? And vegetables, for stir-fry? No problem. Now, I just want you to show me where a few things are and then you can go sit down with Tessie while I take a half hour or so and make you ladies dinner.''

Louise wasn't up for an argument over who would cook dinner, especially when she didn't particularly love cooking. What the heck, she could turn over her kitchen to a bossy stranger.

It was a little harder than she thought it would be. After finding out where the corkscrew and other obscurely placed utensils were, Barbara gently shoved her out of the room.

During all this, Tessie had said nothing, but had found the bar in the cabinet in the recreation room, fetched ice and water in a pitcher, and was ready to offer Louise any kind of drink she wanted. Louise was faint with what her jocular husband called ''guest adjustment,'' those first delicate moments with guests when the hosts found out what they had to put up with. "Why don't I have a nice stiff vodka and tonic?" She was a poor drinker and knew she shouldn't drink at all. It gave her headaches, and sometimes altered her perceptions, as she told Bill. Yet who was there to embarrass? Why, these nervy women might even admire her more if she hung one on and told them all off, tree murderers that they were!

Donna was missing. While Tessie prepared her drink, Louise excused herself and went to hunt down her third houseguest and thwart any evil plans *she* might have.

She found her in Janie's bedroom, which had a large alcove with some sun and therefore housed family plants on glass étagères. Donna was rearranging the plants. Louise gasped at the woman's nerve; she was a little surprised, for she had thought Donna was a more introverted guest.

"I know they may not look so good," the woman apologized, self-consciously brushing her blond hair from her face, "but I just moved them a bit to give them better light."

Louise conjured up a patient tone of voice: "I used Bill's light meter when I arranged these plants, and the differences in light requirements seemed to be insignificant."

Donna reached out and touched Louise's arm in a gesture of repentance. "Louise, it was just an experiment. Let me move them back to their former positions."

Louise pressed her lips together. It was a moment of truth: she was either going to hate these women or love them. "Really, it's okay; let's not bother. We should go back. Tessie is making drinks."

As they passed her kitchen, she gave a nostalgic look in, as if she were someone who had been banned from the premises. "Hi-i," said Barbara, as she heard them pass. She didn't bother to turn to them, but simply gave them a little wave with two waggling fingers raised in the air over her shoulder. Her long curly hair was bobbing above a cookbook she apparently had brought with her, for it looked like none of Louise's. Things were boiling merrily on the stove and the oven was on preheat.

Louise's shoulders sank. Talk about being taken over by enemy hordes. Genghis Khan had nothing on these three. She and Donna went to the recreation room, where Tessie awaited her; she was ensconced in the recliner chair, drink and snacks at her side, a stenographer's notebook and pen in her lap. "Now, Louise, we can't waste a minute. I want to interview you for the story we're doing on you as Plant Person of the Year."

Two could play this game. "Excuse me a minute." Louise went and got herself a notebook and pen out of her Windsor desk, collected her vodka and tonic, and sat near Tessie.

She drank for a moment in silence, thirstier than she thought, downing about a third of the tasty drink. "Okay, Tessie, when you get through asking me questions, can I ask you some?"

"About?"

"Everything I don't know about the Perennial Plant Society, and the perennial plants of the year, and how they're chosen. And how you people get that way, anyhow."

Much later, the Perennial Plant Society people were tucked in their beds and Louise stood alone in the silent living room. Actually, she felt safe and well fed, and was grateful for the company, since Bill was gone and so were most of her neighbors. Nora's somber warning had stuck in her mind. Though it was easy to discount the spooky side of

Nora's nature during the daytime, it was harder at night, especially with strangers hanging around her house.

As she went around locking up the house, she couldn't help giggling. Her three women visitors had taken over house, kitchen, and garden. They had discovered almost everything about her home and yard, including the toolshed and its contents, and the existence of a fake rock near the front door that held a door key. They learned a few things about her husband, her children, and her farming ancestors, including her darling old grandmother. And it turned out these P.P.S. people knew how to clean up a kitchen. They made hers shine as it had never shone before, following a delightful dinner served stylishly at ten on Louise's best china—an appetizer of delightfully sautéed morel mushrooms, chicken Florentine, a salad with tiny, fresh garden vegetables, plus a tart from heaven: there were ground-up black walnuts in its buttery dough, and it was filled with mangos and fresh apricots.

She hadn't worried about Jay McCormick all evening, and before she threw herself in bed at one, she looked out the front window at the Mougeys' far across the street. The house was dark. Good: The man was getting some rest.

Chapter Twelve

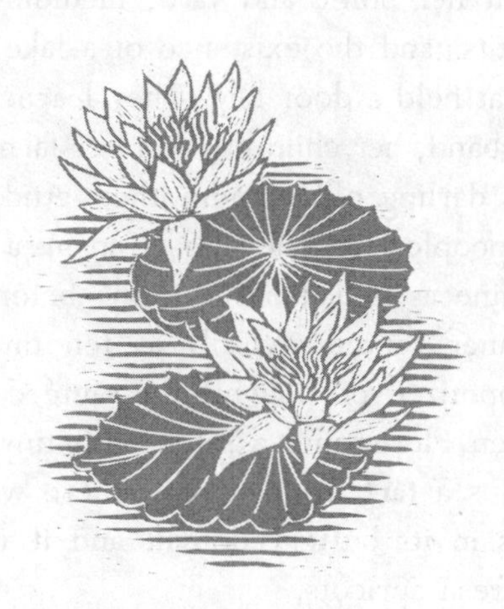

"Yo, Louise!" cried the frisky John Batchelder, his big smile showing as he waved at her from across the Hilton's lobby: her cohost was a happy man. She walked over and joined him and Marty Corbin and the Channel Five crew. They had just arrived and were standing with their camera and sound equipment, ready to get to work. She had just done her duty by having brunch with the officers and board members of the P.P.S., hoping they considered her a worthwhile choice for ''Perennial Plant Person of the Year.''

John had been lukewarm about this show, but his spirits revived when he heard from Marty that he was interviewing the koi doctor. Slouching gracefully like a statue of the young David, John looked down at Louise with dark-fringed hazel eyes reminiscent of the young studs roaming the squares of Rome or Florence. ''I like this Gil. We got together for breakfast this morning and have things pretty well worked out. I bet I know everything there is to know about koi.'' For her part, Louise was glad John would not be accompanying her on the shoot in the exhibition hall, which involved talking about dozens of special plants that growers had brought with them; it would have been awkward to have the two of them exclaiming about every new variety they came across.

''So, how are your houseguests? Pretty nice people?'' In spite of his exotic looks, John was a person from plain midwest origins with plenty of common sense. Illinois was a place where being ''nice people'' counted. When he broke up with his last girlfriend, Cheryl Wilding, a manipulative Washington TV newswoman, Louise knew that he was on the right track as a human being.

She gave him a droll look. ''Actually, those gals remind me of you. Remember how you visited our house and suggested we topple about half the trees in the yard?''

''Yeah, but I didn't mean to offend. Don't forget, I come from a place where they don't exactly have woods. If you like living in a forest, well, hey, that's your choice.''

''These women were twice as opinionated as you. Of course, I was supposed to listen, because they're experts. But don't get me wrong: I like them. They just have unbelievable chutzpah. On the plus side, one of them cooked a divine dinner, and they made me sit and put my feet up while they cleaned up.'' She grinned. ''They didn't want me to be tired and ugly when we taped the program today.''

''I help clean up, too, Louise, when you invite me to dinner,'' he pointed out plaintively.

''I know, John. And I appreciate it.'' She gave him an encouraging smile. He was at the top of his form, just where they all wanted him, ready for a good interview with the fish doctor. Marty, however, was much less good-natured. His dark bushy eyebrows were pulled down in a dark valley of a frown. His brown eyes were wary as he watched her approach. He stepped up to her and put a placating hand on her arm. ''Louise, honey, I've been thinking things over. I even talked to the G.M. yesterday. This program on the environmental bill—we gotta tread carefully. The G.M. doesn't like the idea of politicizing *Gardening with Nature.*''

Damn. Why did Channel Five's general manager have to get in on this? ''But, Marty, the environment is at the very heart of our program—''

''Yeah, I know, you've said that before.'' He gave her his most sympathetic look. ''Louise, you know I love ya, and I love your work. Okay, G.M. be G-damned, I'll go this far: We'll get a script from our clever Rachel, one that doesn't fawn all over the President. If we were to rerun this program later in the year, the G.M. doesn't want us to look like fools if Fairchild loses and the Congress rolls back all these drastic new proposals they just passed.'' He shook an avuncular finger in her face. ''That's the problem, my dear, in a nutshell. And it ain't gonna go away too easily. It's all up to what Rachel is able to do.''

''Okay. But if worse comes to worst, could we pull the program?''

His frown deepened. "We'd catch all sorts of flack about that. We don't have that kind of money to waste."

She sighed. The pitch of life was growing faster, and it wasn't even ten A.M. The day had started quietly. Subdued guests sipping black coffee at the antique pine table, nibbling tidbits of sweet buns. With Louise driving Bill's Camry, the trip to the Hilton also started out quietly, but by the time they reached the Memorial Bridge, the women's motors had switched on; by the time they reached the hotel, they were revving. Nothing like a big convention to get one excited: seeing old friends and associates from all over the country, taking part in programs, getting up on stage and describing a new plant one has been hybridizing or propagating, "partying down," as they termed it, at lunch and after the day's events are over.

She knew one of the places they were partying down tonight was at *her* house. Barbara had prepared tray upon tray of snacks, encased them in plastic wrap, and shoved them in Louise's refrigerator. Louise had no illusions about a quiet Wednesday evening.

But now she had to tread the long exhibition hall and talk about plants with dozens of different plant exhibitors. She went with the crew for a preliminary walk-through, and stood at the entrance for a moment. The space was enormous, filled with cubicles displaying hundreds of varieties of plants and plant materials, and smelling much better than the normal large hotel space. Earthy, fresh as a spring day.

It only took her five paces inside the hall to fall madly in love. It was a gray stone urn filled with an eye-stopping combination: *Heuchera* "Pewter Moon," *Salvia argentea,* blue-flowered Russian sage, and tradescantia, with a pale pink-flowered, scented geranium tucked in the middle. She went over and touched a heuchera leaf, which was a miracle of good design. The cameraman trailing her had caught up, and his eye, too, was caught by the splendid plants in the gray pot. She told him, "Let's put this one on our dance card."

After a feverish three hours of taping, they were at the last booth in the exhibition hall. With Marty satisfied, they were ready to call it a day. It was only then that she noticed a familiar figure standing in the wide corridor, watching her.

Her jaw dropped; it was Franklin Rawlings, his skeletal face stretched into his trademark smile. He gave her a courtly, faintly mocking bow. Of all the people she would have expected to see here, Goodrich's campaign manager was the last.

He strolled over, as if he had all the time in the world. "Mrs. Eldridge. Why did I know you'd be here?"

"I don't know, Mr. Rawlings. Why?"

"Because this is just what you should be doing: telling the uninformed public more about perennials."

"Are you a gardener? Is that why *you're* here?"

"Surprised? Do you think I've gotten to where I am being a one-dimensional man?" He put out a long, thin hand and touched her arm. "But let's not the two of us bicker. I was, uh, in the neighborhood. You won't believe it but there was a political luncheon here today. Just decided to see if you were hanging around at this convention. As I said at that fund-raiser, I hope a major media outlet like Channel Five doesn't yield to political pressure. The environment is sacred to Congressman Goodrich, just as much as it is to our flawed President. Don't go out on a limb, young lady. The political winds are changing."

With that he turned on his heel and strolled down the exhibition hall. She watched him. He stopped and touched plants in various exhibits, chatted with exhibitors, accepted handfuls of freebies from the plant people, and looked for all the world like an ordinary garden enthusiast and not one of the big political shakers in Washington.

Louise, too, came home laden with sample perennial plants that the growers eagerly thrust into her hands. They occupied two flats that weighed at least twenty pounds each. She carried them separately up to the front porch and set them neatly near the edge, wondering if she would have time to put them in the ground before her guests returned. Tessie, Barbara, and Donna had stayed at the convention, telling her that they would get a ride out with Gil.

She brushed her hands together to wipe off traces of dirt, then looked at her watch. Suddenly, fatigue caught up with her; it had been a tiring day after a late night. In lieu of putting the perennials in the ground, she would go in and take a long nap. Otherwise, how would she ever keep up with these energetic plant people?

When she crawled into bed, she fell immediately to sleep and she dreamed. Strong, muscled women, her P.P.S. friends Tessie, Barbara, and Donna, decked out in military-looking uniforms and yellow hard hats, held chainsaws in their hands as if they were machine guns and ran around her beloved yard like soldiers with a cause, ready to buzz down her trees. "No, *stop*!" she heard herself crying out loud, as she awakened with a jolt. It took her a few moments to come back to the real world. The bedside clock said it was seven o'clock. Time to get prepared: There was going to be a party here tonight.

Chapter Thirteen

IT WAS ONE OF the most amiable parties Louise could remember. Almost twenty Perennial Plant Society members gathered in the rooms of her house and flowed out onto the patio and into the bamboo garden. Like her trio of houseguests, they seemed to feel at home immediately with Louise. Many had met her during the day as she and the Channel Five crew went through the big exhibition hall taping the show. She gave tours of the yard and gardens, illuminated now with just a few outside lights so any imperfections fell into the shadows.

Inside, music was playing; a few danced. Others sat around with drinks and talked shop: new automation systems for nurseries, new methods for hybridizing plants, arguments over the use of native plants, new ideas brought up by speakers at the opening day of the convention.

Gil Whitson, Louise noticed, was well-respected by all, as both a leading garden designer and an author of and contributor to garden books. He moved easily from group to group, like a host. Tessie ran the bar, and Barbara and Donna distributed refreshments. In fact, Louise needn't have been there at all, except to give yard tours and bask in the glory of being next year's Plant Person of the Year.

Gil finally made his way to where she was sitting talking to a grower. Taking the seat next to her, he said, "I liked that John Batchelder. He did a great job with the interview. By the way, you said your neighbors have a koi pond. Any chance I can go look at it?"

"Yes. It's straight across the street, and it's a fairly well-lighted yard, but you'll still need a flashlight. Come, I'll get one and go with you; a friend's staying over there." She led the way to the kitchen and got the light.

"You don't need to come. Just point me in the right direction. I always like to see a new pond and be sure the situation is good for the fish."

"Mary Mougey, whose pond this is, told me to keep an eye out to see that the raccoons don't eat them."

"She must have been joking. You would have to sit up all night to guard them from that predator. Anyway, if the pool is deep enough, raccoons won't jump in and swim after koi. They *will,* however, stand on those underwater plant ledges, and with their feet firmly planted, take a swipe at a fish.''

She oriented him toward the house across the cul-de-sac, which had its usual yard lights on, as well as a light in a front window of the Mougey house. Jay was probably buried in his work, for he'd wanted to finish that story before Friday, which was only two days away. Remembering how jumpy Jay had been, she returned to the house and rang up the Mougeys to warn him that Gil would be coming. There was no answer. Oh, well, Gil seemed like an unobtrusive man, who probably wouldn't disturb her busy writer friend.

She went back to the party and selected a compact disc filled with Tony Bennett songs; Bill's mother had brought it as a gift when she came to visit earlier in the summer. Then, for a change of pace, she brought out a Charlie Mingus CD to play next. Bennett's fourth song was playing when Gil returned. She remembered, because she thought he was taking a long time to look at a fishpond in the semidarkness. The first thing she heard was the front screen door slamming shut. She turned, and there he was, looking disheveled and angry, the flashlight hanging in one hand like a club, the other hand jammed in his jacket pocket. His jacket collar was flipped up, and thin wisps of faded blond hair over the top of his head were out of place. The man's catlike eyes were narrowed with rage in his reddened face.

She got up from her chair and walked quickly over to him.

''Gil, what's the matter?''

Tessie approached, too, sensing trouble.

''Plenty,'' he barked, throwing his hands out to either side in an extravagant gesture. He paced in a little circle near the piano, where a P.P.S. member, bored with Bennett, had been softly competing with ''Tea for Two.'' He quit when

Gil started his harangue. ''I've had a tiff. I damned well *hate* to have such a thing happen.'' His loud tone began to fray the edges of the congenial group. Conversations halted.

Louise had a sinking feeling he had run into Jay McCormick. ''Did you, uh, run into my friend there? Are—the fish still all right?''

''Good questions, both of them,'' Gil answered, in acid tones. ''Yes, I met someone, and I gather it was your friend. Louise, he was a *boor.* He knew nothing about fish.''

That sounded like Jay, in his present mood.

''What, uh, exactly, was he doing?''

Gil plucked a cigarette out of a pack, and Louise could see he was dying for a hit of nicotine, but forbore since no one was smoking inside. ''I went straight to the back of the house where you said I'd find the fishpond. He was there, crouched down next to the pool. Louise, I think he was loaded. Said something about how it was time to celebrate. But what infuriated me was what he was doing to those fish.''

''What did he do to them?'' she asked, catching her breath. She had visions of hundreds—no, perhaps thousands—of dollars' worth of koi floating on top of the water, dead.

Gil got a handkerchief out of his pocket and mopped his brow, keeping the other in his jacket pocket. ''He was crouched down near this crazy crane statue next to the pool, and then he got up and he had this plastic container in his hand filled with remnants of fast food: cheeseburger, pickles, greasy fried potatoes, *apple pie*! Next thing I know, he had thrown the whole mess into the pond for the fish to eat!''

''Oh, *no.*'' She didn't know exactly what fish ate. The only words that crowded into her brain were off the wall: *''Do not feed the fish,''* a line from a Dr. Seuss book she used to read to her little girls that always sent them into attacks of giggles.

This was not funny. ''Um, is that food going to hurt Mary's fish?''

''Look, fish will eat anything you give them, but it's not necessarily good for them. It was just the principle of the thing. What would he have fed them next? That guy should not be allowed anywhere near marine animals, especially ones as valuable as koi. And those were a particularly fine group of fish. Who was this jerk, anyway?''

''Actually, he's a visitor who's staying there because he got bumped out of this house.'' She put a placating hand on Gil's arm. ''I'll go over there tomorrow and tell him not to feed the fish.''

By this time, others had gathered round, attracted by Gil's angry tone.

''Come on and have something to drink,'' offered Tessie.

''I don't need a drink,'' he growled, and Tessie backed up, almost as if she feared Gil would strike her.

Louise continued to press. ''There's a comfortable seat right here on the couch, Gil. Why don't you take it?''

His face was stormy. ''I don't think so, Louise. In fact, I know there's plenty of room in the other cars for people returning to the city, so I'm going to get out of here and go back to my hotel room. I need a little alone time.''

He hurried out the front door and she trailed after him, still apologizing. When he reached his van, he turned and gave her a haunted look and a grunted ''good-bye,'' then gunned the motor and sped off.

When she returned to the house, the party had resumed its normal pace and if anything had grown livelier. She glanced at her watch and saw it was getting on toward midnight; she marveled at the youthful capacity of the group. Hard work gave them the strength for hard play.

No one seemed surprised at Gil's behavior. One amiable man made an awkward try at explaining it to Louise: "You wouldn't believe it, but Gil designs the most serene gardens you ever saw. But in his personal life he's always been a little hot-tempered, and it comes out at parties. You know, like Satchel Paige said, 'Social ramble ain't restful.' With Gil, it's always after a couple of drinks he probably shouldn't be drinking, and it's mostly talk besides."

That was fine, but now she was left with the embarrassing task of reprimanding the errant Jay, the most unrewarding houseguest she had ever entertained.

How to Put Serenity into a Small Garden

AMERICANS HAVE A TENDENCY to admire many things and want everything. This can be particularly true of gardeners. If the garden isn't quite full, why not tuck that new *Penstemon digitalis* ''Husker Red'' into the back corner, and try that new white marigold in the six inches in front? If we fulfill our dreams of owning every plant, the overall effect will be ''chaos-theory'' gardening. In both large, but especially small, gardens, there should be a feeling of calm, not chaos. Serenity in the garden is reached by stopping before we have gone too far, not destroying our views or *allées,* and remembering that less is sometimes more.

Garden designers will tell you that the small garden or yard is a greater challenge than the large yard, and small spaces are what most gardeners must work with. Perspective is a sometimes-forgotten consideration. Mastered by the Japanese for centuries, it concerns itself with the close-in, the middle distance, and the far distance view. By the placing of objects in these spaces, we alter perspective. We can use both our own trees, rocks, and walls and our neighbors' to provide these accents and defining borders.

If a yard is wide and shallow, parallel vertical lines of plants will give it more depth. Conversely, a deep, narrow yard can be broken up and widened by interrupting the view from front to back. This is where the concept of garden "rooms" can be put into action: using barriers of trees, bushes, or partial walls to create interest in what is to come next.

A small yard needs no more than a few simple elements:

- An interesting tree. River birch *(Betula nigra),* with its peeling white bark; the unsurpassable Japanese maple, *Acer japonicum;* or a species of cherry would be good choices.

- A focal point, such as a rock with a depression that makes it a good birdbath, or a generous-sized decorative garden pot.

- Several small evergreens, such as dwarf mughos or pines; and a couple of skeletal plants such as ornamental grasses, Apache plume, sagebrush, or yellow or red dogwood.

- One or more ground covers to unify the plantings, such as liriope, epimedium, carex, ginger, sweet woodruff, ivy, or lamium. Within this ground cover could be planted an irregular drift of early spring bulbs; the ground cover will conceal its dwindling foliage.

- Several ample clay pots submerged in the ground in the dramatic center of the plantings. They would hold colorful plants to accent different seasons. In spring, the pots could be filled with primroses; in summer, tuberous begonias, petunias, or geraniums; and in fall, they could be replaced with chrysanthemums or anemones.

Even a small space can contain a water feature such as a scaled-down waterfall or pond; this becomes the yard's central feature. Such a minimal pond should be planted with miniature water flowers. Simple changes in the grade can enhance perspective, even without water; this is done to good effect in western gardens where "dry bed" streams are imitated in a rocky descent of just a few feet.

The famous English gardener Gertrude Jekyll wrote in one of her books that garden design was all about making ''pictures of living beauty.'' The paths in her woodland gardens led from one living scene to another. The use of color was important to her designs, and she was known for using it in great bold swaths. Other times, she used it in the most delicate ways, and once described coming upon this view: ''A pleasant mass of color showing in the wood-edge on the dead-leaf carpet,'' intertwined drifts of just three flowers, white daphne, red lenten hellebore, and yellow dog-tooth violet. The colors were what old-fashioned garden writers used to call ''sad''—flower tints of secondary strength, and as beguiling to the eye today as they were then. Combined with the other tones Jekyll valued so much—the tans, browns and grays in tree trunks and bushes—these splendid and finely designed flowers in their faded hues formed a perfect garden picture.

Chapter Fourteen

SINCE TESSIE, BARBARA, AND Donna were anxious to make the nine o'clock session of the convention, Louise had no need today to employ her handy formula for "speeding the parting guest." First, it was something she and Bill had only joked about, after a gaggle of guests had strung out their departure for more than half a day. Then she tried the formula and found it worked, and it involved only a little lying. There were four rules. Number one was to make the guests a hearty breakfast, but only to brew up a limited supply of coffee, and not the guests' favorite brand. Second was to put a scribbled schedule for the day in a visible place so they could see that she had lots of things on the to-do list. Third was to allude the night before to a possible doctor's appointment for an undisclosed minor ailment. Fourth was attitude: to be friendly, and at the same time businesslike and brisk, so guests knew she didn't *need* them, that she had already made the psychic break and was ready to go on with life without them.

None of the rules applied this morning. She made the Perennial Plant Society women a fluffy omelet with watercress and black raspberry jam on the side, and brewed a big flagon of kona coffee. She had become quite fond of these women, and they loved her kona coffee. They were the ultimate in guests, intelligent, witty, and helpful. They had cleaned up every sign of the late party and given up talk of taking down trees. She drove them to the Huntington subway station, where a train would whisk them to central Washington, D.C., in ten minutes. This time, she used her aromatically enhanced station wagon. "This car is proof that I'm a serious gardener," she joked.

"Our bags are back there where the manure goes, I suppose," said Barbara, with mock suspicion in her voice.

"I hope no little remaining particles adhere to your luggage, but one can never tell."

"Don't worry, Louise," said Donna. "We all have cars like this. Not one of us is a priss."

When they reached the station, she promised she would keep in touch, and as they embraced each other, she almost felt as if she were bidding good-bye to sisters. If she had had sisters, she doubted that she would be as compatible as with these three opinionated characters, who in the end were as open-minded as they seemed bossy at first.

Once she was home again, there were touchy matters to resolve after she gave the house a quick once-over, which was easy, since her guests had remade their beds and cleaned the bathrooms. It was Thursday already, and more than a week since Tom Paschen had pressed her on the issue of an environmental program. She needed to call him at the White House and give him the mixed message from her producer: Channel Five might do the program, and then again it might not. It would all depend upon what kind of magic Rachel the writer could do with the script. Louise was counting on the thin, intelligent Rachel, who spun words so well, to uplift such a program into a lofty theme of environmental preservation without the sticky political strings attached. Otherwise, she could see Franklin Rawlings being a major source of trouble.

It wasn't easy to get through to the President's chief of staff, but after a ten-minute wait, she heard his voice on the line. "Louise, tell me you've succeeded."

"Well, not one hundred percent."

"Aw, you can do better than that, I know you can." He paused, and Louise wondered if he wasn't looking through sheaves of papers involving much more important matters than whether or not *Gardening with Nature* would do the show. "Uh, look, Louise," he said, "I find a little hole in my schedule tomorrow. I've got lunchtime free. How about coming here and we'll grab a bite in the White House mess? No, wait. Better still, since I have to be at the Rayburn Building at ten for a hearing on the budget, maybe you'd like to eat in the Capitol. We'll meet there, and another newsperson might join us. Then, we can hop the underground train and go to the members' dining room. You might like that: It'll give you a chance to scope out people like Goodrich and his men. I hear they lunch there a lot. And I'll give you a copy of the President's bill.''

And you will twist my arm, thought Louise. She said, ''That would be great fun.'' She would enjoy contact with the political center of Washington, but she didn't want to get herself boxed in by the hard-driving chief of staff, since Marty had not yet given the nod to a program he had jokingly titled ''Wilderness Regained.'' This was touchy business: Paschen was pushing her one way on this issue, and Franklin Rawlings the other way. They were like animals scrapping for a bone that had already been picked. Was a Channel Five program that powerful? If she handled this wrong, she would injure her reputation at Channel Five forever, and Marty Corbin's as well.

Pouring the last of the leftover kona coffee into a cup, she stood in the kitchen and considered her next action: Giving the fish a morning feeding, and talking to Jay. In the bright light of morning, the whole episode involving Jay McCormick and Gil Whitson and the fish seemed ridiculous. How much was she required to tolerate for the sake of an old friend, who was a friend that she had only known for one summer? She impatiently gulped the last of the coffee, rinsed the cup, and headed out to do her unpleasant task. First, she changed into her gardening clothes.

As she went out the front door with a plastic container of fish pellets, she guiltily examined the two flats of perennials sitting on the porch. With her metal-toed boot, she shoved them closer to the front door so she wouldn't forget to plant them. As for this fish brouhaha, she would make short shrift of it. Most likely, Jay had finished his story last night and felt free to get drunk; that would account for his reckless behavior.

Then she remembered Richard Mougey's fabulous wine collection, and groaned; some of Richard's bottles were worth hundreds of dollars. She only hoped Jay hadn't plucked out one of those. Tonight, all would be well because Jay could move back to her house and stay out of trouble on his last night in the Washington area.

The cul-de-sac in late morning was a pool of sun, the neighborhood, deserted. Thankful that no strangers lurked about today, she walked slowly into the Mougey yard and saw Jay's old car tucked back in the driveway behind a huge viburnum bush. The man had not wanted to be seen once he reached Sylvan Valley, although he certainly poked about Washington a lot.

She went up to the front door, which had a sideways orientation like her own, and rang the bell. With a finger, she straightened the elegant little wreath of dried pastel flowers that hung on the door and rang again. Even if he drank too much last night, she doubted he would sleep this late. Walking to the back of the house, she could see the koi pond shimmering in the distance. It was set in an elaborate planting area of which several bronze statues were the accents. One, at poolside, represented a crane with his foot-long bill in the air. Another, set ten feet away near the edge of the woods, was problematic for Louise: a young girl with her hand thrust out in the air, swaying to some unheard music. It was a kind of poor man's Degas. Still a third was the one Louise was most uncertain about: a bronze deer, hooves thrust out and leaping up as if it were escaping through the woods toward Nora's house.

Was this deer politically correct? Wouldn't the onslaught of deer that was overpowering the United States be here soon enough, without replicating the animal in bronze? The overpopulated animal was doing millions of dollars of damage to gardens and crops, plus aiding the spread of Lyme disease; it was just a matter of time until this metal deer was joined by dozens of real ones.

She went to the back door and knocked. The only sound was the squawking of some big birds. She looked up and saw they were crows.

Doubling back the way she came, she headed for the pool, wondering whether or not the fish had digested their dinner scraps. The path to the pool was lined with a stylish variety of grasses, tall, medium, short, striped, the fountain grass showy maroon with tassels. Mary's landscaper had done a polished job, just a little too pat for Louise's tastes, for each little combination was repeated several times along the path.

She was ten paces away before gaps in the landscaping allowed her a glimpse of the pool itself. In preparation for feeding the koi, she took the lid off the pellets and walked closer. All the fish, probably two dozen of them, were busy on the bottom of the pool.

Down there, bobbing against the bottom, was a body, with the fish busily dodging in and out, nibbling on its face and head.

She knelt at the edge of the pool and peered into the blood-pinkened water. She recognized the light hair, the shirt and pants, even the worn loafers that remained on his feet: Jay McCormick, her friend, her houseguest; the man with the graceful body and pale skin and pale eyes whom she had held in her arms and cherished a lifetime ago.

The four feet of cool water had kept him looking quite lifelike, and he had not even lost the color in his skin. The tender parts of his face, his eyes, and the area around his eyes and his mouth, had been bruised and reddened by the nibbling fish. But the largest concentration of them were engaged at the back of his head, and she feared to see what was there. Reaching down and splashing the surface of the water, she cried, "Get away!" and flung the fish pellets far into the center of the pool.

They retreated swiftly toward the food, streaking the pool with color. Unmolested now, Jay stared up at her through his bruised and eaten eyes. A pale billow of pink still emanated from his head, and she knew there was a terrible wound there that had killed him.

For a long moment, she could only stare, but soon a dizziness swept over her, and she sat back on the flagstones. Now there would be no closure, no respite from the guilt she felt for hurting him twenty years ago, and for failing to connect with him again when he came to her house for refuge. No father to take an eager Melissa back to her home in California. And no answer, perhaps, to the mystery of what he was doing here in the first place. She pressed her cheek to the flagstones and cried as if her heart would break.

Chapter Fifteen

DETECTIVE MIKE GERAGHTY GAVE her a long look. It was sympathetic, but firm. It was a look that said, "I know you and like you, but if you know something, you'd better come clean."

She didn't really care what Geraghty was thinking, what anyone was thinking. She had the air of detachment of someone coming out of an anaesthetic. The detective and the other policemen had found her in the Mougeys' living room, and she could tell by their expressions they were worried about her. ''Is this woman flipping out?'' they were probably thinking. For she was slumped on the fawn-colored silk couch, staring fixedly and meaninglessly at the Mougeys' antique Queen Anne highboy. Since then, she had straightened up, but was still too weak to engage in a normal conversation.

Yet Geraghty was inexorably there, sitting in the upholstered chair placed at a right angle to the couch. He had taken his notepad out and placed it on his large knee; his pencil was poised and ready. As a defense mechanism, her mind focused in on Geraghty, seeking anything to delay having to think about Jay's ghastly corpse beneath the water. The big detective seemed to have lost weight, down from the stratospheric poundage of a truly heavy man to perhaps only two hundred pounds; this brought out a certain Irish handsomeness. Nor did his usually florid face above his curly white hair seem so red, but more healthful-looking, with the blue eyes vivid and sparkling and lacking the old bloodshot quality.

''Did you hear me, Mrs. Eldridge? I'm talking to you. And you're lookin' at me, but you're daydreaming.''

She shook her head. ''Oh, I'm so sorry.'' She had slumped like a baby in a car seat, so she straightened herself again.

''So you found this house wide open and you phoned us. Tell me you haven't touched anything.''

''I haven't touched anything.''

His words hurt. They were too personal, too cynical, as if she were a rookie cop who was a bit of a screwup. That was because she and Geraghty had been thrown together twice before. Both times, they had found a personal affinity with each other, always marred by the fact they were involved in the tense business of murder investigations. In fact, the last time, she had been one of his prime suspects.

It was hard to completely forgive the big, white-haired detective for all those misunderstandings from the past, but his marblelike eyes were full of kindness. ''Now, Mrs. Eldridge, this has been a terrible shock for you. I know you could have nothing to do with this, and I just want you to tell me, nice and slow, everything you know, with no holding back.''

Holding back, and not being believed by the police, were the twin pitfalls of her previous experiences with this man. ''I have always tried to cooperate with the police,'' Louise said in a voice that even to her reeked of self-righteousness.

''Umm. Well, just as long as we get off on the right track this time, and don't get crotchety with each other. So, let's get started. To your knowledge, who is the man in the pool, and just how did you come to be over here to find him?''

Her answers were mechanical. She told Geraghty almost everything, of how she knew Jay McCormick and of how he'd stayed at the Eldridge house for a week. She spoke of his writing and of his daughter in Washington and the situation with his ex-wife, Lannie Gordon. She told him why Jay had to move out and why she came here this morning, to check on him and to feed the koi. As she talked, she looked out the far living room window and saw a quick gleam of sunlight on bronze. It suddenly struck her that what happened to Jay could be nothing more than a macabre accident. She got up and walked over to the window to look out. ''You think this is murder, don't you?''

The detective had followed her across the room and stood behind her, as if protecting her from something. He said, ''Not necessarily.''

''But Jay's death could have been an accident. He could have fallen against that whooping crane out there, gashed his head, and fallen into the pool.''

''Our very thought, Mrs. Eldridge,'' he said. ''Come on and sit down again. You've been through a terrible experience here, and I don't want you to get faint or anything, especially since you tell me Mr. Eldridge is out of town.''

''An accidental death,'' she murmured, liking the sound of the words. Resuming her seat on the couch, she crossed her arms on her stomach and hugged herself to keep from trembling. ''I wonder why the Mougeys, who are thoughtful people, didn't think about the danger of that bronze bird.''

''They might have,'' said Geraghty, ''if they'd had small children. Otherwise, people put the darndest things in their yard and call it art. He could just as well have killed himself on the statue of the child, too. Her hand sticking out that way is another lethal weapon, to say nothing of that deer's hind leg, kicking out back the way it does.''

''Detective Geraghty, I'd be so glad if it's an accident. This has made me feel so guilty.''

''Guilty?'' he asked, frowning. ''Why?''

Her words came out awkwardly, through trembling lips. ''He was an old friend, and I kicked him out of my house and *made* him move here. Otherwise, he would be alive right now.''

He shook his head. ''You'd best not take on the blame for this, Mrs. Eldridge—it's not your fault. And right now, help me if you will. We want to be thorough and rule out other possibilities beyond the obvious one of an accident. You call him Jay McCormick, but he has identification in his wallet that says he's John McCormick.''

''That was his given name.''

''And he's from Sacramento. Know what he was doing here?''

''He was writing something, I don't know exactly what. He'd been in Washington for about five months on this project. I'm not sure who he was writing for—maybe himself, or maybe for the newspaper he used to work for out there, the *Sacramento Union*." *In fact,* she thought to herself, *if I ever get my strength back, I'll call that newspaper myself and talk to the editor.*

Geraghty looked at her dubiously. "Five months? Seems to me that's a long time to work on one story."

She raised her shoulders in a semblance of a shrug; it was easier than talking.

Geraghty sighed. "Okay: Let's look at it from another angle. If this man wasn't even from the Washington area, it doesn't make a lot of sense to think that he had enemies here. As far as you knew, was that true?"

"I'm not sure about that. Actually, he seemed sort of paranoid, trying to avoid somebody. Just yesterday, he said if people were to hunt him down, they would be 'suits.' "

"Suits."

"Yes, you know, *'suits.'* "

" 'Suits.' Okay," and he wrote that down on his pad.

"He wasn't worried about the stranger."

"The stranger?"

She told him about the dark-clothed man who intruded in her yard, and how she disposed of him and called 911, as well as about the big gray car that appeared to be surveilling the cul-de-sac.

Geraghty's eyebrows went down in a frown. "So you're sure you don't know what Mr. McCormick was writing about?"

Louise remembered the daily frustration she had felt because she had no idea of what Jay was pouring out on his computer. "He wouldn't tell me, and we're—we were—friends. I think it was one of two things: something political about the upcoming presidential election; or something about the Supreme Court brouhaha about prisoner rights that's got people excited out there on Constitution Avenue. He used to be very big on investigating death row crimes.'' She looked down at her hands sitting helplessly in her lap and felt the tears coming again. ''He was a very good man, Detective Geraghty.''

The big detective had the good grace to say nothing, and let her cry in peace, merely handing over his worn linen handkerchief for her to dry her eyes.

Several other officers had been scouting around the yard and now had entered the house to begin looking for evidence; among them was Detective Morton, and at the sight of him, Louise wished she could disappear into the couch. She couldn't handle Morton right now. He was Geraghty's partner, and a man whom Louise had learned to dislike. Maybe it was because he had actually believed Louise might have murdered her Channel Five colleague. He had dark hair, a well-boned face, and a muscular upper body, so that from the waist up one might have thought him the perfectly formed man, but appended to his long trunk were a pair of short legs. This gave him the scary aspect of a monster; she had an inkling Morton knew it, and tried to live up to it in some perverse way.

''What did you find back there, George?'' called Geraghty. So it was *George* Morton. And to her he said, ''Detective Morton is second in command on this investigation. Just wanted you to know that.'' Morton doubled back and, without greeting Louise, whispered something in Geraghty's ear. Then he impassively gazed at her, his expression saying, ''Here again, are you, Mrs. Eldridge? Well, with me, you're guilty until proven innocent.'' Morton was the rudest cop she had ever met, and unfortunately, she had met quite a few since moving back to the Washington, D.C., area.

''Hello, Mrs. Eldridge.''

''Hello, Detective Morton.'' Then he disappeared into the bedroom area of the house.

Geraghty, left with the job of overcoming the bad resonances of the other detective, pulled himself forward in his chair to bring himself closer to where Louise sat on the couch. Detecting 101, she figured: Make nice with witnesses from whom you need information. ''Uh, you say this McCormick was writing a story. What was he writing *with*? We've searched the house, and we found a computer upstairs in the bedroom, all nicely covered and shut off. Do you mean that one?''

''That's probably the Mougeys' computer. I doubt that Jay would have used that. He had his own; it was small and black. Not very fancy. Some generic brand. He always kept it with him wherever he slept.''

''We checked the guest room on the first floor, where he appeared to be staying. The door was wide open, and there was a mess of coffee cups and dirty clothes all over the place. A pile of typewriter paper. But no computer, no disks, not even a typewriter, or scraps of paper with writing on them. How do you think that happened?''

The enormity of it hit her: Jay didn't die a simple accidental death by losing his balance after polishing off a bottle of Richard Mougey's wine. He was murdered.

''It's futile,'' she said faintly, looking at Geraghty.

''What's futile?''

''Trying to find a simple answer to Jay's death. It wasn't an accident; it had to be murder. Jay McCormick guarded that computer and his writing with his life, and that's apparently what he did last night.'' And then the tears began to fall again.

Chapter Sixteen

THE LINEN HANDKERCHIEF ENDED up in a wet ball before her tears finally stopped. She looked around and began to take in the activity around her. Mike Geraghty still sat near her, solid and silent. Morton bustled back and forth, growling fussy directions to patrolmen who were helping search the house.

In an economy of motion, Geraghty caught Morton's eye and with a tip of his head signaled him to come over. When he did, the lead detective tilted his head meaningfully toward Louise. The master of nonverbal communication.

Morton nodded.

Louise looked at the two of them. ''What—''

''George here is going to walk you home,'' said Geraghty. ''You're pretty shook up.''

''Really, there's no need to do that.''

Geraghty tapped his pencil against his big knee and gave her another close but kindly look. ''Mrs. Eldridge, you may have seen death before, but it's different when it's somebody you care for. You're white as a sheet, and you look like you have about the strength of a . . . a wet *noodle.*'' Not given to colorful speech, he flushed with surprise at his own words. ''Well, something like that. All I know is that you need to go home and rest if you can, especially since I need you to come into the station to talk again later.''

He straightened up in his easy chair: no more forays into the world of metaphors and similes for him. ''You'll talk to Detective Morton, because I'll be working on another case. I'd like you to make it there by four, if you could.''

She proffered the soaked handkerchief. ''I'll have to launder it for you.''

He cocked his head a little, as if to say, ''Keep it.''

She and Morton left the Mougey house together, and for a wild, whimsical moment she wondered if Geraghty had done this on purpose so that the two of them could become more compatible. Not friends, just not venomous enemies. Morton picked up speed crossing the front yard, and soon she found herself two steps behind like a Japanese wife, trotting to keep up with him. How could those short legs move so fast? He sped across the cul-de-sac and up her front path. Once on the front porch, he turned to her with a knowing look, then turned back and tried the door. ''Aha,'' he said, "just like I figured." The door was open, the way she had left it. He shook his head in angry disapproval. "You go around this neighborhood leaving your house wide open?"

"Sometimes."

"How long you been gone—an hour? Anybody could have walked in here: a rapist, a murderer, a thief. Better stay behind me." He entered the house, his hand on his gun, and looked in every room and closet before he was satisfied.

Then he returned to the living room, gave the antique furniture a suspicious look, and shook his head again. "Mrs. Eldridge, I know this is a nice neighborhood, but it isn't *that* nice." He cocked his thumb toward the Mougey house. "Now just look what happened over there—plus you know what happened to you a coupla other times. Would you please put your house key in your"—he waggled his finger hopelessly at her, standing there in her compartmentalized shorts and T-shirt—"well, somewhere in those shorts. And lock up when you leave the house!"

With that he stomped out. She ran after him and called, "I'll do that, Detective Morton, I promise."

He had heard her, for he turned his head and shot back an expression of total disbelief: "Huh!"

So much for trying to communicate with the man.

She went inside the house and stood stock-still in the middle of the living room. Her stomach churned, her head ached; she felt utterly miserable. If only Bill were here, or Janie, or one of her close neighbor friends, Nora or Mary. She longed to share her grief with someone. Even her newly acquired P.P.S. friends would have sympathetically listened. In fact, they probably would have thrown themselves into investigating the murder, whether she wanted them to or not.

Her first task was to call Mary and Richard, and tell them a dead man had shown up in their fishpond. She went to the Rolodex and found the number for their Caribbean villa; she needed to phone the police station with the number, for they, too, would call the Mougeys. A housekeeper answered and informed her they had taken off for an overnight sail with friends. Louise didn't want to leave the macabre message with the woman. She would leave it to the police.

Wandering inexorably toward the kitchen, she didn't know what made her feel worse, the guilt or the sorrow. When she sighted a sweet bun sitting on the counter, she realized part of it was hunger. Munching the bun, she went to the refrigerator and took out the last of the leftovers from Barbara's dinner and popped them in the microwave. Taking her food to the patio, she sat at the glass-topped table and ate, thinking over the situation in which she found herself.

She had to get rid of her guilt, which was piling up inside her like a thunderhead. But how? It was guilt for being annoyed with Jay because he was a lousy houseguest and because he kept all his secrets to himself. Guilt for sending him away in the first place, when he would have been safe with her. But it was too late for guilt and for throwing herself down on the ground again and crying. What she needed to do was to think.

She had sent him across the street on Tuesday evening, and it had taken him only a little more than twenty-four hours to end up dead in Mary Mougey's koi pond. "Oh, Jay," she murmured. "Why?" What had happened since he left her house? Before he went, she had told him of the mysterious man who had skulked around Dogwood Court earlier in the week and he had been undisturbed. But she had not mentioned the big gray car. Would that have been a warning to him?

Tuesday evening, when her plant people arrived, Louise had seen Jay leaving in his old car, looking almost as if he were wearing a disguise. Where was he going then, back to watch his ex-wife's activities, or somewhere else that was more dangerous? She had been working Wednesday and didn't see him at all during the day, and only heard about him that evening from Gil Whitson.

Gil. She suspended a forkful of food in midair, as she conjured up the memory of that angry man standing in her living room Wednesday night. She tried to remember the details of what Whitson had said that night. He had barged back into the party like the proverbial bull in the china shop, ranted back and forth, and made a spectacle of himself. He was almost incoherent with rage over the way Jay was treating those fish. He had even explained himself in an incoherent fashion, stuttering and stumbling about for words.

Then, she recalled an ominous detail from Gil's ravings: he had referred to Jay in the past tense. Her stomach tightened with anxiety. She didn't really think Whitson was a killer. Yet Gil had to have been one of the last people to see Jay alive, for the police told her that her friend had been dead for around twelve hours when she found him. She had not told Geraghty about Gil, and it was just the kind of information the detective would later accuse her of withholding on purpose. Or at least Morton would; Geraghty always forgave her for her blunders, but George Morton never would. Next time she saw the police, she would mention Gil.

With a start, she realized there also was Charlie. Impolite, utterly arrogant Charlie Hurd, who had been in a power struggle with his older employer over the issue of sharing information. Why hadn't she even thought of him when she talked to the police? The reporter was the closest person to

Jay McCormick in the past week. Hurd had talked to Jay far more than she or Bill had: he was in the loop. And she realized this eager young man had everything to gain, and nothing to lose, with Jay's death. Why, he could simply gather up Jay's disk and take major credit for the story—whatever it was.

She heard a sound in the woods. Normally she would have attributed it to a bird or small animal scrabbling through the brush, or even a child traipsing through the leafy paths that wound through Sylvan Valley. But now a keen sense of danger overcame her. She was truly vulnerable here, all alone on the patio of her wide-open house, with a killer again loosed upon the neighborhood. Detective Morton, despite his crabby ways, was quite right: she should be more careful. No better time to start than now, she thought, and she went into the house, rinsed her dishes, and locked up. Her house key went carefully into the watch pocket of her gardening shorts.

But after just a few minutes, it was intolerable being locked indoors. A little gardening, she was sure, would purge her guilt and help her think straight, being fully as good for her as the solution of confession to a priest was to a Catholic. It was two o'clock now, and the Virginia air was growing close and breathless. Big clouds had piled in and were playing hide-and-seek with the sun, so that the woods had moments of brightness followed by periods of deep gloom that transformed friendly trees into macabre forms capable of hiding enemies. Her eyes darted around, looking at the army of huge sweetgums to see if anything was concealed behind them.

She had to get a grip on herself. Jay's murder had little connection with her, and at any rate, a killer would hardly lurk in the woods at two in the afternoon. With firm strides, she crossed the distance to her toolshed to retrieve her shovel and a pail of potting soil. She threw open the door, and out poured the aromatic smells of the good earth.

If there was anything that ruled Louise's life, it was order in the house itself, and blithe disorder in the garden. Before her was a picture of order, each tool in place against the back wall, shovels, picks, hoes, pitchfork, and cultivators hanging against another, pails of peat moss, soil, perlite, and soil mix like a row of soldiers ready for service.

But something caught her eye, something out of order. It was the corner of a piece of plastic protruding from underneath the pail in the corner. She picked up the pail and uncovered a see-through plastic folder containing papers.

In the woods, a bird called and there was a distant roll of thunder. A shudder rolled through her body as if it were an echo of the rumbling sky. Quickly, she grabbed the folder off the floor, replaced the pail, and withdrew from the toolshed. She went to the back door and tried the handle, and felt real panic when it didn't open.

Was the door handle broken? Had someone inside locked her out? In an instant, she remembered she had locked the place up; she shook her head for being such a silly fool. Taking the key from her shorts pocket, she let herself in and carefully locked the door from the inside. So much for safety: It was time-consuming and nerve-racking to have to lock herself in and out of her own house.

She looked down at the plastic sheaf, and tears welled in her eyes as she remembered those fleeting summer days of long ago with her clever friend at her side. The minute she saw the papers, she knew that Jay had prevailed: hiding the things that needed to be hidden, and delivering the goods in the end, just as he had done years before.

• • •

A wizard had written the memos. They contained no names, just game plans. At the side of each recommended plan of action were three numbered boxes. No initials, but all the boxes on the first page, at least, were checked, in different pen strokes, which presumably meant three people had signed off on the specifics.

The papers outlined specific steps in a dirty tricks campaign. It had to be the blueprint for the assault against President Jack Fairchild, though neither Fairchild's nor Congressman Goodrich's names were mentioned anywhere; instead, there was reference to the "opponent" and his family. There were dates, ranging from earlier in the summer to as recent as ten days ago. The first missive, Louise noticed, came out about the time Goodrich had prevailed in the California primary and assured himself the nomination.

The first memo set out a plan to co-opt the media, especially the tabloids and conservative talk shows, and included a proposal to reward news outlets that used the campaign's information in an effective way. Another made recommendations for planting derogatory stories in tabloids about the candidate's "spouse." This memo concerned a DUI conviction from years ago and purported information about her treatment in a rehabilitation clinic. All had been done according to this paper, Louise realized; the tabloids had eagerly taken up the story, with the reluctant major media outlets following suit. There was even a brief, cruel synopsis of ways to denigrate the children of the family by dredging up teenage incidents that resulted in minor scrapes with the law.

The one that stopped her eye sketched out the scenario

for tying the "opponent" to a political assassination, including his part in a cover-up murder. Louise knew this must refer to the story about Fairchild's purported part in the assassination of President Diem and the subsequent murder of an army file clerk.

The last memo made her scalp tingle. It tersely stated that there could be a mole in the campaign. The memo recommended ways to check this out, uncover the mole, and perform "damage control." One recommendation was to give all campaign staffers lie detector tests. This had received the checked approval of the three anonymous readers. Another was to reexamine all employee files to assure that they were authentic. A private investigator was to be hired to track down the residences of all employees and see if there was anything suspicious about their home lives.

Louise thought back on the man in the dark clothes with the bulge in his suit jacket. That could very well have been a private detective checking out Jay McCormick.

The final recommendation on this page regarded moles. It suggested that if a mole was identified, a task force should be sent out to retrieve all "purloined materials to assure that the infiltrator has no more opportunity to peddle stories either to the opposition campaign or to the press." Interestingly, this last recommendation had received a hearty check from two of the three people who signed off on the item, with the third check being lighter, showing less conviction. Alongside it she found the only handwriting on any of the pages: a scribbled few words that said plaintively "Can't we avoid violence?"

The answer to that was no.

Jay McCormick had to have been the mole, the political plant, and he had started arousing suspicions. He had come to Washington, D.C., after Goodrich's strong win in New

Hampshire, and parlayed his experience as a political writer into a job on the congressman's campaign staff. From the little Jay had told her, this timing made sense. Being from the West Coast, his bland face was unfamiliar to most Washingtonians; knowing Jay, he might even have added a few disguise elements to his appearance for additional insurance. His wife, Lannie Gordon, would have been the only one who could have identified him.

And not being an advance man or in some other high-profile job, Jay probably stuck to the office and did his work out of the sight of the public. Being smart and a good writer, he had probably made himself invaluable, gaining access to both these memos and the campaign's deepest secrets.

She riffled through the sheets again and felt a sense of disappointment. When she found them, she had felt the thrill of discovery, as if they would give her all the answers. But the memos themselves were sketchy outlines. They didn't prove much. They just laid out a plan for the Goodrich campaign that was like a reenactment of Nixon's in 1972. And Nixon won then by a landslide, she recalled.

The very idea of a concerted dirty tricks effort was odious to fair-minded Americans—or was it? Were Americans, jaded now by over two decades of political scandals, too cynical to care? And telling the dirty truth about a politician wasn't against the law. She wondered if these were dirty lies, or dirty truths.

It wasn't the lurking stories about Mrs. Fairchild's past alcohol problems, the President's character, nor being involved in Diem's murder that dogged the President. It was the alleged murder of the army clerk, bringing forth the horrid question, "Did the President kill to cover up his past?" That single rumor was drawing Fairchild down in the polls, day by day. No one, not even Tom Paschen, who often was the President's front man with the media, had been able to do anything so far but issue angry denials.

The picture became clear: Jay witnessed the sleazy senatorial campaign managed by Rawlings in California. When the man became head of Goodrich's presidential effort, Jay's outrage drew him back into investigative journalism. He came to Washington and rooted out the truth over the past five months. And then a murderer had come along and killed the political plant, taken his computer and his disks, and with them, the most important story of Jay McCormick's life.

Or was she wrong: Did the clever Jay hide both his computer and his disks, as he felt ever greater pressure to get his story done?

Following One's Native Instincts: Natural Gardening Goes Mainstream

A BOTANIST ONCE JOKED that America's native plants went over to England, got themselves an Oxford education, and then came back to us as cultivated perennials. The British seal of approval was needed to convince Americans their native species were worth digging up from the wilderness.

Things have changed dramatically since those early years of the republic. We proudly grow native species in our gardens, and the federal government virtually dictates their use for America's roadways and federal projects. This has created a supply problem that challenges the conscience of both suppliers and gardeners, to see that they are not raping the American wilds of plants the explorers found here centuries ago.

When Europeans left Europe for the voyage to America, they were careful to pack within their goods their favorite seeds and plants from the Old World. But the plant traffic going the other way was even heavier. The discovery of the immense American continent soon created a voracious appetite among the Europeans and the British for its plants. Masses of them crossed the oceans on ships, often strapped to the deck to weather the salt spray; many were droopy and dead on arrival, with the hardier ones easily identified by the end of the trip.

By the middle of the eighteenth century, American flora had overwhelmed the Europeans' ability to keep track. Carolus Linnaeus, a Swedish doctor and one of the many famous botanists of that century, solved the problem by devising a system of classification on which all our plant names are based, called "botanical Latin."

In America, adventurous, science-minded people like John and William Bartram traveled through the wilds of the East Coast on horseback, collecting plants and seeds, including rarities like the Franklinia tree, *Franklinia altamaha,* that grew in only one place in the world: Georgia. While foreigners treasured the American plants, only the wealthiest settlers in the New World had time to dabble with ornamental gardens, the rest being concerned first with survival. And soon, another flower fad emerged in Europe:

a Dutch naturalist brought back tropical plants to Europe from Asia, and the fascination with native American species gave way to a delirious love affair with "bedding plants," begonias, impatiens, and other annuals that still strike our fancy. Americans took up this fad, which may have further delayed an interest in the wondrous plants that were growing in their own forests. Among the exceptions was Thomas Jefferson, who adopted the natural look that had just come into vogue in England. His farm, Monticello, became a *ferme ornee,* or ornamental farm, an enchanting naturalistic setting for both continental and American native plants. Natives made up one quarter of the total.

Things have changed since then in America, and today, native plants and a natural, relaxed gardening style finally have become mainstream. In the past five years alone, it is estimated that five hundred additional native plant species have come on the market. They are being eagerly sought after by home gardeners.

This brings up hard questions about preserving our national plant heritage. Not only the growers, but also the gardeners, must face these issues. Lady Bird Johnson started things when she agitated for the 1965 Highway Beautification Act, which banned billboards and called for beautifying landscapes. In the 1970s, the Garden Clubs of America stepped in to help promote the use of native

wildflowers and grasses. And in 1994 the federal government made a bold move, declaring that regional plants should be used in all federally funded landscaping projects. A new umbrella organization, the Federal Interagency Native Plant Conservation Committee, joined together private and public plant conservationists to continue the effort to preserve native species. There is a downside to the 1994 government action, however. The demand for native plants from the federal government has exceeded the supply. It is feared this encourages the collection of plants in the wild. It also creates problems for nursery operators, since some natives are hard and expensive to grow.

Instead of just rushing out and buying any newly offered native plant, home gardeners should deal only with responsible dealers and sources, or they could be contributing to the loss of native species. There are even more complex problems involving the fate of other countries' natives: pretty little plants we put in our gardens may result in the obliteration of plant species from foreign lands. This is happening in Turkey, where popular bulbs like snowdrops, hardy cyclamen, and sternbergia are being ripped from the wilds by the millions and sent abroad, many to the U.S. Our country is now trying to help Turkey learn methods to cultivate these bulbs commercially.

The gardener may wonder what exactly is

meant by *native.* A better term is ''regional,'' for what grows well in one part of the U.S. does not necessarily thrive in another. When people plant, they should seek out specimens that are part of their regional ecosystem. That doesn't mean they shouldn't try other varieties, including exotics. Even the most diehard proponents of natural gardening have come around to the view that there is nothing wrong with using exotics. It is interesting that Frederick Law Olmsted argued the same thing in 1863. Even while he was establishing an ''American Garden'' in Central Park, he was telling the knee-jerk nativists of his day that there were many worthy, low-maintenance foreign plants for use in the U.S.

Natural gardens are comfy settings for plants, because we can let them go and do their own thing, multiplying as they will. But beware, for some can grow out of control. Check the growth habits of any plant carefully before you buy it, and keep watch once you put it in the ground. Horror of all horrors, even some of those handsome ornamental grasses that are standard items in every nursery can seed themselves! Natural habitat or not, you don't want a jungle out there.

Chapter Seventeen

LOUISE HAD BEEN RAISED in a home with a stubbornly honest father and mother. Straightforwardness was honored, and lying was out of the question. But that was more than two decades ago. Since then, ambiguity, indirection, and just plain lying had come to seem less odious in her eyes. After her exposure to Bill's world as an undercover agent, she began to think of lying as a pragmatic tool. Agents, after all, had the "right to lie," provided it was "in the best interests of the United States." An agent's wife could not help but yield to this culture.

Bill had occasional troubles melding an ethical personal life with his job as a spy. Now, the scum of prevarication and deceptiveness had splashed onto her, and she didn't even recognize it as wrong, except at certain moments. Sometimes, when she sat in the Presbyterian service on Sunday and listened to her minister talk about honesty and truth, she could make the fine distinctions, and her heart would cry out for the simple, good old days of her youth, when black was black and white was most definitely white.

Now, she sat in the gloom of the family room, with the wind outside pulling in a major storm, whipping the trees and throwing small debris against the windows. It seemed only appropriate that it should storm on the day that Jay was found dead.

She was locked in the house all by herself, safe from everyone but herself. Crucial evidence sat in a folder on her lap and she knew the honest thing to do was to turn these papers directly over to the police.

But her past all came together. The police's misreading of evidence that had put her in jeopardy in the recent past. Her growing penchant to handle every situation for herself. And a looser personal standard.

These were the reasons she was going to tuck these papers away for a few days until she had a chance to think about who killed Jay McCormick. After all, what was the alternative? She could picture the stolid Morton querying her on the folder: "How do I know you didn't put these papers there yourself? When did you find *this*? Why didn't you know they were there?" By the time he was done, she would feel as if she were the perpetrator.

But that wasn't the worst thing that could happen. The police might not take this evidence seriously, for it reeked of anonymity. Her friend's murder could go unsolved if the police discounted it, and that was what she was afraid they might do.

Clutching the folder, she got up, unlocked the door, and went out to the toolshed, the wind battling her all the way. There, she took a shovel from its place and went to the garden. If Jay could hide evidence, so could she.

She needed Jay's story, and hoped against hope he had made a backup disk and left it somewhere around their property. Starting with the house and then moving to the addition, she searched in every nook and cranny, including in her and Bill's plastic disk containers, and behind pictures. Remembering her friend's nightly peregrinations around the outside of the house, she knew she should check the yard, too, and was grateful the rain had not yet started. With the wind buffeting her, she made a thorough search, hoping to find any little clue, even a bit of disturbed mulch, that would indicate someone had hidden something.

She even wandered down to the bog garden with its robust skunk cabbages still flourishing and eager for rain, their golden spathes glittering whenever brief rays of sun shone through. No, it was too swampy for anything other than a bullfrog to be hidden here. Returning to the front yard, she looked longingly across the street. Yellow police tape still surrounded the Mougey property. She had to get over there and search, but how and when?

Her cordless phone rang and she pushed the "talk" button. "Hello?" No one responded, and then there was a click. She stood dead still. The click confirmed the fear in the back of her mind: Just by being Jay's friend and by giving him room in her house, she was more involved in his death than she had been willing to admit.

The enormity of being mixed up in another murder made her feel faint, and she headed for the Stonehenge bench that Bill had fashioned for her out of three thick flagstones. Sitting with shoulders drooping, phone still in hand, she felt a sense of entrapment. It wasn't fun, being scared first in her own backyard and now in her front yard only twenty feet from a suburban street. In a few moments her strength had returned and the faint feeling began to subside. She tucked her phone away in its pocket and walked slowly back to the house. That's what she got for carrying a damned phone anyway: not a measure of safety, as some women thought, but an opportunity for crank calls from God knows whom.

As if to mock her, it rang again as she was entering her house. The wind slammed the front door closed behind her and she jumped in alarm. Furious now rather than frightened, she barked into it, "Give your name, coward."

"My name is Martha Eldridge, and I'm not a coward. Hi, Ma. What's the matter, are you on the rag?"

"Oh, *God,*" said Louise, and went over and sank down on the living room couch. "Martha, darling."

"Ma, don't say 'Oh, God.' You sound like Diane Keaton in a Woody Allen movie. Come on, I know what's wrong. I knew the minute I heard a story on the noon news report about a murder there. The words 'violent death,' 'northern Virginia,' and 'fishpond.' It was all I needed to figure that you could be involved. And then there it was, a mention of where they found the body, the backyard of a house in 'trendy Sylvan Valley.' Why, Ma?"

Another rebuking child. Her nineteen-year-old sounded like a stern judge in a courtroom, and Louise felt very much like a defendant. ''Martha, it was none of my doing, I swear. I simply discovered the body. They didn't put my name in that story, did they?'' If the radio news had used her name, that may have been the reason for the crackpot phone call just now.

''Your name wasn't mentioned. So who is this guy John McCormick? It rang a faint bell, but I couldn't remember. Isn't he one of your old beaux?''

''Yes. Don't you remember the time you and Janie asked me if there were other men in my life besides your dad? And I told you about some sweethearts, including Jay.''

''Jay. Yeah, now I remember. He was one of the more interesting-sounding ones. Didn't you do antiwar stuff together back in the seventies with him, and make out in art theaters?''

''Kissing, only kissing.''

''Oh, yeah? Too bad a guy like that had to be killed.''

''It's very mysterious, Martha. It could have been an accident, but I don't think so. I'm so glad you called because I have absolutely no one to talk to about this except the police. The rest of the world has gone on vacation, and your father is in Europe. But home tomorrow, thank heavens.''

''Now listen to me,'' said her eldest, with the insightful tone befitting a young woman who knew it all without experiencing much of it, ''I want you to promise me right now. Stay out of this one. Just keep your nose clean, as that police detective friend of yours might say. Try to stay alive until Dad comes home. Is Janie there to goad you on, or is she still hammering nails in Mexico City?''

''Janie comes home with your father. And she's loving pounding nails. Meanwhile, I am perfectly safe. All sorts of police are working on Jay's death. It was just such a shock,

Martha.'' The tears threatened to fall again, but she straightened herself on the couch and refused to give way to them.

''I bet you need to lie down. Can you do that? You know you're always better when you get enough sleep.''

''Thank you, dear, I agree. I need a nap. Now tell me what's going on in Detroit.''

''It's fabulous,'' said Martha, and Louise could picture her, a tall girl with long brown wavy hair, actually resembling Louise quite a bit except for her father's blue eyes, her lean frame hunched over the telephone, because Martha never relaxed when the day was still on. For a while, a tireless social butterfly; now, a tireless seeker after worthy causes. ''Father Harrington's a saint, he gives no quarter to assholes, and I love and admire him. I definitely am relinquishing my idea of women's studies to focus in on urban studies.''

''Oh.''

''Granted, there are still a lot of women's issues, but I'll let someone else solve them. It turns out I *love* big cities and all their problems. I'm reading Daniel Patrick Moynihan and William Julius Wilson: you and Dad ought to read this kind of thing instead of whatever you *do* read. If we don't solve the problem of cities, then we can't do much for America.''

''I agree.''

''Here in Detroit where I am, almost everybody's black. Mostly poor and black, I might add, and really wonderful people. The only whites are some of us volunteers and Father Harrington. And people are struggling to find work.''

''Are you safe, Martha?''

''My body's not always completely safe from harm. But obviously, neither are you in Sylvan Valley. Or at least your old boyfriend wasn't safe. My mind and spirit are safe, and that's the most important thing, isn't it?''

After they hung up, Louise reflected on what a wonderful girl her daughter was. She hoped Martha's physical envelope survived so that she could pursue those dreams.

She decided she would take her eldest's advice and crawl into bed for a much-needed nap. But then the clock in the living room chimed three and she knew she had to change her clothes and go to the police station and talk to George Morton. First, she went to the refrigerator and took the bucket of earthworms to the toolshed and measured out a wriggling mass, closed her eyes, and chopped them with a butcher knife.

The patrolman at the Mougey house looked at her strangely, but assured her they would throw them in the pool for her promptly at four.

Chapter Eighteen

LOUISE, SERGEANT JOHNSON, and Detective Morton sat facing each other in the cramped administrative offices of the police station. Johnson, superior officer to both Geraghty and Morton, was a quiet, intelligent black man whom she had met on the Madeleine Doering case.

Louise lost no time in making a clean breast of it; she told them everything that had happened between Gil Whitson and Jay. It was one thing to delay giving police the ambiguous papers she'd found in the toolshed, but she wasn't going to keep silent about anyone who might be responsible for his death. In fact, she was even having second thoughts about holding on to the memos.

Since she hadn't wanted to implicate Gil, she added a strong caveat: "I can't believe he killed Jay, and if he did, I am sure it was a total accident. He might not have reported it because he was too scared. But that wouldn't explain Jay's missing computer—unless he hid everything, computer and all."

Detective Morton, who was recording her words in a formal statement, said sourly, "No need to draw conclusions about anybody, ma'am. That's what the police and the courts are for."

Sergeant Johnson leaned forward and gave her a kindly look, as if to soften Morton's impact. "We appreciate your input, Mrs. Eldridge. Now, is there anything else that you think might help us?"

"Well, then there's Charles Hurd . . ."

"Charles Hurd? And who is he?"

As she described what she knew of the young man's role as researcher and legman for Jay, the sergeant's eyebrows elevated. "Seems you know more about Mr. McCormick's affairs than you first indicated. I suppose we can reach this reporter at his newspaper."

She nodded. "I guess I should have told you all this before, but I was pretty upset after I found Jay. Sorry."

"We understand, Mrs. Eldridge. We'll follow up these leads. Now I need to tell you something. We had tried to contact Mr. McCormick's former wife, Lannie Gordon, because of the daughter you told us about who has to be informed of the death of her father. When we finally got through, Ms. Gordon was pretty concerned. She wanted to come and see the body, so she's gone on her own to the medical examiner's office, and then we asked her to drop by here to talk to us.''

Closure, Louise supposed. After all, she had been married to the man for fifteen years, and probably sensed he still cared for her.

The sergeant cocked his head toward the interior office window, which had a view through to the hall. ''I bet that's her right now, George. I'll finish with Mrs. Eldridge, if you want to talk to her.''

An important look suffused Morton's face as he got up and hurried into the hall; he obviously hoped that any new twist, even Lannie Gordon's arrival, might provide him a major break in the case. Louise turned around in her chair and saw her. Lannie Gordon was tall, with shoulder-length red hair and wearing a pale-green suit with gold buttons. Even from a distance Louise could identify it as a Chanel. Although Lannie's eyes had traces of red from crying, her face was smooth as a mask, her expression unreadable.

How could Jay have married this woman, who was so hard and smooth? As Lannie looked into the office, she and Louise exchanged long, unsmiling glances. Then, Morton hustled her away down the hall.

Johnson cocked his head in the direction in which they had gone. ''You're sure you don't know her? She seems to know you.''

''Only from what Jay said about her. And he shared quite a bit with me. There was a lot of competition over the child, Melissa, but I think Jay was fond of Lannie. That didn't mean he trusted her, exactly.'' She told him of the outcome of the custody battle that had stretched out for years between two people who still appeared to have feelings for each other. ''You might say that Jay won the battle,'' she said, not realizing the irony of the statement until the words came out.

Sergeant Johnson made a note of it. After she answered a few more questions, he seemed satisfied. He escorted her to the door of the office. A tall man, he smiled down and said, "Now, Mrs. Eldridge, play fair with us, okay? If you find out anything, we need to know, to solve this crime. Remember, it was your friend who was murdered. You should have the largest stake in finding the perpetrator."

The words brought tears glistening to her eyes again, but she blinked them back. "Of course I'll share anything I learn."

"And I think we had better make a search of your house, too. We'll do that early tomorrow."

Her heartbeat quickened, and an image of the carefully hidden memos came to her mind. She had done an expert job; they would never find them in a million years. In fact, only a dedicated gardener like herself would ever uncover them. "I'll expect you. But of course I thought of that possibility, of something being left in our house. I have checked every room and even in Bill's and my computer disk containers."

He smiled. "Then we'll just give it a once-over ourselves; I'm sure you don't mind that."

By the time they had arranged a time for tomorrow's search, it was almost seven. She stepped out of the warren of offices, went down the hall and into the front office. Through the windows, she could see that the dark northern Virginia skies had opened. They let down a colossal rainstorm with winds that whipped against the glass in splattery sheets. Gully-washers that would probably soak the basements of many area homes. She looked down at her thin cotton-lawn flowered dress. Without raincoat or umbrella, she was going to get soaked on the way to the car.

Clutching her shoulder purse close to her body, she was

about to step beyond the shelter of the little porch, when a large gray BMW cut close in front of her and stopped in an exhibit of quiet control. The driver's side window slowly rolled down.

Framed there was the face of Lannie Gordon. She, too, must have forgotten an umbrella, for her red hair was plastered against her oval face. Her tear-streaked amber eyes stared at Louise with such intensity that Louise shrank back.

"It's Louise Eldridge, isn't it?" she said in a smoky voice. "Hop in for a minute. In fact, I'll do you a favor and drive you to your car so you don't have to get as wet as I did."

Louise was impressed with the woman's civility. And now she had a chance to relieve her curiosity by talking to the hard-driving Lannie Gordon. For her curiosity was as acute as Lannie's: They were probably the only two women that Jay McCormick had ever loved.

Lannie bunted the car as close to the porch as she could so Louise could climb into the passenger seat without getting wet. It was a sumptuous car, with leather seats, luxurious legroom, and fine music playing out of special speakers embedded in the rear. It smelled of cigarettes. In fact, Lannie had one cocked in her left hand.

"I'll crack the window," said the woman, seeming to read Louise's distaste. Or had her nose wrinkled up unbeknownst to her? With one hand, Lannie maneuvered the car slowly ahead. "Where is your car?" she asked.

Louise pointed to the aged station wagon not far away and Lannie guided her BMW to an empty slot alongside it. They sat there, with the BMW motor purring quietly.

"Thanks so much, Lannie," said Louise, turning to look at the woman. "And let me just say that I'm very sorry for your loss and Melissa's loss." Here was Jay's former wife, carefully made up and wearing the most elegant clothes Louise had seen in a long time. She could hardly picture the two of them together, but a much different-looking and -acting woman probably fell into the arms of the idealistic young Jay McCormick two decades ago.

''Actually, his death has shaken me a lot more than I thought it would. We were together fifteen years, you know, and viewing his body was the most horrible thing I've ever had to do.'' Louise could see the woman's chest heave, and she was afraid Lannie would burst into tears. ''His eyes,'' Lannie said. ''I hated looking at what happened to his eyes. They said it was the fish, sucking.'' She shook her head and quickly bowed it.

Louise remembered, too, and tried to restrain a shudder. Just then, lightning cracked outside the car; a huge boom of thunder followed. ''Lannie, this storm is making me awfully nervous; I have to get home.'' She groped for the door handle, but before she found it, the woman's trembling hand reached out and touched her arm. She could feel the long nails pressing into her flesh. ''Oh, don't go yet, Louise. It would be a comfort to talk just a few seconds. And I hope you don't mind me calling you Louise. I feel I know you from your television program.''

She was surprised at that statement. With those long fingernails, painted peach today to complement her suit, Lannie didn't appear the type of person who grubbed in the soil.

''I can stay a minute.''

The woman exhaled a stream of smoke and said, ''I have a wonderful garden—and gardener, of course, since I have five acres on the river. I watch your show for its sheer entertainment value. A bit of light stuff on a late Saturday morning before I leave to go back to work.'' She smiled graciously at Louise, and there was no apparent malice in her words. "You have a most *engaging* sense of humor and your delight in plants is obvious. But I really don't subscribe to your organic views in the least. They're so off-the-wall that sometimes they make me laugh." Then she took another big drag on her cigarette.

"Somehow I didn't think you would be organically inclined." The woman didn't think smoking was bad for her lungs, so why should she be interested in chemical-free gardening?

Lannie smiled. "Because I'm a smoker? You don't understand smoking, Louise, and why I fight for tobacco, although you should, because"—she cast a look at Louise's dilapidated car in the adjoining parking space—"I'd guess you're a liberal. It's a rights issue: *We're,* in a sense, fighting for your precious First Amendment rights."

Louise kept silent and tried not to inhale.

Another drag, and then Lannie snuffed the butt out in the ashtray. "Oh, but let's not argue over that. What I really want to know, Louise, is what Jay was doing in your house."

"In my house? What made you think he was in my house?" It seemed crazy, but this woman sounded jealous.

Lannie tapped her nails nervously against the steering wheel. "Recently, I discovered Jay was in Washington and secretly meeting with Melissa; I'm sure he was paranoid about the custody decree and whether I'd skip the country with our—wonderful child. Since he chose to drive an old heap, he was ridiculously easy to identify in our neighborhood, where people tend to drive new cars. I followed him and saw him park in back of your holly hedge."

No, Jay hadn't been hard to follow. Belatedly, Louise realized the gray car circling the cul-de-sac was Lannie Gordon's. "All right. He stayed with us for a week."

"I thought so," said Lannie. "Look, I know what you

meant to Jay back in those old bygone days at Georgetown before the two of us met. You were always the passionate, committed type, the way Jay told it, until you tossed him aside and left him a mere half of a man. I restored his ego eventually, but it took some doing."

Louise pulled her breath in sharply.

"First, I thought the two of you might be getting together again, except you and your husband both are listed in the phone book. So I gathered he was just a guest in your house. Now he's died in this horrible accident. And I can tell that you're the type who would keep his secrets for him now, out of guilt if nothing else."

"Wait a *minute,*" said Louise, flustered.

"No, you wait a minute," Lannie said in a shaky voice. "I am concerned about Melissa, Louise, and that is all. What I want to know is this: Did he leave anything with you? This isn't for me, it's for our daughter. If you have any of his possessions, a Pulitzer-prizewinning story, maybe, that's what I think it is, since he's been apparently working around here for months. Or anything else he might have left around, I want it. It doesn't belong to you: It belongs to Melissa."

"But that couldn't be right," said Louise, shaking her head. "The police would want it first—"

"Why would the police need it?"

Louise looked at Lannie; the woman had no clue that Jay had been murdered and that this was a police affair from now on, nor had Detective Morton apparently divulged it to her. "Well, if there is a story, there's the question of ownership by his newspaper."

"I know the law better than you, and you are wrong," Lannie said, her voice rising sharply. "You probably already know I am a damned good attorney, Louise. Being in *my* job means I know when to settle, and when to *sue*—I know how to sue someone's *ass* off!'' Looking wide-eyed at Louise, she flinched, as if expecting to be hit. Then, without warning, she burst into tears.

Louise stared at the woman in complete bewilderment. Finally she understood. She reached over and patted her softly on the arm. ''I guess you still loved him.''

Lannie nodded, still crying.

Louise felt faint; this was just too much for her to handle. ''Lannie, I'm upset, too, over Jay's death, but I don't know anything I can do for either one of us. I wish you'd stop threatening to sue me; I don't even think you mean it. I feel terribly sorry for you and Melissa, but I can't really help you. Only time is going to do that.''

Fighting tears herself, she turned to grope with the door handle again, and finally got it opened. Quickly climbing out of the car, she slammed the door shut without thinking, though it had only needed a velvet touch.

As she looked back through the rain-smeared windows of the BMW, she could see only the silhouette of the woman's dejected face.

Chapter Nineteen

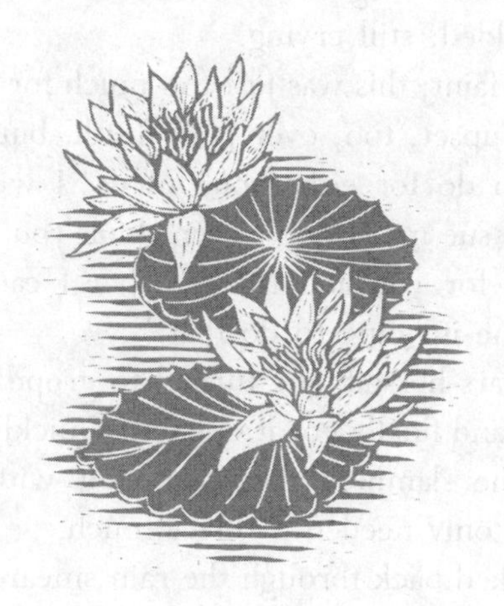

HUNCHING OVER THE STEERING wheel and straining to see through the driving rain, Louise tried to sort out her thoughts: They were as tumultuous as the weather. It seemed to her that Lannie Gordon was grieving mightily over an ex-husband; the old romantic fire had still burned in the woman's heart.

Why was she so anxious to obtain the story that Jay was writing? Did she, like Louise, believe it was a story about the presidential campaign? Louise tried to piece it together, and parts of it fit: Tobacco interests and Congressman Goodrich's opposition campaign went together, as the old song said, "like love and marriage." In the media, there had been stories of big contributions to the congressman from the embattled tobacco companies. There was plenty of incentive for the industry to support Fairchild's opponent, since the President had declared war on the industry and successfully fought its efforts to promote cigarettes with kids.

Being a political junkie, Louise knew big contributors got very close to the candidates they supported. Lannie Gordon might be in tight with the Goodrich campaign. Could she have inadvertently tipped the Goodrich people to Jay's whereabouts? Once Lannie discovered Jay had been killed and not died accidentally, what kind of reaction would she have if she found she had led murderers to her former husband?

By the time she reached home, the rain had slacked off, but Louise's neck was stiff and her body ached with fatigue. No wonder: With only six hours' sleep the night before, she had lived through one of the grimmest days of her life. Discovering her dear friend's mangled body, then discovering his cache of puzzling evidence. Weathering both the questions of police and the emotional meeting with Lannie. And to think the day had started so amiably with the departure of her Perennial Plant Society buddies. It seemed ages ago. Now, she was so tired that all she wanted to do was to crawl into bed and go to sleep.

Though the misty twilight was deepening, she had no trouble seeing the car that butted rudely into her driveway entrance. It didn't surprise Louise that it was one of those presumptuous sports cars with a spoiler on the rear end that always passed her quickly on the highway to avoid the shame of cruising behind a relic. She squeezed by it in her bulky station wagon and pressed the garage door control, triggering the faint but welcome overhead light. When she got out of her car, a young man no taller than herself was standing beside her.

''Oh, *God,* you startled me,'' Louise gasped, clutching the damp bosom of her lawn dress. She stood perfectly still. Another stranger to deal with: She hoped he didn't have a gun, but was too tired right now to get excited about it. She looked him over. He wore an expensive tan summer suit over a white shirt with tie. His dirty blond blown-dry hairdo was a little damaged at this point from the rain. Arrogant eyes peered shrewdly from a narrow face dominated by a sharp nose. His hands were stuck in his pockets and he stood in a well-practiced slouch position.

All he lacked was a hat with a press ID stuck in its band, but that, of course, was passé, and Charlie Hurd was anything but passé. She was looking here at a predator, the modern-day cub reporter trying to get ahead in a shrinking industry.

''You've *made* me,'' he said, grinning, and she smiled back for the wrong reason, amused at his use of gangster lingo.

''Hi, Charlie,'' she said resignedly. ''I take it you *are* Charlie.'' After a day like today, and the kind of life she had been living lately, she wasn't going to bother to call him Charles.

''So Jay called me Charlie, did he?''

She leaned wearily against her car, then realized belatedly that the back of her skirt would pick up the film of mud on the side and imprint her buttocks like a photo negative. ''Sure. Isn't that your name?''

His mouth went into a little pout, and then he seemed to

think the better of it and mustered a smile. ''I prefer Charles, but that's not important. You must be Louise.'' He stuck out his hand and she reluctantly shook it. Perhaps his fingertips were toughened from tapping on computer keys, but his hand was soft as a lady's.

''I suppose you're here because you heard Jay's been murdered.''

''*Murdered?* Jay?'' The young man stepped back dramatically, a little over-dramatically, Louise noted cynically. ''The radio and TV just said he died from a fall in a fishpond, so I thought he tripped and hit his head or something. Now the cops think it's murder—I'll be damned!''

He was saying the right words, but something didn't quite jibe. Then she knew what it was: Charlie expressed no sorrow for his colleague's death. Hadn't he been working closely with Jay for the past five months? Had no bond of friendship or respect been forged between the two men in that time? Or was she being as judgmental as the people in Camus' *The Stranger,* who indicted the stranger for failing to weep at his mother's funeral?

Coolly, she said, ''There's some outside chance it was an accident, but I don't think so. I gave the police your name, so they'll be questioning you. I just came from the station myself, so I've done my part.'' Then she straightened and walked out of the garage. Charlie followed. His presence behind her was not comforting.

''But wait, Louise, I need—I mean—we all need Jay's story. Where's his story?''

She pulled in her breath. How did he know that Jay's story was missing? Tightening her grasp on her ring of metal keys, she swung around and confronted him. ''You don't expect me to give you information about Jay, do you? If I did know about his story, my first inclination would be to give it to the police—or maybe that paper out west, because I'm sure he must have been working for the *Sacramento Union* again. With all due respect, Charlie, I don't know *you* from a hole in the ground—I've only had a couple of conversations with you, and those were pretty unrewarding."

"You think I'm a prick."

She folded her arms across her chest, keys still tightly clutched. "Maybe."

"Well, then, the hell with you, Louise. You're not helpful, and you say you're an old friend of Jay's. If you can't help me get his story, I'll find someone who *can.*" And with that, Charlie Hurd turned and sprinted back to his car. He started it with a roar and screeched out of the cul-de-sac.

What on earth did he mean by that? Shaken, she turned up the mossy path to the house and had only gone a few steps when she felt a touch on her elbow. She gasped again, turned, recognized the tall figure, then exhaled. It was Chris Radebaugh, from across the street. "It's you! One more scare tonight and I'm going to have a heart attack!"

With his usual grace, the teenager apologized. "Sorry: the *last* thing I wanted to do was to scare you, Mrs. Eldridge. I just came over to see if I could help. Who was that guy who went off in such a rush? I saw him go into the garage after you, and it looked a little suspicious to me. The neighbor kids told me when I got home from work why the yellow police tape was up around the Mougeys' house—I'm real sorry about your friend Jay."

She took his arm companionably and they continued up the path to the house. "You wouldn't believe how horrible it was, finding Jay's body staring up at me from that pond . . ."

"Must have been pretty bad," agreed the young man. "Uh, you'll probably hate me for this—"

''For what, Chris?''

''For asking you something—in the name of science, of course . . .'' If anyone was interested in science, it was the eighteen-year-old Chris, who was going to major in biology at Princeton. ''I wondered if the body was floating. I mean, how long . . .''

Louise gulped. ''He'd been in the water about twelve hours. Actually, he'd sunk to the bottom.''

Chris nodded soberly, as if that tallied with everything he knew about corpses in water. ''And then, of course, those fish . . .''

She shuddered. ''Some other time, Chris, not tonight.''

''Sorry. Just curious about those things—don't mean to be disrespectful. Jay seemed like a real good guy that time I met him. So what about that character who just blew out of here in his sports car?''

''That's Jay McCormick's researcher, Charlie Hurd, poking around here trying to find out where Jay's story has gone.'' She turned to the teenager. ''You realize, don't you, Chris, that it was no accident. Jay was murdered, right next door to your house. He probably was killed for his story.''

Chris whistled. ''Heck, the story that's going around the neighborhood is that he tripped over that stupid bird statue. Look, Mrs. Eldridge, I know Janie and Mr. Eldridge get home tomorrow, because I'm picking 'em up, but is there anything I can do—I mean, do you have anything going on?''

The tall teenager had an eager expression on his face. He and Janie had been helpful in the past in finding out things about murders. Maybe he could help.

But, no, this young man was off to college soon and the last thing he needed was to be involved in some murky mystery about an investigative reporter who had obviously probed too deeply for someone's comfort.

"The police will have to find out what happened to Jay. It's not our job, and I won't have time, because after a couple of days' reunion with my family this weekend, I have to go back to work full-time."

Hands in jeans pockets, he shook his blond head. "That's like me, Mrs. Eldridge. I'm getting loaded up with things to do for going away. Especially since my folks are gone for twelve days and my mother left me a list of stuff I have to pack."

"Then don't worry about Jay's death, Chris, I'm sure the police will find the answer." She wasn't so sure of that, but it was something that had to be said.

She went in the house and found several messages on the machine, including a commiserating one from Laurie Kendricks next door, who knew Jay was her friend and had been her houseguest. Another was Channel Five business. The third one puzzled her; it was from Gil Whitson. A stuttering, disjointed message: *"Louise, I'm just taking a minute between convention sessions here. I'm so sorry for making a fool of myself at your house. I hope I didn't ruin the party. I'm sorry I lost my temper with your friend, sorrier than you will ever know. Can you forgive me?* Please *forgive me. I hope you don't think I'm crazy, making that fuss about the fish. But fish are part of my life, maybe too big a part. Well, anyway, I hope someday we can meet on a happier note."*

She leaned against the kitchen counter, folded her arms, and frowned. Gil Whitson was a wild card. Could he have come in before or after another person and figured in Jay's death and the disappearance of his writing tools?

She was so tired and hungry that her body was near collapse, and yet she needed to find out something right now from Tessie Strahan. To fortify herself, she grabbed a peach out of the fruit bowl and poured herself a glass of milk, which she spiked with chocolate. Then she placed the call to Tessie's room at the Washington Hilton.

Tessie was a know-it-all, and that meant knowing it all about Gil Whitson.

''Sorry to take so long answering, Louise,'' she said, ''but I was in the tub. You only caught me here because I've found two nights of partying in a row is all I can handle. I must be failing; I used to go three nights in a row with no trouble. I'm going to bed right after we talk, so I can live to fight another day. Now I'll answer your question.''

A veiled hostility had entered the woman's voice. ''I don't understand how you can think Gil had anything to do with your friend's death. Listen, don't think I'm not sorry your friend died, though I hadn't heard anything about it or I would have called you and offered my condolences. But believing Gil has anything to do with it is pretty far out.''

''Tessie, it's not that I believe anything. It's just that everything has to be checked out. I didn't want to, but I told the police about Gil being over in the Mougeys' backyard and having an argument with Jay.''

''I don't know why you had to do that.''

There was a chill in Tessie's voice, and Louise realized how little she really knew the woman. ''I couldn't *not* tell them. That would be illegal.''

Louise figured this would ring a bell with Tessie, the soul of probity. Her staccato voice softened, from machine gun to typewriter volume. ''When you put it that way, Louise, I guess I can understand. And then, this man was your old friend.''

''And Gil is my valued new friend. The very worst thing that could have happened, Tessie, is that Jay and Gil had a shoving match and Jay accidentally fell on this weird statue that stands right next to the koi pond. Then, maybe Gil became too scared to tell anyone about it.''

''Oh, yes.''

''Yes, what?''

''Well,'' said Tessie with a reluctance that sounded like it came from her very toes, ''I hate like the dickens to drag this up. But of course, we've known Gil for years. Years and years. And Louise, let me assure you, we all have warts—I bet even you.''

''Yes, indeed I do.'' Louise was excited. This woman knew something that might unravel the mystery of Jay's death.

''Gil Whitson is a kindly man, we all know that. But he's very high-pitched. He takes a drug to help him stay balanced.''

''Lithium?''

''Yes, but that's very confidential. It enables him to bring out his artistry in his work, and not get into those extreme highs and lows he used to experience.''

''I've heard it's a wonderful drug.''

''Now, back some years ago, about seven years, I think, a terrible thing happened to Gil. There was an incident with another designer, who was found mysteriously *dead*. Gil underwent a great deal of questioning, but there were no charges brought. He said it was just a, you know, quarrel between friends, and then the man died of a heart attack. But let me tell you, Louise, there're lots of hot tempers among artists, you know that. And Gil is an artist, no doubt about it. Although he is quick to anger, and we see that occasionally just like the other night, I don't think he would hurt a flea. Especially not your friend. Actually, the very reason he became a koi doctor was because he discovered working with fish soothed his soul."

"I could feel that sensitive side in him. A sensitivity and a gentleness. Even my cohost, John Batchelder, spoke of it after he interviewed Gil at the hotel's koi pond."

"Yet there was that incident . . ." mused Tessie, and Louise could hear the worry in her voice. "I suppose that would come up if they look into Gil's past very closely."

"I can't thank you enough, Tessie, for being so frank about this. I know how hard it must be for you."

"I just hope the police find another answer."

"I think they will, Tessie. I can't go into it, but there are others who are likely suspects in Jay's death."

"Thank heavens for that," said Tessie.

After she hung up the phone, Louise realized that she was concealing the very evidence that might give police a lead on these other suspects. But she didn't feel too guilty about it. She had already clued in the police to the possibility that Jay was writing about the presidential campaign. And she would relinquish those papers in the plastic folder after she had checked out a few more leads.

Meantime, she was puzzled by Gil. There was Tessie's story, and more importantly, there was Gil's remorseful voice pleading with her in the telephone message to forgive him. Forgive him for what?

Covering Up: All About Ground Covers

GROUND COVERS WERE ONCE thought of as neat soldiers—tough, disciplined, and eager for service. Myrtle, ivy, pachysandra, and ajuga were in their front ranks. But the list has expanded to include many other plants, from specimens with tiny leaves that grow no higher than a few inches to shrubs such as rhododendrons and azaleas, and perennials such as daylilies, sedums, *Coreopsis* ''Moonbeam,'' as well as native geraniums, roses, and potentilla that literally have been bred to spread.

Any low-growing plant, when used in profusion, can become a ground cover, and last the whole season if its mass of seedpods is left in place for winter effect. There is no excuse for open ground in the garden, for

the selection is enormous—of both flowering and nonflowering varieties and new forms of old favorites.

The English were fond of underplanting big rhododendrons with mayapples, and this simple plant, which starts with tightly furled umbrellas that open into little fringed parasols, will proliferate and add a charming effect to an empty garden corner, or underpin larger plants. But we are talking here about fertile, moist shade. In sharp contrast, a dryland dweller could try the recently developed dwarf rabbitbrush, which will grow in the exact opposite conditions of mayapple. This plant has lacy foliage and big yellow flower clusters for over a month in late summer and autumn. Its big tan seedheads and casual form give it an interesting winter silhouette.

Scores of other possibilities exist, including the tried-and-true ones mentioned. Although some dislike the look of pachysandra after a hard northern winter, it soon recovers and gives forth little white flowers. Ajuga, in contrast, seems to look good in all seasons. It comes in several varieties and colors and makes a delightful show of upright flowers. Others prefer epimedium, with its heart-shaped deep green leaves and delicate pastel flowers. It does not spread as prolifically as some, such as lamium, which seems to grow as you watch it. *Lamium* "White Nancy" is one of those useful plants with white veining in the leaves that brightens

dark places. Irregular drifts of white tulips can be planted under its gentle cover to make a glorious combination. Lamium is easy to handle and pull up if it spreads too far, but stoloniferous varieties such as ivy are a tussle to deal with.

Nothing is quite as perfect as the European wild ginger *(Asarum europaeum)* with its rounded, shiny, kidney-shaped leaves. It has little hidden flowers, which are the more fun for that; it is always good for dividing and giving pieces to friends. Now there are new varieties, including the small-leaved *Asarum* "Callaway," and the large-leaved *Asarum splendens.* The latter has long, narrow, heart-shaped leaves marked with showy bands of silver that light up the shade. Truly delightful is the nonhardy wild ginger snapdragon, *Asarina procumbens,* which forms thick mats of foliage hardy in zone seven up, and has sprightly pink snapdragon-type flowers. If you live north of there, you can use it as a charming, ever-blooming houseplant and patio plant. Also tender but beautiful are the rosy Chinese fountain grass, *Penissetum orientale,* and the spiky, glaucous blue senecio, *Senecio mandraliscae.*

You have to keep your eye on it, for after all, it is bamboo, but the silver-edged dwarf variety, *Sasa veitchii,* spreads like a grove of very small palm trees, and is a perfect foil for lilies, or fritillarias that pop up amidst its foliage. The English use many plants—iberis,

corydalis, tiarella, anemone sylvestris, lungwort, notably the white variety, *Pulmonaria saccharata* "Sissinghurst White"—for undercover work.

For a flowery expanse all season long, nothing is any better than the true geranium. These geraniums fan out in colorful masses to cover a lot of ground in a stunning display of little flower faces. Some of the best have darker centers, giving surprising depth to the picture.

Daylilies have long been valued as cover plants in garden areas. They may look like a lot of work, but with an electric trimmer it is easy to clear off the spent blossoms, and then repeat the process when the leaves need cutting back in September. Sprightly light green fountains of new growth soon make the ground cover interesting again.

Anyone who has raised *Sedum* "Autumn Joy" knows that its virtues cannot be exaggerated. It has a compelling lime color earlier in the season, and then its flowers begin their interesting progression through shades of pink, red, brown, and finally tan. These seedpods last the winter. The plants grow and spread and fill in space nicely. Other sedum varieties also do well as ground covers. Roses have always been well bred, and now some have been bred as ground covers, but other tough varieties also can serve this purpose—rugosas, for instance—and will even hold a hillside nicely.

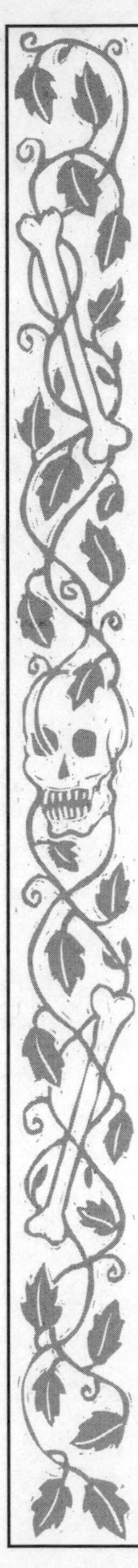

Chapter Twenty

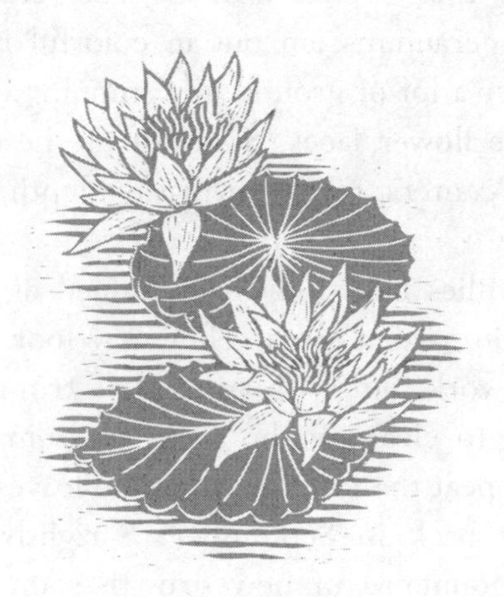

THE STREETS OF DOWNTOWN Washington on this late Friday morning were filled with hurrying people dreaming of the approaching freedom of Friday night. Most were yuppies, with a few unhurried, sun-saturated homeless folks mingling in the crowd and inexorably slowing it down. Louise had taken the subway downtown, staring out the blank train windows into the gray half-light and brooding about Jay McCormick. Now, as she walked the few blocks to the Capitol, she trudged the streets with the memory of her friend's murder dragging on her like an anchor dragging on a boat.

After what seemed an hour but was only minutes, she reached the hulking, graceless Rayburn Building where she was to meet Tom Paschen. Jay's death had thrown a pall on what otherwise would have been an exciting and memorable day: luncheon with the chief of staff for the President of the United States. And she was late, because when the police had come that morning to search her house and yard, she had found it awkward to leave. Finally she told Morton where the key was in the fake rock if he needed to reenter the house. Disapproving of the rock, naturally, he bade her a gruff good-bye and she hurried off to the subway station.

She was approaching her meeting with Tom Paschen not with a sense of anticipation but with grim determination. It would be a fair swap: Paschen would press her for a progress report on the environmental show, and she would pump him for leads to Jay's killer, without revealing that this was her intention, of course. She meant to find out everything she could about the Goodrich campaign and about Lannie Gordon.

Tom was an authority on political campaigns and what happened behind the scenes; "behind the scenes" was where her friend Jay had met the people who probably killed him. And he undoubtedly knew something about Lannie, since she was a Washington player with a high-stakes hand.

She went to the second-floor hearing room to which he had directed her, and saw that she was late: The proceedings were just breaking up in the high-ceilinged chamber. Paschen looked like a small figure, standing behind a table facing the elegant curved wooden dais at the front of the room. Two uniformed police hovered near, apparently to protect the chief of staff from harm or the intrusions of the public. Half a dozen members of the House Budget Committee were gathering papers and getting ready to leave. The banter between the chief of staff and the congressmen was familiar and without rancor. No one was fighting or delaying action, Louise realized, in this week before Congress adjourned so members could hit the campaign trail, seeking money and votes.

Tom turned. His eyes searched the big room and he spotted her. Smiling, he strode over, checking his watch as he approached. ''A little late, aren't you? But it's okay; we'll go right over to the cafeteria.'' He gave her a once-over. Like a lot of other women in Washington today, she was wearing a linen suit with flats, her suit a pale green that she always thought brought out the color of her eyes and hair.

''You look very nice.''

''Thanks.''

They took the elevator to the basement and followed the sign to the subway. ''I've always wanted to ride this subway,'' said Louise.

''I usually walk alongside. Better exercise. But if you want to ride, let's ride.''

They came to the open blue-and-gray cars with their high Plexiglas sides, and sat in the front one on a seat facing backward. Louise noticed there were only four cars, so some people indeed had to walk the distance. Sitting across from them was an elderly congressman with a lithe young woman, obviously his aide. They sat close together, bodies touching, while she talked straight into his ear about something: a bill he had to vote on, perhaps; or what they were going to do later tonight. Even from four feet away, Louise could smell the young aide's intriguing cologne and wondered at its effect on her companion: It must be breathtaking.

The woman was giving a verbal massage. Louise could

tell from the expression in the congressman's eyes. He looked happy and victorious, like a puppy having its stomach scratched.

She looked at the other cars behind them, and saw that they, too, were occupied by congressmen with their staff members in somewhat more pedestrian attitudes. Yet the women were attractive if not beautiful, the male aides dapper in suits and expressions of deep self-satisfaction. It was all told in the expressions: the interchange of glances back and forth between congressmen and aides. Louise could practically smell the sex, arrogance, and power that permeated the place.

The congressman in the opposing seat came out of his agreeable reverie for a moment and recognized Paschen. Louise was amused to see that the chief of staff's presence brought him to immediate attention. In an instant, the congressman had adopted a sycophantic air and opened a conversation about a piece of pending legislation. Paschen mostly just smiled and listened. Some of the walkers alongside the train wanted Tom's attention, too; they had to be content with a waved greeting.

They got off the train, and Louise was amazed when person after person continued to seek out the President's man, this man with the uncontrollable sixth-grade-boy's cowlick, and pipeline to the most powerful leader in the world. It continued even as they went up a ramp, its low head space causing tall men to hunch but no problem for the diminutive Paschen. As they traveled through a warren of low-ceilinged passages, she felt a sense of awe: They were in part of the original Capitol building, most of which was destroyed by fire during the War of 1812.

They reached the elevators, and went up two floors to the members' dining room. All the way, Paschen fielded questions and comments with good grace. "Yep, that's right, we're down in the polls, but not for long. Look for a significant news release in about five days." "You liked the President's speech last night? Wait until the convention; he's got a dynamite acceptance speech. He's going to outline a future for the country that will make sense to you and every other American." "Doubt the President can help you with that right now, but give it a few months. Let's talk about it after the first of the year." "Terrific idea. Call the appointments secretary—we'll get together on it next week."

Ironclad confidence and self-assurance, like an old dreadnought from the turn of the century. But the dreadnoughts, if she recalled correctly, were not impervious to being sunk; she wondered if that wasn't what was going to happen to President Fairchild, along with all of his people, including Tom.

When they were seated at a table, one of the better ones in the room, they were suddenly left alone, as if they had acquired a communicable disease. Tom explained this phenomenon. "It's an unspoken rule that once you arrive here with your lunch guests, you are given privacy while you eat. So don't worry. We'll have a chance to talk. You can order the classic bean soup if you want to, or anything else you want, fish, roast beef."

He looked at his watch. Louise could read the Rolex label. But of course he would have a Rolex watch. Again, she was reminded of the harried rabbit from *Alice in Wonderland*. "We don't have a lot of time. You already know that, right?"

"I understand, Tom." She smiled at him, wishing he would relax; it was a strain being in the presence of a busy man whose right eye tic was now in full operation. He was beginning to make her feel both nervous and guilty. "Tom, I'm honored to have been invited here, and I promise I won't overstay my welcome."

"Now, now," he said, with an embarrassed grin, "you know I didn't mean that."

"Yes, you did, and it's all right, believe me. As a matter of fact, I don't have much time, either. You probably don't know this, but I lost a friend yesterday."

"A friend."

"Actually, it was on last night's news. Jay McCormick. Or, as they called him, John McCormick."

"Oh, yeah," said Paschen. "Heard about that. Speechwriter. Used to be a reporter for some California paper. Gashed his head and fell in a fishpond, didn't he?"

"That's what the reports are saying."

"That's not what happened?"

"I don't think so. I'll tell you about it."

Her stomach was churning, just thinking about the fact that her ship had left the dock, so to speak: She was launching her own private probe for Jay McCormick's killer. Or maybe the launch was yesterday, when she sat in the gloom of her family room, the storm threatening outside, and decided to withhold evidence from the police. "Maybe we had better eat first. I'm feeling awfully hungry."

His gray eyes lit up. "Want fast service? A girl after my own heart! Let's go get in the buffet line."

The buffet table was sumptuous and she loaded her plate. Tom looked over at it with approval. "I can tell. You're the kind who doesn't come back for refills, right? Me, neither." At the table, he piled food onto the back of his fork, continental style. In between bites he lifted his head to say, "Thought if we hurried, there would be time for a quick tour around the White House gardens. Would you like that?''

Surprised, she stuttered, ''I—I'd love it.'' Louise began to feel better in spite of herself, the pain of her friend's death yesterday being diminished by the very fact that she could look forward to the adventures of today.

But she needed to handle things right. As she delicately cut into her rare roast beef and added a dollop of horseradish sauce, she realized the luncheon mood would be soured if she came right out and told Tom that the environmental show was in doubt. Instead, she started out by pumping him about the opposition campaign.

He gave her a vignette of the various players and where they came from, with the focus on Rawlings and Upchurch and his men. There was no doubt in his mind that Rawlings, though buffered from direct contact with the more outrageous campaign charges, was the author of these charges.

Although she had seen at close hand how tough Rawlings could be, she couldn't buy it. Her expression apparently revealed her skepticism, for he said, ''You don't believe me, Louise, but you should. That guy is an old street fighter who knows every dirty hold and sucker punch in the repertoire. I told you, he's orchestrating this whole goddamned thing, and it's going to fly in his face in no time at all.''

She must have looked dubious, for the expression in her companion's gray eyes had hardened. ''Okay, I'll prove it. I've researched Rawlings, right back to when he was a little thug in grade school. Talk about early criminal records of presidential children: This guy had a long rap sheet by the age of twenty, when just by accident some pol saved his ass, got him into college and then into politics. Huh. Shows you how close crime and politics have always been. What gets me is that everyone thinks he's such a pleasant, straight-up guy.''

Tom even knew something about Goodrich's campaign headquarters and about Nate Weinstein, the man who ran the office; Tom apparently respected Weinstein, regardless of their party differences, as a hard-working and honest political worker. At that, she put down her fork and pulled a little pad out of her jacket pocket and jotted down a couple of notes.

Paschen paused with a forkful of food midway to his mouth and looked at her curiously. "Now, just what the heck are you going to do with that information?"

"Oh, probably nothing. I just like to know what's going on and who's involved." She smiled. "You know better than most other people that being in the know is important in Washington."

"Hmm. Well, Louise, just remember, as I give you this primer on national campaigns: Not all the people involved in them are running on the same wavelength. There are the Indians and the chiefs. And in the Goodrich campaign, there are other distinctions to be made as well. For instance, between the seasoned professionals and the crazies. That's what I call Upchurch and his gang. In fact, if I know some of the campaign workers there, and this probably includes the man who heads the office, they're ashamed to be involved in the disgraceful stories those guys have been peddling."

She was afraid he wouldn't answer her questions regarding the murder charge against Fairchild. But he did. His face colored with refreshed anger and his voice was low. "Right now, we have a lot of people working on that one. The evidence they purport to have is from over thirty years ago, and it's these army records that supposedly contain the investigation of the President's involvement in the murder of this file clerk. Well, hell, Louise, it's a pack of lies. We know records can be faked, and this is a good job of fakery, no doubt. That's why we need to get hold of the records themselves. We've demanded to see them, and I think it will happen''—he raised his arm and consulted his watch again—''about two hours from now.''

''That's great; I hope you find out the truth. Tom, can I ask you another question about the Goodrich campaign office? Would they hire anyone that they didn't know well?''

He looked at her speculatively. ''I don't know why the devil you want to know all these things, Louise. But the answer is maybe. They're just like our campaign office, and I'm sure you know there's always a main office downtown, with subsidiary offices around the metro area. We'd take on a hotshot outsider, a speechwriter, advance man, somebody like that, whom we didn't know. He'd have to have a dynamite rep and we would vet him well, believe me, and so would they. There's nothing worse than having unreliable people in your national campaign office.''

His eyes glittered mischievously, and together with the wild cowlick, the grade school boy was very much in evidence. He gave just the slightest wink. ''Campaign offices are filled with secrets that you don't want given out to the general public.''

She put her fork down, through with eating, for she could hardly suppress her excitement. She was more convinced than ever that Jay McCormick had done just that, infiltrated Goodrich's campaign. She even had a way to prove it now. She *had* to find his story. Then, just as fast as her spirits rose, they fell, as she remembered that the person who killed Jay had the story.

Or maybe not.

Knowing Jay, there had to be a backup somewhere. A backup disk or hard copy. Or had they found that, too?

Tom was nearly finished with his meal, and she had run through most of her questions. Casually, she said, ''I bet you have the inside dope on everybody in Washington, don't you?''

His jaw tightened. ''If you mean are we checking their FBI files, no way. The Fairchild administration has stayed clear of that one. But there are other ways of checking people.'' He smiled knowingly.

''Now tell me what you know about a woman named Lannie Gordon.''

Paschen looked faintly annoyed. ''How come you're so interested in all these people who are the President's worst enemies?''

''Oh, Lannie, too?''

''If I weren't a gentleman, I might have a name for her. She's a worthy foe, let's put it that way: Preps those tobacco company presidents and the whole industry—and God knows they need her more than ever, since they made that big settlement to avoid lawsuits. Naturally, she hates the President's guts because of his antitobacco initiatives.'' He leaned toward her. ''Now, Louise, just why do you want to know about her? She is a tough character—I'd steer clear of her, if I were you. She might sue you, and if she did, she'd win.''

''She's Jay McCormick's ex-wife.''

''You don't mean it.''

''Yes.''

''Interesting,'' said Paschen. Louise could see him trying to factor it all in. ''Lannie's one of the toughest infighters in this town. Hands out money to Goodrich's campaign in pots. It appears to be legal, until someone reforms campaign financing again. Actually, it stinks like fuckin' rotten eggs,

Louise, but we both court big money. The rules are Byzantine, and if I know her, she follows the rules. Sorry for the lapses in language; sometimes I forget you aren't just one of the boys, but then, I don't know how in hell I could forget," and he smiled fondly at her.

"Thanks for all that information. Now I need to talk to you about our proposed two-part program on the President's bill." It seemed as good a time as any to slip in the fact that Marty Corbin and the Channel Five general manager continued to drag their feet on the project. "There are problems, I'm afraid."

"Two parts? More than one show?"

"We'll divide it into two segments, if we do it."

"But not more reservations," he said crossly. Having finished his lunch, he wiped his mouth with his napkin, neatly folded it beside his plate, and gave her his full attention. She felt intimidated; the whole reason for this lunch was for him to hear the words that the show was a done deal. And she was going to tell him something quite different.

"However, the writer is preparing scripts that may be able to overcome the difficulties they foresee."

His lips compressed in an amused, cynical line. "Difficulties? What a handy euphemism, Louise. You mean, Corbin's afraid Fairchild's a dead duck, right? And then where would these silly programs be, if the whole bill gets watered down or overturned a few months after it was aired?"

"Oh, it isn't quite like that."

"Oh, yes, it is. That's what you're thinking. You and your reruns. Do you guys think the environment is going up in smoke if the President loses the election? Christ, Louise, I get impatient with Channel Five. That bill is sound; it is going to take more guts than Congress possesses to nullify it, even if Fairchild does go down the tubes.''

The fretful expression still on his face, he picked up a spoon and tapped it impatiently on the white tablecloth. ''Why, I even expected to have another media person here today. Cheryl Wilding of Channel Eight's real hot for a story on the environmental bill. She had to cancel because she was sent out on a breaking story.''

Cheryl, her cohost John's rejected girlfriend, was beautiful but unscrupulous; she had fabricated evidence that nearly sent Louise to jail for murder, but was never charged with anything and was still a popular TV anchor. She was probably ten times more important in Tom Paschen's eyes than Louise, with her humble public television gardening program.

Now the luncheon fell in context: Tom was trying to kill two media birds with one luncheon. She felt less important than ever.

Then he reached down into his briefcase and produced a thick booklet, which he plopped on the table between them. ''If it's any use, here's the bill itself. Show that to Corbin and your general manager.'' He slipped in a quick smile to soften the words: ''See if it impresses them in the least.''

If only Paschen had made his case directly with her producer, she wouldn't be in this mess. She looked him straight in the eye. ''Tom, I'm sorry about this, but that's really all I can say at this point.'' She patted the big stack of paper beside her. ''And thanks for this. I am really sorry about the uncertainty. But I'm still hopeful.''

Hopeful wasn't good enough for the chief of staff. He frowned and hunched over his coffee. He wouldn't be happy until the Channel Five powers that be said yes, and until then, he would be bugging her, not Marty, not the general manager. Whether she liked it or not, she was still in the middle.

Then, they were distracted by what could only be described as a grand entrance. Paschen acknowledged it with a disgusted grunt. At the doorway of the dining room stood Fairchild's opponent, the possible next President of the United States, Congressman Lloyd Goodrich. He was a handsome, white-haired man with highly colored cheeks.

Tom practically sneered at the legislator's dramatic arrival. "Look at that sickening expression on his red face. He thinks just because he's dead even in the polls with a sitting president three months before the election that he's going to win it."

With Goodrich was an entourage that included Franklin Rawlings, Willie Upchurch, Ted French, and several prestigious-looking individuals. "Who are those others?" Louise asked.

"Big donors, most likely. They like to bring 'em here; it makes them feel as if they're on the inside. It's even better than visiting a congressman's office or watching him show off in a hearing room."

As the group passed their table, Paschen's eyes covertly watched each one. When Rawlings veered off to approach their table, he sat up straighter. "Franklin," he said coolly.

"Tom." An insincere hand on Tom's shoulder. And then all Rawlings' attention was directed to Louise.

He said, "I see you're being courted again, Mrs. Eldridge. I hope you keep looking at the big picture." A warm smile suffused his face. His tan suit, although well cut, did nothing to enhance his sallow complexion.

"I think you've made your point, Mr. Rawlings."

"I hope the point is taken," he persisted amiably, but she

noticed that his smile seemed forced. Giving her a little wave, he sauntered off toward Goodrich's big round table.

Paschen hunched forward again toward Louise, his eyes blazing. "What the hell does *he* want from you?" he asked her in a stage whisper.

"The same thing you want: to sell his candidate's position on the environment."

"Louise, they're poles apart. Goodrich doesn't care a flying *fuck* for the environment!"

"I know that, Tom."

But they weren't done with the Goodrich crowd. Suddenly, Ted French doubled back and stood looking down at the two of them. "Hi, there. Tom, you can't keep this woman to yourself, and I see Franklin has met her. I demand an introduction this time." He slid his hand onto the back of Louise's chair and leaned his large, broad-shouldered frame over, giving her an uncomfortable sense of being smothered by his sheer bulk. She looked into his sharp-featured face and met the blue eyes, that indeed had been taught to feign friendliness upon meeting a new person.

Since she could not escape him, she twisted back in her chair to provide a little distance between them, and extended a hand. "I'm Louise Eldridge."

He looked at the seething chief of staff, bowed over her hand, and said, "Ted French, and I'm charmed, just the way Tom is. I see you two together quite a bit these days. What gives?"

She gave him a droll look, and when she spoke, her voice was husky. "That's because we're having a torrid romance. It occupies Tom morning, noon, and night."

Paschen looked startled, then broke into a pleased grin. French straightened up to his full height. "Well, I know you're putting me on."

"French, just what the hell do you want here?" demanded Paschen.

The other man smoothed his blond hair back in a nervous gesture and said, "I just thought you'd want to know that another story's coming out on the Diem matter."

Paschen interrupted him. "Look, I don't care about those stories; they'll be shot down soon enough. Now I wish you'd go away and leave us alone."

At that moment, a distinguished-looking older man at the next table tweaked French's tweed coattails. Then he got serious and gave them a sharp tug. In a shaking voice, he said, "Sir, do you have no scruples?" It was an echo of a famous remark out of the political past, and Louise struggled to place it and then did: the Army-McCarthy hearings.

Tom grinned. In a low voice he told Louise, "Congressman Robert Fulton, who, incidentally, sponsored us here for lunch. French is in for it now."

The stern-faced congressman looked up at the Goodrich campaign aide through thick trifocals and said, "This dining room is sacrosanct, young man. Those who come here yearn for and deserve privacy in which to conduct their business. And you, you are abridging the very rules under which this place was instituted, back in the days when lawmakers and their associates were thought to be gentlemen. So, would you kindly leave Mr. Paschen and his companion alone to *finish* their luncheon, and prove that you have some semblance of those old-time and still-revered values?"

"Well, uh, yessir," said French. He gave Louise an uncertain wave, and quickly retreated to the safety of the congressman's table.

Tom leaned over toward Congressman Fulton. "Thanks, Bob. Set that puppy right, didn't you?"

The legislator grinned. ''Didn't I, though? Stole from Joseph Welch, but Joe wouldn't mind if he were here.'' He cast a curious but polite glance at Louise, but was in no position now to ask for an intrusive introduction himself. Then, in a most courtly manner, he said, ''Sorry my table was too crowded for us to sit together.'' Then he nodded to her and turned his attention back to his companions.

Louise's attention had turned to the Goodrich table. It was a quiet unfolding drama. French had just sat down next to Franklin Rawlings, and the older man immediately launched a quiet diatribe in his ear. She could tell from French's face, not Rawlings': The young aide had bounced from one chewing-out to another. The campaign chief's face was chalk white, and his expression had lost all the random goodwill it once possessed: It was toxic with controlled anger. All did not seem well between Goodrich's merry men today.

A shudder ran through her. Maybe Tom was right about Rawlings.

As they left the dining room, they stopped at the adjoining table and Tom gave Congressman Fulton the introduction to Louise that he'd so obviously wanted. ''She's got a wonderful program on WTBA-TV: gardening. You have to watch it. She's interested in doing a two-part program on the President's environmental bill.''

Fulton held her hand overlong in his clawlike fingers. What was it with these older lawmakers and younger women? ''I voted for that bill,'' he said, his voice shaky and righteous. ''It's what this country has needed for years to ensure the environment survives. I'll look forward to seeing that program.'' He patted Tom's arm. ''Tom here will tell me when it airs.''

She slid a glance over at Paschen as they left the room, and he caught her at it. He gave her a big grin. He didn't feel the least bit guilty; he was going to pressure her every chance he got until the environmental show became reality.

As for Rawlings, she had no idea what he would do next—maybe invite her out to lunch.

Chapter Twenty-one

Just as Tom Paschen expected, his limo driver was waiting under the portico at the side door of the Capitol building, and quickly got out of the car to assist Louise into the backseat. Tom settled in next to her with a satisfied sigh, his bulging briefcase resting beside him. "Only takes five minutes to get to the White House," he explained. "Once we get there, we'll have exactly twenty-five minutes for a garden tour."

She sat there hugging the voluminous environmental bill and smiling in anticipation, like a child about to enter a candy store.

"I guess I act like a train conductor who's trying to stay on schedule," he said by way of apology.

"Sort of, yes. But you do have to stay on schedule, don't you?"

"Unfortunately, yes."

When she began to talk about a book she had read about the White House gardens, his mind was safe to drift. He found Louise Eldridge very attractive, but irritating at the same time. For one thing, she asked too many questions about the President's worst enemies. Why did she need to know about Lannie Gordon? Lannie scared him: She had access to the kind of money that could ruin a candidate in the last two weeks of the campaign, with dirty ads that one couldn't counter fast enough. Lannie had every reason to see Fairchild lose at the polls. Her very job was on the line, after all the dough that had been plowed into Goodrich's campaign.

He guessed Louise wanted to know about the "tobacco queen," as Tom had privately dubbed her, because she had once been married to that second-rate speechwriter who apparently was Louise's friend back in college. But it was a mystery as to why she needed to know so much about the Goodrich crew. She was particularly interested in where they lived. Hell, he didn't know where they lived. She probably would have liked it if he had been able to offer her a psychological profile on each one of them. How far did the woman think the President's chief of staff could reach to find out things about people? Contrary to what he had told her in so pious a tone, he *had* secretly obtained FBI files on Rawlings as well as Upchurch and his men. He had sent them back in a prompt, efficient fashion before any damage was done.

As for Louise, there was something a little too forward about the woman. It was high time Bill came home and controlled his wife. If she were *his* wife, he wouldn't allow her to barge around asking those kinds of questions. Or at least he would want to be damned sure he knew how she was using the information. Bill had told him once that Louise had a nosy streak; that was evident in the way she had gotten herself in such bad scrapes in the past. Paschen hoped he hadn't told her too much today. He liked her, maybe too much, and he didn't want to be responsible in any way for putting her in danger. After all, someone killed that friend of hers out there in the Virginia suburbs, and it was cheek by jowl, apparently, with where Bill and Louise lived.

He wondered: Could the murder have something to do with the Goodrich campaign? Louise had not tipped her hand on that. Damn her, she was just like every other woman, a dissembler. If that was the case, and that half-assed writer had dug something up about the Goodrich campaign and she knew about it, he needed to know what it was. Well, that made two things he would have to keep pressing Louise on. Not bad duty, though, he reflected, and glanced over again at Louise's attractively flushed face and wavy chestnut-colored hair.

Not many women had appealed to him since his wife left him earlier this year. Women had suddenly become like hand grenades, very hard to handle, very apt to blow up, and then claim him as part of the wreckage. Funny how his family back in Boston had reacted to his separation, after twenty years of marriage. His mother was cool and unsurprised, and so was his sister. "Darling, you just weren't raised right, and I'm sorry," said his whimsical mother. "You always were a kind of a genius, especially at understanding government and things like that. But you have yet to cultivate the skills that ordinary human beings need.'' Then she had hugged him close, and told him that she was just making another of her broad jokes. But Tom didn't think she was kidding; he pretty much agreed with her. He was a lousy specimen of a human being, loving work and loving the game, hating leisure. Probably treating his wife badly over those two decades of marriage. *Face it, Paschen,* he thought, *you handle a congressional caucus better than you handle a woman.*

And it was beginning to get him. The tic in his right eye bugged him a lot. It was like a harbinger of what was to come: maybe high blood pressure next, then a heart attack or stroke.

Too much work and no leisure. He was trying a little leisure right now, though, trying to relax by taking the leggy Louise for a quick tour of the White House gardens. More than anything in a long time, he had enjoyed his little interlude at the Art Gallery last week. The trip up to the tower with Louise, unself-conscious and astoundingly beautiful with her long swath of hair with its red highlights, strolling around in that sexy black pantsuit and high heels and trying to make an art convert out of him.

It was fun, and fun wasn't something he was good at. If he had a woman like her, he knew he could learn. It wasn't only her enthusiasm and the way she threw herself into things that he liked: She went after things; and she was smart. Too bad she was married to a man he knew and thoroughly respected.

Anyway, something told him Louise wasn't available, though there was always movement with women. For instance, it hadn't taken his own lissome wife very long to make a new alliance. He had heard from reliable sources she was dating the CEO of her firm.

The knowledge made his stomach knot.

They were driving in the White House gates now, and a glance at his companion showed she was on excitement overload. Her excitement unexpectedly communicated itself to him. They were let off at the front entrance, with Tom advising the driver to return in exactly thirty minutes. He told Louise, ''He'll take you right to the subway station.''

They had walked onto the front porch before they heard the limo driver bring the car to a halt with a screech of brakes, and saw him race over to them. ''You wouldn't want to be without this,'' he admonished, thrusting Tom's briefcase at him.

''Thanks,'' said Tom, shaking his head. ''Can't believe I did that.''

At the enormous white facade, Louise acted as if she were entering a holy shrine, although he knew she had been here before with Bill at receptions involving Bill's job with the State Department. ''I always love to come here,'' she said, smiling at him. He noticed her eyes were pure green now, not just hazel anymore, and decided it was a reflection of what she was wearing.

He dutifully went into his guide mode, for he had taken a couple of people on this little tour, his mother and his sister. ''First, we have our usual red geraniums in pots. Lots of pot gardening around here, inside and out.'' Guiding her into the residence, he added, ''I want to show you the Rose Garden and then we can walk onto the south grounds. It's more private. The public tours take people through the East Garden, so maybe we won't go there.'' As they entered the residence, uniformed guards greeted them. He introduced Louise, whose visit was expected, then handed one of them his briefcase and asked him to see that it got to his office, and gave another Louise's packet of papers to hold on to until their return.

They drifted through the first floor and passed an enormous Victorian flower arrangement on a long bronze table. He could hardly get her past it, and he knew there was schedule trouble ahead. If she was going to dally at the very first spot of interest, she would throw his tour schedule down the toilet. Nervously, he glanced at his watch.

"How utterly romantic," she murmured, circling the table to view the arrangement from every side. He trailed after her. "It's like a gardener's dream, all those full-blown pink and yellow roses, the delphiniums and the lavender statice. And those swags of smilax, like ribbons binding it all together."

He eyed the floral grouping with suspicion. Overdone, in his opinion. "Don't particularly like it, myself, Louise, but your taste is better than mine. And that's certainly the current fashion at the White House. But I did hear Jackie Kennedy hated roses like that; liked spring things instead. Anyway, let's step lively."

He took her arm firmly and soon hustled her out the south entrance. He could tell she had wanted to spend more time in the residence, but he just didn't have more time. Then they headed for the Rose Garden. Anchored by huge old magnolias, it was a large green expanse bordered with lush beds. "I never look at the flowers," he confessed, "because I'm always here with the President for a public ceremony."

So she told him what the gardens contained. "Those are boxwoods outlining the beds. And in with the roses and the lilies they have placed all those old-fashioned varieties—asters, hollyhock, mullein, black-eyed Susan, phlox. What a wonderful mix."

"Check out the gardeners," said Tom, as they approached the far corner of the Rose Garden. "They're always doing that. A plant barely has time to bloom before these guys come along and yank it out and plant something else.'' The crew was pulling out the summer plants and refertilizing the ground for a new crop of fall flowers that were standing near, ready to take their turn.

They were installing a flower that even Tom knew the name of. He showed off for Louise: ''I know what those are: they're chrysanthemums, topiaries and just plain ones. I like them better than what they're taking out.''

She smiled. ''You like everything neat and tidy, don't you? That's more or less the opposite of me. I like everything irregular and wild.''

Then they wandered over to the East Garden, in what was a lull between groups of public visitors, passing trees that were gifts from the early presidents up through Jack Fairchild. He was able to point out a few to his visitor. His eyes lit up.

''Now let's go to one of my favorite places. Haven't been there for a year or so, but even thinking about it gives me a little sense of peace and quiet.''

They walked down the lawn toward the southeast corner of the property, and he took her to sit on a cast-iron garden settee resting under a huge oak tree. Tom said, ''It's a great place to come to get away from it all, and get a real feeling for the history of the place. Except I never have time to come here. This bench was bought for Millard Fillmore back in the 1850's by his gardener. Anyway, that's what they say.'' He looked up at the large bower of leaves above them. ''In fall, these leaves are fantastic. They turn bright red.''

She looked up, too. ''Scarlet oak, probably. And that's an old horse chestnut next to it; I bet these two trees have seen a lot of history.''

He smiled over at her. "Nice spot, isn't it? It would be a great place for a man to propose to his beloved."

She smiled faintly and clasped her hands together. "I think so, too. For all we know, someone did."

He shook his head, wondering if he were becoming soft-headed. "Sorry, I didn't mean to be so maudlin." He hoisted up his arm and checked the time. "Our twenty-five minutes is nearly up." His other arm was still on the back of the settee, barely touching her back. For the first time in as long as he could remember, he wasn't anxious to get back to work. "Louise, I really enjoyed this. Maybe next time you come, I'll have learned more about the trees and stuff."

She gave him a warm smile that threatened his resolve to leave. "It was very nice, Tom. I can't thank you enough."

Then he leaned forward and propped his elbows on his knees, and gave her a knowing sideways glance. He could feel himself slipping out of his relaxed mode back into the controlled frenzy he had adopted as a necessary function of his job. "Oh, you can thank me, all right. And you know how: Just get that show off the ground at Channel Five."

Pushing her again, pressuring her. He could even see the turnoff in her beautiful green eyes. She was hurt. And she had reason to be. She wasn't the one responsible for the final decision at Channel Five, so why did he box her into a corner? Why the hell couldn't he learn to be a human being? And once he was into it a little, why did he have to revert to an uptight bureaucratic prick?

Politically Incorrect Plants, Conceits, and Follies

SETTING A TRIO OF flamingos in your front garden amidst the marigolds sends a jaunty message: "This is kitsch: take it or leave it." Americans have unique ways of expressing their most personal views on gardening, through columns, arches, urns, statues, baubles, balls, and bells—otherwise known as conceits and follies.

A conceit is "an extravagant, fanciful, and elaborate construction or structure." Not all conceits and follies are politically correct. For example, do we really want to tread on frogs inset into concrete garden stepping stones, or hang in our ornamental cherry a birdhouse fashioned in the shape of a cat, with its mouth the birdhouse door? Then there are the gazing balls to set in the gar-

den: Does this mean we are supposed to hold séances among the flowers? And incredible as it seems, garden stores still sell those statues of men reaching out to hold the master's horse, that hark back to the days of slavery. Americans will exercise their freedom of expression in the garden.

By far the most seriously politically incorrect ''folly'' is to buy invasive plants and release them into our ecosystems. Such plants as lythrum, which is banned in some states, autumn olive, Japanese honeysuckle, Oriental bittersweet, multiflora rose, and crown vetch are threats to our environment, harming crops, wildlife, and waterways. The grossest example is the kudzu vine, which was imported from China to control erosion, and now drapes the Southeast with its unwelcome presence. Gardeners should read up on the subject and learn which plants are invasive, and not only avoid them, but tell their nurserymen not to sell them. Many of them are still sold as ''quick'' garden solutions.

Perhaps the greatest error in adding objects to the garden is leaving them out there to fend for themselves. That four-foot-high Greek statue of the ''young man'' that you came upon in the Athens market and had shipped home. That strange urn you bought at the antique emporium for way too much money. The old horse trough you picked up at a farm auction. The gazebo made out of real wood, for which you paid thousands of dollars. All of them will make the grade, provided you give them company. Make them part of the garden, not stand-alones that demand our undivided, and sometimes embarrassed, attention. The Greek young man will look his best when set among a little group of trees or perennials. The horse trough could turn into a winner if you overgrow it with plants such as chartreuse lady's-mantle *(Alchemilla mollis),* sprawling true geraniums in pale pink or lavender, and some Queen Anne's lace for the appropriate country touch. Likewise, the gazebo should be landscaped. Try a shallow garden around its circumference, or for a more formal look, anchor it with evergreen shrubs set out equidistant from its corners.

Eighteenth-century English gardens were replete with replicas of classical ruins, with broken columns tops in popularity. Only the most fearless or artistic gardener would feel comfortable doing that today. Upright columns still work, though, and are fine places on which to perch urns of plants. Go beyond a column, obtain two, and put in a four-foot crosspiece to form an arch. A designer did this, and even the most amateur carpenter could replicate the feat. Another do-it-yourself idea for adding architecture to the garden is a homemade pergola to cover the garden walk, made of slim poles with crossbars.

Columns are not for the informal gar-

dener, whose numbers are legion. They like to add eclectic elements of all kinds, including rusty pieces of junk: After all, what are gardens for, if not self-expression? And who is to challenge their taste, for one of the winning exhibitions at a recent Chelsea flower show was the overrun grounds and neglected greenhouse of a famous British plantsman, moved intact into the exhibition space. So we know neglected, rusty, and ruined objects have made it in the world of garden design. Those who want to try this might start small on a small scale with a rusty water pump, and plant it up with a few clumps of grasses and some lyrical native flowers, such as daisy-flowered *Tanacetum niveum* and rosy penstemon and purple sage.

What is called going too far, and surely is a piece of political incorrectness, is using an abandoned toilet and decking it out with flowers. But, in fact, someone is doing that, in an otherwise sedate suburb of Chicago.

Chapter Twenty-two

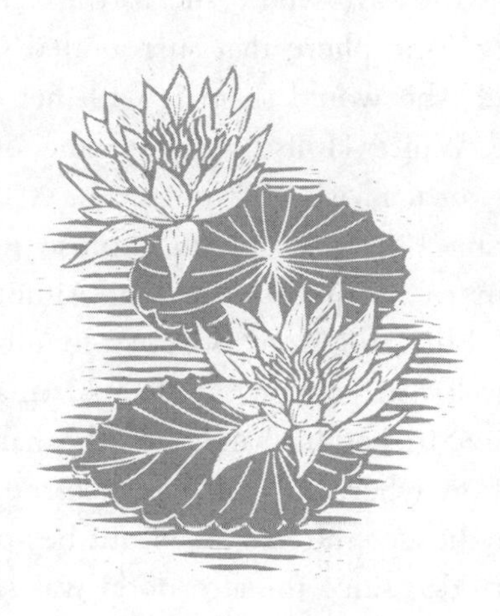

LOUISE MAY NOT HAVE been as busy as Tom Paschen, but she, too, had her important jobs to do. She needed to get home and make a few phone calls, the most important one to Jay McCormick's former newspaper. If Jay was back working as a reporter, the editor would know what Jay's story was about. He might even have a duplicate disk or hard copy in hand.

It had been an interesting day, with Tom Paschen alternately pleasant and provoking. She wondered if he had always been this way, or if his recent marital troubles had thrown him off stride. He reminded her of a wily but predatory animal: a fox, perhaps, gentle in protecting its own family, fierce in battling enemies.

And it was an eye-opener for Louise, especially that trip on the Capitol subway, where she had a chance to experience the heady atmosphere that surrounded Congress. First chance she had, she would share it with her husband.

As for the White House gardens, she only hoped she could make a return visit. Maybe the next time, however, she would bring Bill as chaperon. Louise found this feral quality in Tom to be quite attractive. Although a Harvard graduate, like Bill, and from Boston old money, Tom had lost that white-bread eastern intellectual image that sometimes still clung to her husband. Yet she hardly wanted to create a situation where Bill's friend became sweet on her.

On the way home, she had taken out her pad and made a list of things to do, since the afternoon was still young. The key to Jay's death must be the mysterious story on which he was working. Exactly what the story said, she didn't know, but she needed to talk to everyone involved and pursue every single person who was interested in it. Tom Paschen had also given her a valuable lead into the Goodrich campaign. She was determined to do what she could to find Jay's killer.

First, she poured herself a big glass of iced tea, and took the phone and pad onto the patio, sitting in one chair and propping her feet on the opposite one. She dialed Jay's paper in Sacramento and she speeded the process of getting through to the editor, Al Kirkland, by telling the operator she might have knowledge about Jay's death.

While she waited to be connected, she glanced around her patio garden. The plants were perking along nicely, like happy little soldiers. They were making remarkable growth progress after the maraudings of little Sally. Her eye focused in and recorded a remaining bare spot. She'd have to fill that in with a clump of liriope.

It took a lot of talking to convince Kirkland that she was who she said she was. She ran through her credentials, including how she met Jay in graduate school at Georgetown in 1975. At last he believed her, and the suspicion in his voice disappeared.

"He spoke fondly of you, Louise," said the editor. "But you understand I don't immediately trust everyone who calls me about Jay. We're not dealing with some minor affair here. This is a story with the dimensions of Watergate . . . . well, I may be exaggerating a little, because it doesn't involve constitutional issues, as Watergate did. Yet it's going to be significant enough to ruin a presidential candidate—and the country's top political consultant, too."

She repressed a gasp. That packet of memos she had found in her toolshed was only a tiny clue: Jay must have gotten to the very heart of the matter.

The editor's voice was dry and unsentimental, but she could tell it was a cover-up for some deeper feelings. "Now we've lost Jay, and I can tell you I'm sick about that. And we've also lost his damned story. The detective out your way, Geraghty, said Jay's computer and all signs of his research are gone. No hard copy. Nothing."

Louise's heart sank. "Didn't he ever send *you* anything?"

"No, that wasn't Jay's way of doing things. I knew the story concerned the campaign and named people like Rawlings and Upchurch—we got a good look at them when they were out here managing that fall senatorial race. That's when Jay first got a line on how they operated. When Rawlings went to Washington with Goodrich, he knew something like this was bound to happen in the presidential campaign. He became filled with righteous indignation, just as he used to when he was a young reporter. He asked to come on board again as a reporter. Of course, he wanted to keep an eye on his daughter out in D.C. anyway, so I rehired him and sent him there. He infiltrated, essentially burrowed right into the guts of Goodrich's operation."

"My God, that took nerve."

"And under his own name, too: John McCormick. Of course, with us, his byline in the *Sacramento Union* was 'Jay McCormick.' Jay didn't want to get hired by Rawlings under false pretenses, for fear the paper would be ruined by a big lawsuit: Juries today have zero tolerance for reporters getting stories by lying about their identity—even when it involves heinous crimes."

"He went under his own name and took his chances."

"Yep. Jay got in the door because he had the highest recommendations from his boss in the PR firm out here. He told the Goodrich people that 'John,' as he went by in the public relations business, was a quiet guy who detested the spotlight—that's so they didn't put him on show like a Peggy Noonan—but that he was the best speechwriter since Bill Safire. And he was. Yet Jay didn't share the conservative view, as you know. Once in, it was frustrating for him, because he wrote some good speeches for the congressman and knew they were aiding his cause. Meanwhile he was writing his own story about Goodrich's dirty campaign and hoping to bring him down."

"I only wish he'd sent you some hard copy, or given some to Charlie Hurd, that assistant of his."

The timber of Al Kirkland's voice changed; it became sharper, suspicious. "*That* guy—you know him?"

"I just met him once. He's not very pleasant."

"He phoned me yesterday. He's too eager by half—in fact, seems to me he's almost ghoulish in his disregard for the fact Jay is dead: I don't trust him any more than Jay did. On the other hand, Jay couldn't have done the story without someone like him—it's just too big."

Louise recalled the uncomfortable meeting she had with Charlie Hurd in her garage last night. "Quite a contrast between the two of them, isn't there? Hurd acts like a bald-faced opportunist, while Jay was a kind and wonderful man."

The editor's voice had become a little more ragged. "I knew Jay for twenty-three years and he was very much like a son to me, if you must know. It took a lot of guts to give up a high-paying PR job and go back to reporting, but the story was going to be the crowning point of his career—a story that would really make a difference."

She felt as if she knew the man at the other end of the phone. "Al, I want to do what I can here. For instance, when did Jay call you last?"

"Wednesday night."

"Did he say anything that might give you a clue as to who was involved in this?"

"Nope, not that night. But the night before: Tuesday, I'm pretty sure. He'd already changed his car, ditched the rental car and got an old clunker, I think for cover, because he thought someone was tailing him. Tuesday night, he said he'd changed digs again. Didn't like it much. Jay is kind of messy and disorganized, and it was like asking him to clean up his desk and move to another one."

The old guilt flew in like a hawk and grasped hard on to Louise's shoulder. "I did that, Mr. Kirkland. I made him move across the street."

"Well, it wasn't good timing, Mrs. Eldridge, but I'm sure you had your reasons. I know Jay wasn't perfect."

"But that wasn't why." But he didn't want to hear her convoluted story about not having room enough for all her houseguests.

"Anyway," continued the editor, "he joked about the new place he was staying at. Said it was pretty fancy and he had a whole wine cellar at his disposal. 'Cept that was a joke, because Jay wasn't much of a drinker. Then he mentioned something about how all his efforts were 'ending up with the fishes.' And then, damnit, *he* ends up with the fishes."

Louise noted the phrase down on her list. "Was he serious when he said that?"

"No, not serious at all. It was another joke; Jay used to have lots of jokes." The editor was silent, still grieving, as she was, over a dead friend.

"I remember." She didn't want this conversation to bog down in tears, so she continued briskly: "I'm glad to have talked to you. I'm going to try to find out something about what happened to Jay. I can't stand not knowing, and I don't know what the police can do."

"Mrs. Eldridge, I don't know you," said Kirkland, "but I hope you're careful. You have some pretty dangerous people running around Washington. As for us, we've sent a man out there to check things out, including that Charles Hurd. His name is Paul Mendoza. I'll put Paul in contact with you. We here at the *Sacramento Union* have lost something valuable: Jay McCormick. At least, we'd like his story back."

She was disappointed at Kirkland's lack of information. It would have seemed natural that Jay would have discussed the story with his superior, but instead, like a prima donna—and she got the clear impression that all investigative reporters were prima donnas—he decided to keep the details of the story to himself until the very end. All that was known was the theme: a tale of dirty deeds that could bring down a presidential candidate.

She consulted her list. Nate Weinstein: Tom Paschen had said Weinstein was the office manager at the Goodrich campaign office. Calling him would at least enable her to find out what they were telling people about their missing speechwriter.

Obtaining the number from information, she placed the call. It was answered by an eager Goodrich campaign volunteer. "Hello, I'm"—Louise thought quickly—"Marie Emerson of the Bethesda campaign office. Can I speak to John McCormick?"

"Oh, sorry," said the woman, her voice rising in a determined effort to remain optimistic even though she couldn't produce John on the line. "He's no longer with the campaign."

"Oh, gee," Louise said, "but he was there a little over a week ago. I talked to him."

"Sure you did. John was right here, toiling away on speeches in his little back office, handling lots of little things for Mr. Upchurch. But, gosh, he left, and they told me—uh, just a minute."

The woman put her on hold. When she came back, her voice was subdued. "I'm sorry. I have no information on him. And now I have other calls on the board. Thanks for calling the Goodrich campaign, and be sure to vote November seventh!"

"Wait," said Louise, frantically. "Can I speak to Nate Weinstein?"

"Well, I don't know. Hold on." Someone obviously was giving the woman input. "Yes, actually, you can. What's your name again?"

"Marie, from the Bethesda office."

"One moment."

And it only took seconds. She had certainly stirred up the place. "This is Nate Weinstein," said a cool voice. "Who's calling, please?"

"Marie—Erickson, from the Bethesda office." Damn. She should write it down when she made up names.

"I don't recognize that name. Are you a volunteer?"

"Yes, I am, and I love it." She tried to sound as agreeable as the dynamic young woman who had answered the office's phones. "I'm trying to reach John McCormick."

There was a pause. "Just how do you know John? He didn't go to the branch offices."

"I got acquainted with him in the past few months and we became friends. I understand he's left. Do you know where he's gone? Is he all right?"

Weinstein was silent. Whether or not he was involved in the dirtier deeds of the campaign, he must have figured out that the dead John McCormick found in a fishpond in northern Virginia was the self-same John McCormick who had worked as a Goodrich speechwriter until he dropped out of sight nearly two weeks ago.

"Ma'am, do you read the papers? I'm pretty sure the man you're seeking has been found dead. An accident, I believe, down in some northern Virginia neighborhood."

Tom Paschen had vouched for this man as one of those basically decent political professionals who tried to do an honest job in the face of today's fiercely partisan politics. Who knew what would happen down the line? Maybe someone would need this man to tell the truth on a witness stand.

It was easy for her to call up her grief over Jay's death. In a soft tearful voice, she said, "I was afraid of that. He was an awfully decent man, and I really liked him. So—it is the same person I grew to know a little. I'm so sorry."

"No sorrier than I am. John became invaluable around here, let me tell you. Marie, tell me your last name again."

Suddenly nervous, she hung up, afraid he would ask for more information. She stared at the phone in her hand, and came to a realization that made her temporarily breathless. The Goodrich campaign headquarters might have a naive person answering phones, but certainly not a naive phone system: They undoubtedly had caller ID. That meant they could trace where this mysterious phone call came from.

Rawlings, Upchurch, or French—any of them might know by now that she was bent on learning something about Jay. She didn't know which one of them she mistrusted the most. She leaned her head back on the patio chair and gave a deep sigh. In her haste to sort through all this, she had exercised her usual hubris. Had she also put herself in danger?

Chapter Twenty-three

IT TOOK A FEW moments to recover from the call to the Goodrich campaign headquarters; it was always an effort for her to lie, and worse this time, for her lying had probably done her more harm than good.

With the afternoon waning, she realized she had to hurry on to the next item on her list, namely, the printed question on her notepad, WHO ELSE KNOWS ABOUT LANNIE??? Tom Paschen hadn't given her much additional information about the woman.

She needed to know more. But where to get additional facts?

The answer came quickly to her: Mary Mougey, who knew everyone in the Washington area in a way that was incomparable. Asking people for money, as Mary did, brought out the best and the worst in them, and Louise was certain that the affluent Lannie had been approached to donate money to Mary's world hunger campaign.

Anyway, it was high time to try to reach Mary in St. Maarten and talk over Jay's death. The Mougeys should be back from their sailing trip by now. It was cocktail time in the Caribbean; they would surely be at home, for Richard was an exuberant drinker and Mary didn't mind a few herself.

This would be a dicey call, too. Louise got up from the patio chair and paced the flagstones, phone to her ear. Mary answered. "Oh—Louise," she said briskly. "Hold on." Was her neighbor's voice just a trifle aloof when she found out it was Louise calling? Or was Louise imagining things because she felt so guilty? Was all of this going to come between her and her friend?

But no, Mary's voice was all graciousness when she returned to the phone. "My dear, sorry for being brusque. I had Detective Geraghty on the other line, and I told him you were trying to get through—we were finished talking, anyway. What a terrible thing to happen! I'm *so* sorry to hear of your friend's death . . ."

Louise quickly explained to Mary how Jay came to be staying at her house in the first place. Then, she launched into an effusive apology, almost as elaborate as the Victorian banquette of flowers at the White House.

"Don't apologize, my dear; it's just one of those terrible

things. Detective Geraghty said it could have been an accident, or it could have been . . . *murder*. It's just bad, either way."

"Oh?" said Louise, not following her.

"If an accident, it has to be *Oscar's* fault. If murder, well, then I know you will somehow be involved—and that is not always good, as we both know."

"Now, just who's Oscar?"

"Oscar's the name Richard gave to that dratted bronze bird near the pool. After Oscar Wilde, you know: a silly little association that doesn't make much sense, actually. I had a *feeling* that statue was in a bad place. Detective Geraghty did not mention anything of the kind but I wonder if your friend could have borrowed a bottle from Richard's wine cellar and—perhaps imbibed a little too much."

How perceptive the woman was. Actually, Geraghty *had* found a discarded wine bottle in the kitchen trash. She was thankful it hadn't been Château Rothschild, or Louise would owe the Mougeys a bundle.

"It wasn't an accident, Mary. The man's computer and disks were stolen, and he was onto a big story. Very big. That's another reason I called, to ask you about somebody. Lannie Gordon: Do you know her?"

"Oh, Lannie." The cold but polite tone discounted Lannie and put her in Mary's spiritual trash barrel. "She's a hard sell when it comes to charitable giving."

"But I thought the tobacco people were big givers."

"Bigger than *ever* these days. Various individual tobacco companies give up to one percent of their pretax income to hunger programs like ours, plus arts and education. But Lannie is on a different wavelength. She's working for the tobacco industry as a whole. She's more interested in who's getting elected to office. Tobacco's had a rough go lately, as you well know, and there's nothing Lannie would like better than a president who likes to light up a cigarette."

"Does Congressman Goodrich smoke?"

"I hear he does, and, more importantly, that he's very sympathetic to tobacco interests."

"Lannie was Jay McCormick's former wife. Do you think she is capable of harming someone, an ex-husband, for instance, who has defeated her in a legal suit for custody of a child?"

"Lannie was McCormick's former wife—and there's a child involved? How sad for the child. She is not *bad,* Louise. In fact, I could see liking her if she were associated with someone else. She is just caught up in a business that has its own agenda. She would never get her hands bloodied, so to speak; she has too much to lose. That woman makes close to a million dollars a year."

Louise did a quick mental calculation: Lannie made about fifteen times as much as she did with her two jobs.

"Thanks, Mary. I felt a certain empathy for the woman myself, though I could see she can be tough as nails."

"So you're sleuthing again, Louise. We'll be back home in a few days, and I'll be delighted to go out on the detective trail with you. In the meantime, I want to commiserate with you on the loss of your dear old friend. And there's one more thing I need to talk about." She paused. "Louise, how can I say it? I hear these lurid accounts from police regarding the body, I mean, Jay. I hate to upset you with them, but yet there are the living to be considered. Uh, Jay *floated* in my pond all night, I guess, until you found him. The police also gave me some garbled story about hamburger scraps fed to my koi."

Louise had an intake of breath. Why did they have to mention Jay's fast-food dinner scraps?

''I'm afraid so.''

''Well, if it isn't too crass to bring up at a time like this, how have the koi survived it all?''

Louise realized she hadn't fed the fish all day.

''I think they're doing just fine,'' she answered smoothly. ''But just for insurance, I'm going to have a koi doctor look at them and be sure they're okay.''

Then her call waiting buzzed, and Louise was frankly grateful, for her falsehoods about the fish were stressful. She devoutly hoped that she wouldn't have to manufacture more of them.

''Hold on, Mary, I'll be right back.'' When she put the second call on the line, a quavery young voice said, ''I'm Melissa McCormick, Mrs. Eldridge.'' Louise's heart leaped in her chest and her feet came off the chair.

She scribbled the girl's number down on her pad. ''I will call you right back,'' she promised Melissa. ''Don't go anywhere.'' Then she flashed back to Mary Mougey.

''Hi, Mary, I'm back. A friend of mine is a koi doctor—he's an expert on them. He'll make sure that yours are nice and healthy.''

''I've never heard of a koi doctor. How kind of you, my dear,'' said Mary. ''See you soon.''

''And Mary, that call on the other line—I think it could be a break in the case.''

''Wonderful. Go for it, Louise! But *do* be careful.''

Chapter Twenty-four

SHE TAPPED IN THE phone number that Jay McCormick's daughter had given her. The phone rang only once before Melissa answered. "Hello!" Breathless. A small clattery noise indicated that someone else had picked up another extension.

"Hello—"

"Hold a minute," interrupted the girl, as if talking to a friend. She was a canny one, just like her father had said. Louise could hear a pleasant conversation in the background, obviously a smooth attempt to assure the other person, perhaps a housekeeper, to stay off the extension phone.

How did this thirteen-year-old become so crafty? Was it genetic, straight through from father to daughter?

Melissa returned to the phone. Still as if talking to a girlfriend, she said loudly, "It's cool you called. Gotta see you. Can we get together?"

"Well, I'm in my home south of Alexandria."

"I—hold on another sec." Louise could hear only silence, as the girl perhaps checked out to see who might be listening on the phone extensions. Louise remembered Jay saying that Lannie and Melissa lived in a huge house overlooking the Potomac.

After a couple of minutes, Melissa returned to the line. "Whew! She's gone home. The maid, I mean. I live way out in Great Falls. How will we ever get together?"

"Why don't I drive up right now? It should only take about a half hour."

"You would do that? That's cool."

"Melissa, you have been told about your father, of course."

"Yes." The girl's voice choked. "Mom told me last night, after she visited the morgue to be sure it was him. And now you and I just *have* to meet. I'm following my Dad's instructions."

"He told you about me?"

"Yes. But we can't be seen together, so let me meet you at the beginning of our street, okay? There's a little park where you can pull your car in." She gave Louise exact directions to her house.

"I'll see you there."

Louise hopped into her Honda wagon, rolling down the

windows because the air conditioning had broken down again. She drove through the crowded northbound traffic of Route One, which was becoming more gentrified each year. The two-hour sleazy motels, the halfway houses, the down-at-the-heels trailer courts, the fortune-teller ensconced in an old house, and even the one-of-a-kind Dixie Pig barbecue restaurant with its pig-graced sign were all threatened by encroaching fancy town house developments. It made Louise rather sad. She liked the diverse character of the Route One strip and hated to see the entire area homogenized, the only people left with whom to interact the upper middle class, who sometimes bored her to tears.

Then she caught the Beltway, filled with Friday going-home traffic, until the turnoff onto the Memorial Parkway that would take her to Great Falls.

Things now had been set in motion. No matter what the police had done or not done, she herself had learned a little more today about the people who might have harmed Jay. And now, through none of her own efforts, but rather through the dead man's wiliness, she might get a genuine lead from his daughter.

But an uncomfortable feeling kept dogging her. Paul Mendoza, the Sacramento reporter Al Kirkland had mentioned, would soon be contacting her. And she didn't doubt that other reporters were soon going to make some connection between her and Jay. For one thing, she hadn't asked the police to withhold that kind of information. And just the words "Sylvan Valley" conveyed memories for the media of the mulch murder. Unfortunately, that severed body had been discovered in leaf bags Louise had pinched from her neighbors for yard mulch. It was one thing to try to find Jay's killer, and another to be involved publicly.

She was also quite humble about what she could learn about this affair. For instance, how could she possibly breach the Goodrich campaign and find out which of the three men might have done Jay harm: Upchurch, French, or even Rawlings?

Louise turned off the parkway onto a narrow secondary road. This quiet neighborhood, only a few blocks from the parkway, was protected with signs that kept commercial vehicles and most ride-by traffic out, making it into an almost private enclave. Louise missed a turn, and took the next street, although it was one-way and had a DO NOT ENTER sign. She entered anyway, and within a few blocks saw the small, grassy public park Melissa had described. She pulled her car onto the side of the narrow road.

The girl soon appeared, taking her time, playing a role. Laughable looking, really, with her tinted sunglasses that were so huge that they must have been filched from her mother. Her hair was curly and long, a glorious strawberry blond, a combination of Jay's pale blond and Lannie's red hair, and her thin face behind the sunglasses was pale and anonymous, like her father's. Her slight frame reminded Louise of her own daughter Janie about two years ago, before Janie grew taller and rounded out with breasts and hips. The overalls and T-shirt gave Melissa a kind of small scarecrow look.

With rolling hips, she slouched toward Louise's car like a miniature movie star. Smoothly, she whipped off her sunglasses, only to reveal pale blue, vulnerable child eyes. Then her patina of sophistication abruptly cracked, and she became a kid again. "Mrs. Eldridge, is that you?" she asked timidly.

"Yes. Melissa, I'm so happy to meet you." Louise extended her hand, and the girl formally shook it.

Then she looked around suspiciously and said, "I can't

trust anyone.'' Her eyes opened wider in alarm and she pointed to the glasses. ''That's why I wore these.''

''Hop in right now.''

Melissa hurried around the car and got in the passenger seat. Then she gave Louise a long look.

Louise smiled at her. ''You sound a little frightened. Is everything all right at home?''

Melissa let out a sharp breath. ''As all right as it can be. Nobody's hurting me, if that's what you mean. My mother's always real nice to me.''

Louise stretched out a hand and touched the girl's thin arm. ''First, I want you to know how terrible I felt when your dad died.''

The pale eyes turned to her in anguish, and tears formed and fell onto her cheeks. ''He didn't just die, Mrs. Eldridge. He was killed. I know it. Someone was after him and they *got* him.'' All of a sudden her thin shoulders began to shake. Louise reached over and hugged the girl in her arms and held her tight. After a few moments, Melissa stammered, ''I'm sorry. My dad told me to be strong, that we would start a new life together. And then he went and got killed.''

''And you think he was afraid he would be killed by someone?''

The plaintive eyes looked at her. ''No. He thought they would beat him up or run him out of town and swipe his work.''

''His work. You mean, his story.''

''Yes. It was the best story he'd ever had, that's all I know about it. He swore me to secrecy. I've been sneaking out to see him for months now, ever since he got that custody decree. I'd come here to the park, and he'd pick me up. He wanted to stay close by, because he was afraid my mother would take me away somewhere.''

"Take you away for good?"

"Yes. He was scared stiff. And he had his reasons. She got me a passport, and hers was always ready. It was like a threat, that she'd move us to England or maybe Ireland. She even bought a house there. It's a real cool house; I really wouldn't mind living there, if Dad had been with us. She even had me pack my fall and winter clothes in a suitcase and keep them in the closet."

"And you told your father this, of course?"

"Yes, and that drove him nuts, which is just what Mom wanted, I think."

"That's pretty mean."

The girl's gaze dropped to the hands in her lap. "But you don't understand. My mom loves me. I hurt her feelings when I got up there on the witness stand and told the judge who I wanted to live with. My mother cried, and my mother *never* cries." Again, her voice choked with emotion.

"You told the judge you wanted to spend most of your time with your father?"

"It wasn't that I hated my mother. But life with my dad is so much better."

Louise stared bleakly out into the tall forested neighborhood and wondered how she would feel if Martha or Janie renounced her. "It's a hard thing for you to have had to do, making that kind of choice."

She gave Louise a hunted look, like a small animal. "They fought over me for years. It was terrible. And now look what's happened."

"But you love your mother. And now you'll live with her."

"I guess so. Except I don't completely trust her. She's said too many things about my dad that I know are not true. And now she's even started locking me out of her bedroom, like I was a spy. Not that she's mean or anything—she stayed home the whole morning comforting me.''

She peered at Louise closely again, as if to be sure this new person wasn't going to be another disappointment. ''My father told me that once you and he used to date. And that you and Bill would be my friends forever if anything ever happened to Dad.''

''Indeed we will. We will do anything for you that we can. But your mother will take good care of you.''

''I know. But that doesn't mean I can't do what my Dad wanted me to do.''

''Which was what?''

The girl reached into her overalls pocket and pulled out a computer disk in a Ziploc bag. She handed it to Louise. ''To give you this if anything happened to him. It's his backup disk. Every time he saw me he gave it to me and then he'd take it back the next time. It had his new writing on it. And I would take it and hide it in the tree outside if my mother was home. If she wasn't home, I would hide the disk in my room where the maid doesn't clean. Last week, I think Mom finally figured out that I was meeting my dad, which I'd been doing for months.''

Louise fingered the disk and felt its precious quality, as if it were the Rosetta stone. This was the key to Jay's murder. A great weight seemed gone from her shoulders, for though she may have inadvertently put Jay in danger by sending him from her house, at least now there would be some redemption for her. She could help make his story public. And by doing so, perhaps make some sense out of the loss of her friend.

''Melissa, you are incredible. Do you know how like your father you are?''

The thirteen-year-old smiled faintly. ''Yeah, we're both

sneaky. You should have seen how I convinced our housekeeper I was talking to my friend. My dad and I are just alike. We used to say that it would be fun to live together. Also, we're both slobs, not like Mom. We both have the same habit of hiding things. So, between us, we thought we'd have a fine house, all tucked away with hidden objects. And with soda cans and Dad's coffee cups lying around. And we'd sit around and read books and stuff."

Then she put her head down and began crying again in earnest.

Louise put her arm around the girl, and she leaned into her chest and sobbed. Louise rested her chin gently against the girl's soft, curly hair. After a while, when the crying stopped, Louise told Melissa, "I think you had better go home and try to act as normal as possible. I don't know why, but your mother wants this disk very badly, and you don't want her to know you gave it to me."

"Dad told me not to let her have it." She heaved a big sigh. "Actually, he was still in love with Mom, I could tell, and she loved him, too, at least a little bit. But she would never get back with Dad after he took her to court to get custody of me. Trouble with Mom, she has to win all the time."

She suddenly noticed the old car she was sitting in, and her nostrils twitched. "This car *rules.* Dad said you were a really good gardener; it smells like a farm."

Louise laughed. "It's what I use until some day I get something better, like a pickup, for instance. I haul biosolids in this one."

"He also told me you solved some murders."

"Yes, I guess I helped, anyway."

"I wish you could help find out who killed my dad."

''I'm doing my best, Melissa. I'll turn his disk over to the authorities. And I'll also let your dad's newspaper know that his story is safe. The story might tell us who the murderer is, and it will all be thanks to you.''

The girl looked up at Louise. ''Dad was always more interested in his story than in anything else. Except me, maybe. But no story is . . . worth what happened to Dad.''

Louise's heart went out to the child; she wished she could take her to her own home in Sylvan Valley. Yet Lannie had been a good mother to her, and her mother was with whom the girl belonged.

So she remained silent, and Melissa began to reminisce about her father. The time she spent with him in California seemed to be the highlight of her life, though she seemed to like her private school and her foreign trips with her mother.

''Sometimes Mom takes me to parties and I have to get dressed up and act as if I were all grown up. Company things, sometimes, and sometimes just things that happen in Washington. Tonight, for instance, I'm supposed to go with her to a big reception for Congressman Goodrich. She said it would help me to get out of the house.''

''So you're going.''

The girl stared out of the passenger side window. ''Oh, sure. Political things are sort of interesting, even though I don't like Congressman Goodrich, but he's my mother's good buddy. I couldn't get out of it. You don't know how much trouble it is to get out of things once Mom's mind is made up. She either totally ignores me, or she's all over me like a blanket.''

''Maybe she wants you to like her more.''

''Yeah. As if I could like her as much as a guy who took

me shelling on the beach and fishing in the surf. Y'know, I didn't want to read that story on the disk. Dad said not to, because it could put me in danger."

"So you didn't read it?"

"I started to, but then I felt too guilty, so I stopped at the first page. But I think it's about that Congressman Goodrich."

"I think it is, too, Melissa. But let's keep that to ourselves for now, okay?"

Jay's daughter grinned at Louise, giving her the kind of bright, happy face kids were supposed to have, and which hadn't been much in evidence with Melissa this afternoon. "I might have something else of my dad's that you'll want."

"Oh?"

"Yeah. Don't worry, I'll give it to you, but I just don't want to give up everything I have of his all at once." She reached a slim hand over and touched Louise's arm. "But I'll tell you what it is—a key."

Louise gave Melissa a little hug good-bye. "Be careful, and don't forget, you can call Bill and me anytime, night or day." Then the girl hopped out and waved good-bye and walked quickly toward home, a little bounce in her step, her thin arms stretched out gracefully, as if she were walking on a balance beam. Just a child now, enchantingly innocent, but probably knowing more than she should at the age of thirteen. A child who was trying to cope with loss, but at least knowing she had some friends her father trusted. She headed for an enormous Georgian house perched on the bluff at the edge of the Potomac. More than a home, thought Louise. This was the mansion of Lannie Gordon.

Louise made a U-turn, and as she completed it, she saw the patrol car, its lights ominously flashing. Here it was approaching five o'clock, with about a million commuters in cars going home on Friday night on the nearby GW Parkway. Surely, this patrolman was not going to stop her for wrong-way entry to a quiet neighborhood? But he was, for the way she had been parked was a dead giveaway.

She stopped the car at the side of the road, since he had stopped his opposite. He got out, uniform, boots and all, swaggering over, slapping his ticket pad against his thigh with every other step.

"Ma'am," he said, "you entered this street the wrong way." He poked his head into the window and took a sniff. She hoped he didn't think she was growing marijuana in the back, for the mixed aromas of the residue of her summer gardening were getting fruity.

"Officer, I'm so sorry. I'm not familiar with the neighborhood."

"Let's see your license and your proof of insurance."

"My license. It's right here in my purse." With a little fumbling she found it and whipped it out and put it into his waiting fingers. "Insurance," she mumbled, half to herself, half to the officer, "isn't that the little two-by-five-inch card among those papers at home that I meant to sort?" She shuffled through her wallet for the card. As he looked on with astonishment, she gave the glove compartment door a good hit with the heel of her hand so it fell open. She rustled around in it fruitlessly.

"Oh, gosh, I remember it now. I did a halfway job the other night. Removed the old card from the car, but failed to put the new one in the little plastic container full of papers, because something interrupted me."

"No proof of insurance?" he barked. "Don't you know that's a serious offense?"

"I didn't mean to."

He gave her a disdainful look. ''Ma'am, you better get it together, is all I can say.'' He strutted back to his car and got back in it to write the ticket.

She slumped in the car seat, the heat and fatigue of the day closing in on her. It was such an affront, to be arrested for such a trivial offense. Sitting there in her severely wrinkled linen suit, she had a strong sense of having been treated unfairly. She leaned her head back against the headrest, closed her eyes, and tried to control her growing rage. Remembering all those times she was going to take up transcendental meditation, she wished she had done so. Now it was too late.

Because she was too jumpy to relax, she opened her eyes again and looked in the rearview mirror to inspect her general appearance. That was when she spotted Lannie Gordon, pouncing down on her on foot, wearing high heels and an off-white suit that an ordinary woman would wear for dress occasions, but which Lannie donned for her day-to-day activities as a killer lawyer fighting the war for tobacco.

Naturally, Lannie would have driven her car into the neighborhood by the proper route. She apparently was attracted by the police activity a half block from her house and recognized Louise's distinctive faded brown station wagon. It stood out like Jay's old jalopy must have, when he dared to enter the neighborhood to rendezvous with Melissa.

Before Louise could adequately prepare herself, the woman was at the driver's window, plopping her white-clad elbows onto its dirty expanse, then thinking the better of it and removing them. ''What the hell are you doing in my neighborhood?'' she asked in a throaty voice.

''Is it closed to the public?'' Louise retorted. What *was* she doing in Lannie's neighborhood? For once, she couldn't think of a single lie to cover the situation. She felt like asking what a hardworking person who made so much money and ought to be putting in sixty hours a week to justify it was doing at home at four on a Friday?

Then she remembered: The woman was working again tonight, dragging her young daughter to a big Goodrich affair. Lannie had come home early to get ready for that.

"Are you snooping around my house?"

Louise opened her eyes more widely. "You live on this street? I was having overheating problems with my car, so I pulled in here to give it a chance to cool down. I see you plutocrats have it closed to the bourgeoisie." She grinned. "Just joking, Lannie."

Lannie wasn't buying it. She stood there with her arms crossed. "Do you know Melissa? Have you ever met her? Did Jay bring her out to see you?"

Louise could answer *some* of those questions truthfully. "I promise you, Lannie, that Jay never introduced me to your daughter or brought her anywhere near my house. Now, does that make you feel better?"

"Not much," replied Lannie. "I'd advise you to quit snooping on Melissa. Melissa is well cared for. She doesn't need you." The woman's amber eyes became crowded with tears, that soon were falling onto the breast of her expensive white suit. "She has her mother. Her mother *loves* her, can't you understand?"

Quietly, Louise said, "I know you do. I'm sorry to be snooping." But Lannie turned without a further word, walking despondently back down the road to her house.

The officer, completely oblivious to the exchange, climbed officiously out of his patrol car and made his way back to her. He thrust the ticket at her. She winced when she saw the price of her transgressions.

"And what's your name, Officer?" She gave him her

sweetest smile. ''Oh, never mind, I can see it there on your badge. Officer Strader.'' She stuck her hand out so he was forced to shake it. ''Officer Strader, you have a nice day.''

Kill the bastard with kindness.

Momentarily flustered, he stuttered, ''Uh, uh, you, too, ma'am.'' But in a moment he had regained his supreme indifference and swaggered back to the patrol car.

From underneath the sun visor where she had tucked it, Louise hurriedly grabbed her notepad with Melissa's number; she tapped it in on her cell phone.

''Hello.''

''Melissa, your mother's about to walk in your front door, and she's upset because she saw me here. I am still parked down the street. A policeman stopped me and gave me a ticket.''

''You didn't tell her I gave you Dad's disk, did you?''

''No, of course not. She's suspicious that I'm trying to make contact with you. What else would I be doing in this neighborhood? Will you be all right? Can you pull this off?''

''Yes, I'm a pretty good actress. I've been pretending for months when I snuck out to see Dad. I can pretend again.''

''If I were you, I would deny ever having met me. Remember, you don't know much about me or what I look like. You can say your father mentioned me once or twice. I'm hoping she'll think I was just investigating the neighborhood out of curiosity about where you lived.''

''Thanks, Mrs. Eldridge. I can hear her coming in, so I'd better go. And remember, I'll see you again. We have a reason to meet now.''

''A reason?''

''The key.''

The Enchanting Innocence of the Annual

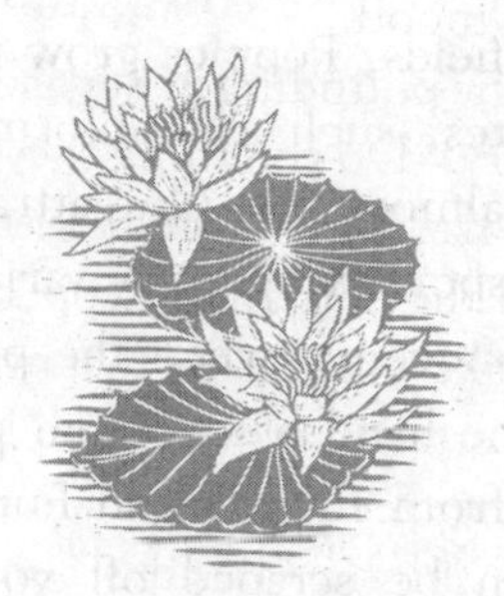

ANNUALS GIVE US WHAT few perennials do: a whole season full of faultless color. They thread through our gardens like the colors in a patchwork quilt, with some quilts being bright with strong colors, and others graced with soft pastels. They fill in gaps and stabilize the garden picture with their constancy and freshness.

There is no end to the use of the annual, whose popularity swept over Europe when introduced there in the 1800s. Americans, always copiers of the British in horticultural matters, also took "bedding plants" to their hearts. This is still the case, as we see millions of plants and annual seed packets offered for sale each year. Fortunately, we can reach beyond the traditional choices of mari-

gold, moss rose, impatiens, red salvia, and petunia to bring new forms and colors to our gardens.

If you haven't grown annual poppies, you should, for they add a true innocence to the garden, reminding us of *The Wizard of Oz* and of classical storybook pictures of children standing in fields. Poppies grow profusely in some climates, such as California, but will perform in almost any. One attraction is the gray leaves sported by many varieties. Maintain your innocence when the police come, but grow the handsome opium poppy; seed is available from English and European catalogs, or can be scraped off your morning bagel. It has blossoms as big as peonies, and imposing floppy leaves. Petite single-poppy varieties in jewel colors make the front of the garden border literally seem to dance: one choice is appropriately called "Ballerina."

Annuals and perennials mix well. The feathery pink-and-gold annual squirrel-tail grass combines beautifully with pale pink perennial phlox or lavender catmint. And the shapely flowers of *Diascia,* rosy pink with yellow throats, are spectacular when combined with the perennial bronze-tasseled fountain grass, *Pennisetum setaceum* "Rubrum."

Perennial herbs like lavender, rosemary, horseradish, rue, or the splendid, shrubby *Calamintha nepeta* add a special refinement to annuals, and are like the arbiters between them and the other perennials.

When we experiment with annuals, we discover some that become our favorites, such as a salvia with special form and color. *Salvia greggii* is not hardy beyond zone seven, but is wonderful for a season, with a small shrubby shape and a cloud of coral or red blooms. It is striking when paired with another underused and striking annual that has coral, purple, or yellow blossoms resembling the alstroemeria; it is called painted tongue *(Salpiglossis sinuata).*

There can be fun as well as beauty in growing annuals. Children will be delighted if you plant sunflowers on the perimeter of a square or rectangular patch of ground. What will result is a sunflower playhouse with towering walls topped with saucer-sized yellow flowers. Kids can use it even as growth starts, and watch the sides ascend to twelve or more feet. To add a Jack-and-the-Beanstalk touch, grow pole beans outside the sunflower house. The big flowers will support their upward progress, and the kids can have the job of keeping the mature beans picked and the giant away.

The annual castor bean plant makes another showy plant, with its large palmately lobed reddish leaves and flowers in drooping panicles. All of its parts are poisonous, however, but this is not the only toxic plant about which children should be warned: Children should not *eat* the garden. There is a smaller castor bean variety, ''Carmencita,''

that fits better in the border and profits from the nearby presence of a lacy gray artemisia. Another taller annual plant is *Nicotiana sylvestris.* It stands in the back of the border, with its fragrant and slightly droopy white blossoms, like a graceful maiden aunt at a wedding reception.

Treat most tulips as annuals and you will enjoy them more and not agonize over their disappearance next spring. Try different kinds—small species tulips, which are more reliable; compact middle-sized varieties; and the tall French tulips that soar so prettily above the iris and columbine. Since you will lose a portion of the bigger ones, especially, plant more bulbs of the same type in that patch. To save your garden from the sorry picture of dying bulb foliage, always plant bulbs in the midst of ground cover.

Snapdragons are one of the clever annuals that seed themselves or overwinter, even in tough climates. Extraordinary colors emerge from some of these seeded offspring. They are delightful coupled with the gray-leaved, salmon- or white-flowered perennial, *Centranthus*—which gets the ultimate compliment that it blooms as long and robustly as an annual.

Some annuals have an intricate delicacy that invites close-up viewing. Love-in-a-mist *(Nigella damascena)* has delicate flowers in blue, pink, or white, held in feathery bracts. It self-seeds, is easy to grow, and improves

the view of leggy perennials like lilies, which are up there in the air with their knobby knees showing. The handsome, horned seed-pods alone make it worthwhile to grow. *Clarkia* is quite another matter, and you may find it only at a florist's, for this beauty, with its four-clawed petals in shades of lavender-red, red, salmon, and white, flourishes mainly in the state of Washington, which some believe has a distinct advantage over most of the other growing areas in the U.S. One northwest gardener put a red variety at the top of an arid stony bank covered with blue-gray woolly thyme and purple-shaded thyme.

A master combination of annuals that is simplicity itself includes blue-flowered borage, chartreuse dill, and airy fennel, mixed in with the arching stems of the cosmos in white or pale pink. The nice thing about it is that three out of the four—all except the cosmos—are good to eat. This includes the cobalt blue flowers of the borage. Candy them or eat them fresh.

Chapter Twenty-five

IT WAS PAST FIVE when Louise reached home. Her neighborhood had grown busier since she left it. A Channel Eight television truck, looking somehow sinister, was slowly rolling out of the cul-de-sac. Children from the Sylvan Valley neighborhood, released from day camp or tennis camp or other life-enriching activities, were on the loose, walking around and gawking at the Mougey house, and because they were small and thought of themselves as invisible, were seriously considering sneaking under that yellow plastic police tape and taking a good peek at the pond where a man was found with his head bashed in.

As she got out of the car, she stared at that yellow tape and realized she herself was definitely going to breach it later on. For one thing, there was no patrolman around, and she had to feed those fish. Going into her home, she carefully put the disk that Melissa had given her into a disk container. If she was going to explore at the murder site, she had to do it now while it was still light, even though there was danger of being caught.

She thought of Melissa and hoped she hadn't put her in jeopardy by getting caught by her mother. The girl now had expectations of Louise, high hopes that she would find whoever had murdered her father.

Louise smiled when she pictured Melissa in her mother's sunglasses, fancying that they and a Hollywood walk would change her appearance. A change in appearance was what *Louise* needed right now. She opened her closet and found what she wanted, a running outfit in faded olive drab; it was heavy, but it was camouflage. It would match the woods nicely, she reflected, as she pulled on her oldest tennis shoes, the ones that were grayed with age. She shoved her long hair back and tied it with a light brown cotton scarf. Then she prepared the koi's afternoon worm dinner, noticing she was hardened now to killing and mincing earthworms.

Feeling a little like a member of the Vietcong, she crouched down and zigzagged her way across the backyards of the Kendricks, the VandeVens, and the Radebaughs. She kept well into the tree cover to avoid anyone seeing her from the street, and was on a constant lookout for child stragglers, little Christopher Robins and the like, looking for mushrooms and toads. Soon she was in the thicket of trees separating Nora and Ron Radebaugh's house from Mary and Richard Mougey's. She slid her way through the young trees and bushes, keeping a close eye out, for the worst thing that could happen to her was that a policeman had been stationed here and would catch her snooping around.

Holding low to the ground, she came in by way of the bronze prancing deer statue, carefully slipped across to the statue of the dancing child, and then crept the rest of the way on all fours down the ornamental-grass-lined path to the fishpond. The koi rushed to greet her and receive their afternoon repast. "Hi, guys," she said, and tossed in the worms.

The state of the koi, she realized, was just as important to her right now as the state of the nation was to a president. She didn't want to lose her precious friendship with Mary Mougey because she had flubbed it with the fish. Once they had consumed their dinner, they seemed to go into low gear, drifting lazily around the rectangular pool. They were dazzlingly bright, dappled, and beautiful. Were they lazy, sick, or just full? She was so unfamiliar with fish that she didn't know what this level of activity represented. If she equated it to her exercise class, certainly low aerobics. A few days ago, when she made her first reconnaissance as fish caretaker, she was certain they had been swimming in a more sprightly fashion about the pool.

Something was wrong with the fish.

She looked up from her kneeling position, right into the chest of Oscar, the bronze whooping crane. She had forgotten him for an instant. There were noises from the street, and though she was at the back of the house and couldn't see people approaching, she could spy another news vehicle making the wide circle of Dogwood Court. She had better hurry. Intrepid TV reporters might decide to breach the yellow plastic strip barrier.

With her knees getting sore from contact with the flagstone, she slid over to a sitting position and clasped her hands around her knees and thought. Jay had told the editor his work, his efforts, were "ending up with the fishes." That was a joke, not a lament, and a joke with Jay, she recalled from the old days when they were sweethearts, meant a trick. Some fact concealed. Something hidden. But where, and what? She already had Jay's backup, thanks to Melissa. What could be hidden "with the fishes"? More hard copy, perhaps, like the sheaf of papers she had found in her toolshed. And could she conceivably find the computer in this yard? It was small, and the opportunities for hiding it in the woods were endless.

First, she looked around her, but she was reluctant to do a thorough search because people would see her if she rose to a standing position. She was surrounded with ornamental grass clumps interspersed with plants of cimicifuga, penstemon, gaillardia, and goatsbeard. Adding a vertical note here and there were Mary's favorite trees, the skyrocket juniper, soaring above the pool and its surroundings. She hoped Jay had not buried things like she had, under a plant, for there were scores of plants in this yard, placed there by a paid landscaper who had gone slightly overboard. Yet she would put nothing past her friend. That might take excavating Mary Mougey's entire backyard.

It rattled the koi a bit when she peered into the pool; the fish thought she had more food, dessert, perhaps, and speeded up their activity. Good, they needed to raise their heart level. Louise doubted a reporter would hide things in the water. Writers were like soldiers: Soldiers kept their powder dry, and writers kept their paper dry.

She was just noticing how rough the stones were on her palms when she cut a finger on a ridge of caulking. As she sucked her finger to stop the bleeding, she reflected that the Mougeys had been taken. Just a year ago they had hired the finest pool company in Washington to install this fishpond, and yet the ravages of Washington's wet climate already had made inroads. The loosened caulking under her fingers was not the only place that had deteriorated. She prodded at the upraised ridge, using her strong thumbnail as a wedge. There was a slight give. With more pressure the flagstone came up; beneath it was a scooped-out area. Not very deep, just deep enough for a three-and-one-half-inch computer disk in a cardboard box. This disk looked identical to the one that Jay's daughter had just given her an hour ago, and when she took it out of its box, she saw it was marked ''Original.''

Wanting to shout with joy, instead she stuck the disk in her pants pocket and swiftly scooped up the worm container and the box. She would forego her hunt for Jay's computer: it would take an unearthing of this whole yard to find it, if it were there. When she looked toward the street she saw nothing. But she could hear something that sent fear through her: two men's voices. She even recognized them: Geraghty and Morton. She had to move quickly, for they were probably going in the house. They would sight her like a hunter sighting a duck through the Mougeys' enormous floor-to-ceiling living room windows. Confronting the police was far more dangerous than encountering some nosy kid in the cul-de-sac. A kid she could always con with some excuse.

Keeping low, she sprinted past the bronze statue of the

dancer, past the bronze deer, and into the thick woods. Once there, she straightened and stood trembling, listening. No one had seen her. But she could see Geraghty and Morton walking around the back of the house, wandering up the path to the pool where she had knelt moments earlier. Geraghty stared into the woods where she stood, and she froze like a deer in headlights. They scuffed around the flagstones a bit, and she panicked: had she put that flagstone back firmly in place? Apparently so. Then, the two men wandered around the house, out of sight.

She let out a big breath and made her way carefully through the backyards again. Now she had two disks, the original and the backup. But there was a danger until the detectives left the neighborhood. She intended to turn over the disks to the police. But first she had to find out what Jay's story was all about.

Once safely locked inside her house, she watched the police from the guest room, which had the best view of the street. Bill's high-intensity binoculars helped; unbeknownst to Bill, she had taken to storing them in the guest room closet, so they would be handy whenever she wished to survey the neighborhood.

She watched George Morton shake his big head back and forth as he talked to Mike Geraghty, and then slam himself into the passenger seat of the unmarked green police car. A frustrated man, his every move told her. Geraghty went around to the driver's side, pausing before getting in and taking a long look at her house and yard. She prayed that they wouldn't decide to pop by, but quickly remembered it wasn't what detectives did. Like the British, they always scheduled first.

She was beginning to read the detectives pretty well, and

their demeanor said several things: that they didn't have a good lead on Jay's killer; that they were going to do another search of the Mougey property and her property as well; and that they wanted to talk to her again.

Louise felt a twinge of guilt for not leveling with Geraghty, but quickly suppressed it. She had work to do.

Chapter Twenty-six

HER COMPUTER WAS IN the addition, which the family had nicknamed "the hut." It was a freestanding building opposite the front door connected architecturally to the house by the grayed redwood pergola, with a view of the bog garden that made it a little like Thoreau's cabin near Walden Pond. It was her writing place, but other family members used it as a refuge when they needed to be alone. When she was riffling through garden books at the library recently, she'd been captivated to discover the renowned British gardener Gertrude Jekyll had similarly named her workshop "The Hut."

In her hands Louise carried a big tray containing the two computer disks, a pot of coffee she'd made in her old aluminum drip pot, a cup, and some cheese, fruit, and cookies. These last would substitute for dinner.

It was almost six, and within a few minutes she would know Jay's secrets.

She bolted the door, then turned on her computer. As she waited for it to boot up, she stared out the glass doors that faced her at the end of the addition and remembered another time she sat in this room and found herself in grave danger. This time she would take no chances: She got up and pulled the drapes on the doors and on the side window so that not even a crack was showing.

As she often had done when working in the hut, and sometimes to her disadvantage, she had left the phone in the house; but right now, she didn't want a phone as a distraction.

She inserted Jay's original disk in drive A and pulled up the index. There was one story only, called "Watergate Revisited: The Dirty Tricks Campaign of Congressman Lloyd Goodrich." Other files were shorter in length and appeared to be research notes.

The main file was dated Wednesday, the day of Jay's death, the time, ten-fifteen P.M. That was about twenty minutes before Gil Whitson strolled over to the Mougeys' to look at the koi pond.

She called the file up on the screen. Its title was apt. It was the story of a dirty tricks campaign, waged by Goodrich, first against his opponents for the nomination, and then against President Fairchild. This was dirty tricks, nineties style, as the author described it. The heart and soul of it depended upon the media, primarily the tabloids and the more sensational ''news'' shows: feeding these sources undocumented stories and rumors that got play often in print, sometimes on television, occasionally both, and became the grist for the mills of conservative radio talk shows.

Jay McCormick had been an effective political plant, documenting Goodrich campaign activities from March through July. As part of the story's lead, he declared that he could prove at least one person had been paid by Goodrich to make false sexual harassment charges against the President, and, even more damning, evidence had been fabricated to hint that Fairchild had been investigated for the murder of an army clerk, purportedly to clear his service record.

To the reporter, the most grievous incident was manufacturing evidence regarding Fairchild's activities in Vietnam. And, as Jay pointed out toward the end of his long story, this charge was having serious adverse effects on the President's popularity. With direct quotes from principals, including Willie Upchurch and Ted French, Jay documented that the story was phony and the army records carefully fabricated by an expert.

Each part of the bizarre smear campaign was approved by the author of the undercover operation within the Goodrich campaign, Franklin Rawlings; and by the executors of the plans, Willie Upchurch and Ted French. Congressman Lloyd Goodrich was said to have known of the effort and to have given it a verbal okay.

Rawlings, mastermind of the operation, was portrayed as a consummate hypocrite. He was described as putting others out front to take the brunt of the ''dirty tricks'' charges. Furthermore, Jay had obtained information about the California senatorial campaign headed by Rawlings, revealing similar dishonest campaigning there.

As a mole inside the campaign, Jay scrupulously recorded, with quotes and examples, the intense cynicism with which the dirty tricks had been planned by this select group. Many campaign staff, including the day-to-day manager, Nate Weinstein, were left out of the loop, not privy to the details of these activities.

The campaign distributed rumors about the President's drinking and purported womanizing, based on sketchy sources that the reporter said were "eagerly embraced, nevertheless." One woman was paid to make sexual allegations against the President, according to the story. A constant stream of rumors was put out to slander Fairchild's wife and children.

Jay went on to detail irregular campaign contributions that bolstered the campaign from its earliest days. Ironically, the efforts were spurred by the reform of campaign rules after the previous presidential election. The reforms changed the system, but didn't relieve the problem: they only made needed campaign funds more scarce, and opened a Pandora's box of devious new ways to get around the laws. These big chunks of money allowed Goodrich to run a heavier television ad campaign than his primary opponents, smoothing the way to his probable nomination at the August convention.

Louise stared in disbelief at the next paragraph: Lannie Gordon, Jay's former wife, was named as a source of hundreds of thousands of dollars in questionable funds. Based on the pattern of previous political fund-raising scandals, Jay calculated that the news media and congressional probes would have not caught up with these facts until after the election and a probable Goodrich victory.

Lannie set up a bogus charitable foundation for children that actually was a conduit to funnel money into Goodrich's campaign. She recognized him early on as the one who would win the nomination, and even before he qualified for matching federal funds, this money source allowed him to pay for crucial TV exposure. Her system was to contact big money people for donations to Goodrich and provide them with a tax deduction because they were handled through this foundation.

Jay wrote that even his ex-wife's fellow tobacco industry colleagues appeared not to know that the operation was outside the law, since it was a one-on-one deal between Lannie Gordon and Rawlings.

Damning words, thought Louise. She sat back for a moment and thought. Did Lannie suspect her complicity had been discovered by Jay? If so, it was no wonder she wanted that disk so badly.

Jay's story was long, probably ten thousand words. At the end, there was an editorial note that said tapes had been made of conversations that took place in the opposition presidential campaign office that proved Jay McCormick's allegations. He said his daughter, Melissa, had a key to a safety deposit box in Riggs National Bank, where the tapes were hidden.

When she reached the end of the story, Louise leaned her elbows on the antique table and put her head in her hands. This was what her friend had died for. And it was pretty clear who would want him dead. Jay had come right out and said that he had worked for the campaign as a speechwriter. Near the end of his story, Jay had written that Upchurch particularly had begun to mistrust him.

Why did they begin to mistrust him? Louise could think of only one reason. Lannie, with her link to these political operators, probably caught a glimpse of Jay, perhaps when he was making a secret visit to Melissa, trailed him to work at Goodrich headquarters, and then tipped someone off:

French, perhaps, or maybe Rawlings. Since Jay was low profile, and almost the perfect man to become a political plant, only Lannie could have put the pieces together.

Louise sighed. Thank heavens, Bill would be here in a few hours. Although that raised other problems: Her husband might insist she turn the story directly over to the police, since he seemed to have a higher standard for her behavior than for his own. She hunched protectively over the computer and frowned, and felt like a mother bear protecting its cub. What would happen to this material if she turned it over to the police?

Her head was swimming with possibilities and scenarios: Willie Upchurch with his ruthless flunkies? Ted French, acting alone, and probably not for the first time? Or Franklin Rawlings, with his amiable public face and Machiavellian ways? Both Rawlings and Lannie Gordon were stripped of probity through this journalistic exposé; Louise was sure Lannie had played some vital role.

Gil Whitson had to fit in somewhere, for no matter how good-willed he seemed, his behavior had been suspicious. And then there was that distasteful fellow, Charlie Hurd: He had a very good reason to remove Jay McCormick, provided he could have found the story afterwards. Whoever killed Jay must be furious at the loss of the disks. And now, she sat here with both copies of the incriminating evidence. If anyone figured that out, she would become the target of the killer. A shiver ran through her. She needed to get out of the hut. It was too vulnerable.

As she quickly gathered up her things, Louise reflected on the irony of being loaded down with information, and with no one to talk to. She had an overwhelming desire to spill it all out to Detective Geraghty. Again, she felt guilty about the big detective: She could even picture him, working after hours in his dingy little office in the Fairfax police station on Route One, fretting over the case just as she was doing. But with less to work with than she had.

But Geraghty would get his evidence soon enough. What she needed were just a few more pieces to put this mystery together. If she didn't find them, she wasn't sure anyone else would.

Chapter Twenty-seven

DROPPING THE TRAY OFF in the kitchen, she grabbed some plastic Ziploc bags and took the two disks outside to the patio garden. These precious objects were going to rest in two separate hiding places, just to be safe. The memos occupied a third. If lightning struck her, she knew, Jay's story would go to the grave with her, for her hiding places were impeccable. *Dear Jay,* she thought, *you would be proud of me.* But she did not expect anything to stand in the way of giving over all this information to her astounded husband in less than four hours. Bill would be proud of her, too, solving a murder, or at least providing clues to the solution of a murder, without getting her own self in serious trouble for once.

Her activity left her a little sweaty and breathless. When she entered the house, she had phone messages, just as she expected. She was surprised they didn't include a message from the Fairfax PD.

Bill had called from the airplane to say they had departed late from Vienna and would arrive at eleven or twelve. She slumped against the counter and sighed. Now she would have to wait even longer to talk over all the things she'd learned about Jay's murder.

Martha had phoned from Detroit. *"Ma, now I've read another little squib about Jay McCormick's murder in the* Detroit Free Press. *This is just a little call to remind you to lock the doors, and don't talk to strangers or do anything rash until Dad and Janie get home. I love you. 'Bye."*

Louise smiled. It was kind of fun being mothered by her elder daughter. And Janie was coming home tonight, and so was Bill, and family life would get back to normal. *Life* would soon get back to normal.

But she was kidding herself. Nothing was going to get back to normal. A gray cloud of anxiety had hovered over her ever since she found Jay's body in the fishpond, and when Bill learned of his death, he would be just as disturbed as she was. There would be no peace until the murderer was found.

The last message on her machine was from Tessie Strahan of the Perennial Plant Society. In the stress and turmoil of the past two days, Louise had almost forgotten her plant friends. But they were still down at the Hilton, talking about plants, listening to lectures from starry-eyed plant hybridizers, and taking tours of commercial and private gardens in the Washington area.

Tessie sounded exhausted: *"This has been* some *convention, Louise,"* she began in her staccato style. *"Too bad, dear, you couldn't have attended these past two days, though we know you have had this sad occurrence with the death of your friend."*

She said nothing about whether the police had talked to Gil Whitson, but knowing Detective Geraghty, Louise bet they had. And if they had, Tessie probably put the blame at Louise's feet, for her loyalty to Gil Whitson ran deeper than her new friendship with Louise.

It was a chatty message. Tessie said, *"Gil's gradually getting the van loaded, and we're leaving for home tonight, but we wanted to come by your house to say good-bye. But just my luck, there may be a subcommittee meeting of growers before we leave, and if there is, it will be too late afterward to come by. So we'll see which way it goes. But we all wanted you to know what a great hostess you were the other night. And don't forget, Louise—next year you must attend again, no matter where in the country we hold it, because we can't be without the Plant Person of the Year at the convention!"*

This was just another blow. Since they were leaving town tonight, it meant Louise couldn't enlist Gil to go over and look at the koi. Tomorrow, perhaps, she would call a veterinarian, if she could find one who made house calls on fish.

It was seven, and she had at least four hours to kill, maybe five. The house suddenly seemed unbearably hot and close. She felt suffocated in here, or was it because of the disappointment of having resolved nothing about Jay's murder? She went to the bedroom and threw off the jogging suit and put on her gardening outfit. Certainly the gardens had been pampered enough because of the P.P.S. visitors, but she could always find one more thing to do out there. Anything was better than staying inside.

But first things first: She grabbed the kitchen scraps and went out into the Washington evening. The air was still moist—good for growing slugs, she thought wryly. Gathering her shovel and pruners from the toolshed, she buried the garbage, then stepped across the garden to prune her new deciduous azalea.

If plants had souls, as some fey people thought, this azalea was trembling at her approach. She had already trimmed it once since she bought it last spring. This time, she went easy, pinching a few inches off a branch to give it better balance or rather, imbalance. She often pruned woody perennials and shrubs asymetrically, since, as she had confessed to Tom Paschen during their White House grounds tour, her standard for flowers and gardens was "irregular and wild."

As she worked, she heard someone call. It was Roger Kendricks, her neighbor, far out in his woodsy back yard.

"Louise, I need to talk to you."

Oh yes, she thought, *do let's talk.* Her desperate need to share her day came surging forth again. She could talk to Roger, the brilliant, circumspect newsman, a man who dropped out of newspapering now and again to lend his brains to Washington liberal think tanks. Roger would keep her confidence, too, in case she let slip more than she intended.

She came across the woods to see him struggling to cut off a one-inch limb with his pruners. "God, Louise, what a sight for sore eyes you are. What am I doing *wrong* here? We're supposed to go out later, but right now I've been sent out here in lower Siberia to cut off 'deadwood,' as Laurie puts it. I'm not too good at it." He scowled at the swamp oak.

She pointed to the branch. "If you save that until tomorrow, I'll come over with my loppers and help you with it."

He breathed a sigh of relief and wriggled the tool loose from the branch. "Gladly." Roger wore shorts and a sweaty T-shirt that emphasized his potbelly, and now he turned to her and she could see his worried eyes under the thick glasses. "Louise, I have to talk to you. Can you come and sit on the patio for a minute?"

"Sure." She trudged after him to the rectangular expanse of flagstone and they settled down into comfortable metal lawn chairs. She held her pruners in her hands and made an effort to relax.

He looked at her seriously. "So you've had a terrible loss, Louise, your friend dying suspiciously in the fishpond like that. Laurie tells me he was your old buddy from college days."

"I hadn't seen him for years, but he stayed with Bill and me for a week before he went over across the street, and we had a chance to remember old times."

"I'm genuinely sorry."

"Thanks." She stared down at the pruners and wondered if that was all Roger had on his mind. She could hardly contain herself, she was so anxious to get to what was hanging so heavily on her conscience. "Roger," she said, "first, let me ask you a tough question."

"Go ahead. You know I'm geared for tough answers."

"I've had a harrowing couple of days, with this murder. . . ."

He leaned back and crossed his hairy legs, seemingly willing to give her time to get out her story. "You think it's murder, too."

"Haven't the papers said that? Or are they still calling it 'a suspicious accident'?" She shook her head. "I haven't paid attention to the news."

"Louise, you must know the *Post* is getting on this story. In fact, I'm surprised they haven't caught up with you yet, because . . . Well, you go ahead. Give me that tough question."

Just how much should she tell him? "Apparently the police haven't revealed this, but Jay's computer was stolen. And, presumably, his disks."

"I gather your friend didn't tell you much about his story when he stayed with you."

"He was very close-mouthed about it. It was extremely frustrating, if you want the truth. But now, I've found something and it leaves me in a dilemma. So this is my hypothetical question: Suppose you had found some—evidence regarding a murder, really important evidence. And suppose the evidence, if you should give it to the police, wouldn't exactly prove who murdered the person—that person being your friend. So, are you entitled to keep the evidence for a while to see if you can uncover more clues? Or are you obligated to turn the material directly over to the police?"

She looked closely at his face to see his reaction.

He chuckled knowingly. "Are they *garden* clues, like the changing color of tulips? The police might ignore them, like the last time around."

"Not garden clues," she said firmly. Just a clue found in the garden, she thought.

He hunched forward. "First of all, let's see what we know about this case: The *Post* called McCormick's paper out West and his editor doesn't think his death was any accident, any more than the police apparently do. McCormick had some kind of inside story about Goodrich and his sleazy campaign."

"I know."

"So, let's assume people in Goodrich's campaign would have a strong motive to get back that story—even to the point of killing the writer." Roger shook his balding head. "Not out of the question—we don't know how many murders there have been to further the aspirations of a national political candidate. But if there isn't some hard evidence at the scene—and believe me, outdoor scenes like the Mougeys' backyard must be hell to work with—your friend's assailant may never be caught. I don't like that Upchurch gang, and there's one in the bunch I distrust more than the others: Ted French. Heard of him?"

"I've even met him. In fact, I saw him just today."

He was surprised. "You saw him? Well, *there's* a loose cannon; French is almost a joke, like Gordon Liddy used to be, except one has to take these jokers seriously. He's the kind of guy who would be capable of violence like this. I think Franklin Rawlings got a tiger by the tail when he acquired French, and now he doesn't know how to get loose. But we mustn't discount Rawlings for reaching the depths of political corruption all on his own."

Her scalp tingled as she heard these unrelenting words. "Rawlings. I saw him, too, and he seemed pretty upset with Ted French about something." What had Jay written about the opposition campaign manager? That he was the commanding general of the reckless dirty tricks campaign. Well, one of his lieutenants appeared to be out of control.

Roger said, "I see you've been around. Rawlings is a man who is always protesting his innocence about everything. And if you've ever met him, you know he is well met: about the friendliest, most amiable, most *available* guy there is. That's why the press loves him, by the way. But the man is unscrupulous. Just between the two of us, the *Post* is investigating that senatorial campaign out in California."

"Oh, is it?" She didn't tell him that Jay McCormick had beaten the *Post* to the punch.

"The only thing Franklin ever really regrets is being caught. And he removes himself three layers from everything, so he seldom gets his name attached to the seamiest deals. If he's behind this murder, believe me, no one will ever prove it. He will have sent someone else to do it. Someone else will be the fall guy."

She thought back on Jay's story, and it came to her clearly: Of all the key figures in it, Rawlings probably had the most to lose, and therefore the greatest motive to murder Jay McCormick. By the same token, Rawlings was probably the most able to avoid disclosure.

And who had the most to gain? It came to her in a flash. "Roger, do you happen to know a reporter around the Washington area named Charles Hurd?"

He frowned slightly and she could see the wheels turning. "The name sounds familiar. Wait—now I know. It's that reporter with the *Arlington Herald*. Someone called his work to our attention and suggested we hire him; apparently he's pretty good—a real comer. What's he got to do with this?"

"He was Jay's researcher. His leg man."

"And you think maybe . . ."

"I'm not sure what I think. Charlie Hurd may be a comer but he's not very nice. I could suspect anything of him—even of doing a deal with the devil: making an evil compact with whoever wanted that story bad enough to kill Jay, and in the end trying to wrest it away from him. Oh, yes, I have my suspicions, but I know *nothing*—at least nothing for sure. This murder may never be solved. And I'm just obstructing things further. What do you think I should do right now? Call Detective Geraghty? Or would you sit on it for a while?"

"If that happened to me?" Roger studied her, leaning tensely forward in the lawn chair as if she might leap out of it at any moment. "I might do just what you're doing, Louise, concealing the—whatever it is you've found in your house. Though have you thought this out carefully? Holding on to something a killer wants so badly may be putting you in terrible danger. In fact, that was just what I was going to warn you about—"

"Warn me?"

"The *Post* had a couple of disturbing phone calls about you late this afternoon."

"About *me?*"

"Yes. One was an acquaintance of the reporter handling the story. The other was someone who refused to give their name. Both callers were trying to establish your link with 'John' McCormick."

She straightened in the chair and gripped her pruners more tightly. "So what did the *Post* tell these people?"

Roger shrugged his shoulders. "Nothing, of course. We don't discuss stories we're working on. But I'd try not to be too worried about it, since your family's returning." He thoughtfully stroked his chin with his thumb and forefinger. "As for the action you should take, I know the best answer. When's Bill arriving?"

"I'm not sure. His plane's late."

"The first thing you should do when he walks in the door is to share whatever it is you have with him. He'll know what to do."

Her mouth formed in a little moue. "And what if Bill were not coming in tonight? Do you think I could possibly handle this on my own?" She could hardly contain her disappointment in Roger. She thought he was an up-to-date guy who knew women were just as competent as men. She felt sorry for his wife, Laurie, who had a mind like a computer and fashion style as well. She ran a flourishing lady's boutique, but could have just as well run any business. Maybe even a think tank.

Roger, sensing a major blunder, raised two hands in front of him, as if to ward off a small, wild animal that threatened to attack. "Wait, Louise. Don't get impatient with me."

"Impatient? I guess I'm disappointed."

"Okay, okay, I can see how you might have misunderstood me." Roger was always the expert, and it never occurred to him that he was wrong, only that someone had misunderstood him. "Here's all I meant. Laurie told me you told her that this Jay was an old boyfriend. That makes me think you may be acting a bit emotionally, instead of completely—rationally."

"I see," she said, coldly. "It's true, women are *so* emotional. Jay McCormick, however, was my boyfriend for six weeks, and that was more than twenty years ago."

"Of course," said Roger, still backpedaling. "The reason for telling Bill, and the reason I think he's important, is that he and you together are going to make a better decision than you alone. Because more than twenty years or not, there's still some heavy emotional baggage there. Isn't there?"

She felt tears forming in her eyes but she wasn't about to corroborate his theory by crying. She stood and shoved her pruners into a front pocket of her shorts. The action made her feel more powerful. "There's always emotional baggage when someone you know dies. I thank you for your advice. You are right, of course: Two heads are better than one, and Bill surely will be helpful."

Roger got up, too. "Louise, I am so sorry. Did I sound like a paternalistic putz? I didn't mean to. It's just that you and Bill operate so well together, you with your intuition, he with his finely honed rational approach from years in the stultifying atmosphere of the State Department.''

He meant it as a joke. She smiled faintly up at him. A year or so ago, she would have apologized to the man at this juncture, graciously retreating, citing her fatigue for her testy remarks. But Roger certainly wasn't standing there thinking he should apologize to *her* for trying to slot her into every existing stereotype there was for a woman. Intuitive and emotional, yes; rational, not really: Leave that part to Bill.

It would be so nice to see Bill, Bill who really understood and knew how to treat a woman. Her honey, who smelled so warm and buttery when she held him in her arms. Suddenly, she wanted to go home and not think about anything, especially not murder and vicious political scandals—and just curl up and sleep and wait for her family to come.

''There's something else, Louise,'' Roger was saying. ''When you tell me you've found evidence in a case like this that could involve the presidential election, you know all my reportorial juices have been released, right?''

''You want the story first.''

He grinned. ''Of course. But rest assured: The *Post* always wants the story first, and usually gets it first.''

Then an idea occurred to her. ''Can we sit down again?''

''Sure.''

She slumped back into the metal chair and crossed her bare, booted leg across her knee. ''What if your paper could help with this?''

He resumed his seat opposite and said, ''Just how would we do that?''

''That political gossip column that you run: How would it be if you plant a little item in there? It could say that someone in the Sylvan Valley neighborhood where the investigative reporter met a mysterious death—a person who had been involved in a prior murder case—had come across his computer disks?''

''Huh,'' said Roger. ''That would make you guys into sitting ducks.''

''Yes, but we could even bring the police in on it. What the heck, Geraghty deserves to be let in.'' She waved her hand. ''We'd find some way to make it foolproof.'' Then she placed her hand on her breast. ''*I,* personally, have no desire to be the target of some political madman.''

Roger stared through her, thinking. ''That's not a bad idea. Provided it was done with a lot of care and thought.''

She made a half stab at a smile. ''Maybe it's something I should take up with Bill.''

''Louise, will you ever forgive me for that? I wonder. And at the risk of being paternalistic again, I urge you to come out with Laurie and me tonight, just to be safe.'' He looked at her earnestly over his glasses. ''Those phone calls made me nervous, frankly.''

''Come with you where?''

''We're going to the big Goodrich extravaganza—heard of it?''

She shoved her disheveled long hair back with a hand; she must look like the wild woman of the West by now. ''Actually, I just happened to hear about that. You mean, get dressed, comb my hair''—she laughed and held up a hunk of it, as if this were a hopeless task—''and go all the way to Washington.'' She made it sound like one hundred miles, not just eight.

''Yeah, but you don't have to get that dressed up; just think of yourself as part of the *Post* press team that's covering the event.''

Knowing she was far too tired to go through all the

required ablutions, she gave her neighbor a smile and shake of the head. "That's very nice of you, Roger, but I'll be fine. I'll lock the house and clutch my phone, and I'll call 911 immediately if I hear any strange noises outside."

She pushed herself up out of the chair. "And now, I'm totally beat; I have to go home. The day started early, with the police searching the house and yard. Then I ran downtown and had lunch with Tom Paschen." She omitted her trip to Great Falls and her emotion-packed encounters with Melissa, the patrolman, and Lannie Gordon. They had taken their toll.

"Tom Paschen? Louise, you're kidding. How did he have time to take you to lunch?"

"It wasn't a long lunch, that's for sure. It was in the members' dining room; that's where I saw all those characters, Rawlings, French, even Goodrich. Tom wants something from Channel Five; I'm his conduit."

"That's very interesting. Your garden show, of course. The environmental bill, I bet. They want you to showcase it."

"Naturally, Franklin Rawlings wants me to deep-six it. He told me straight out that Channel Five shouldn't do it because Fairchild's bill will all be changed once Goodrich wins the presidency." She laughed. "It was like two jungle animals, fighting over scraps."

Roger shook his head. "No, my dear. Media coverage can never be called *scraps:* It's too valuable. Tom's pulling out all the stops, and it's a terrific idea. Fairchild may have major faults, but you have to remember, he has two things going for him. He's a moderate who's kept the economy and foreign affairs under control, and at home he's a strong protector of the environment: He knows the public doesn't want the globe they live on to go to hell."

"Too bad Rawlings's campaign is working, and Fairchild's isn't." Her voice was weary, her motor running down now. "But maybe all that will change soon." She started walking toward her yard, and he accompanied her.

"Louise, you be careful, now. Do you and Bill have a gun?"

She stopped and looked at him, and pulled her breath in with a little noisy gasp. "Do you think I need a *gun*?" She thought for a moment and remembered. Because he thought he might need it, Bill had taken the gun, smoothing the way somehow through all the airport red tape.

"Uh, there's no gun in the house right now, Roger. But I'll be all right." She smiled up at him, and tried to lighten the conversation. "I'll return one of these days and help you prune those trees."

He leaned over and whispered as if the two of them were colluding in a crime, and not trying to solve one. "Once we have these other matters taken care of."

Doing It *Your* Way: Hubris in the Name of Gardening Is No Vice*

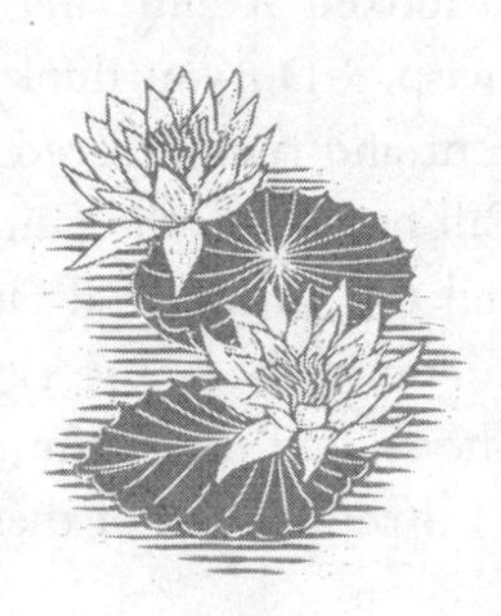

THERE IS SOME REASON why people plant bright red and yellow tulips together; perhaps it's because the Dutch grow them that way in the fields, and we all have a little Dutch in us. But, voilà! The National Arboretum does it a little better. It plants masses of orange-red dahlias next to yellow cannas—but the yellow cannas have red throats to echo the color of their companions. It takes an artistic sense to combine bright colors, and there are other ways than red with yellow to quicken the eye. We can make a bold statement with either flowers, vegetables, or beguiling combinations of the two.

---

* With thanks to former Senator Barry Goldwater

When bright primary colors are used, they can be like the flashy movie star who makes all the other players fade into the background. These Day-Glo tints must be managed: Instead of arraying them in a sunny border across the front of the house, put them in drifts in the garden, or sober them by putting near them the quieting influence of gray plants. Or confine them to pots, where they will seem less intrusive. Nothing is more exciting, for instance, than a group of big orange marigolds crowded into a pot with large fuchsia-colored zinnias. Or pot up some dashing purple *Heuchera* with red salvia, fuchsia-colored dwarf dahlia, and for the eye's relief, a few plants of fragrant white stock. The color of the pot itself should be neutral when we fill it with fierce color: after all, the eye can only take so much.

Vegetables are a fine and surprising element in flower gardens. Okra, eggplant, and artichoke are handsome flowering plants to accent the border. But most surprising is the beauty of the lowly potato. Plant a hill near the hollyhocks or asters, and a flutter of white blossoms will reward you. For another elegant infill to the garden, plant the glowing red-violet kohlrabi, *Brassica oleracea* "Early Purple Vienna." It is a beautiful construction, its bulbous root only half hidden. When it is the proper size, you dig it up and eat it with a smirk—and think of something to go in the empty space: a sprinkling of Bibb let-

tuce or *mâche* seeds, or quick-grown radishes such as "Cherry Belles," which mature in twenty-two days. You can even raise tomatoes in the border. Lace them over with climbing nasturtiums that will mask the eventual decline of some of the leaves over the summer.

Other cheeky and wonderful plantings and practices:

Combining yellow, rose, and deep purple. You can do it with the sturdy shrub, *Spiraea japonica* "Goldflame"—brilliant gold-and-green leaves and rosy clusters of bloom. Pair it with a purple-leaved plant with white spires: *Cimicifuga racemosa* "Atropurpurea."

The tall, hardy bold red *Crocosmia* "Firebird" will enliven a throng of paler perennials without harshness. The long-lived flowers are arranged on stems like wide opening fans. It is without parallel in front of a purple background, such as the hardy smoke bush *Cotinus coggygria,* or the tropical sword-leaved *Cordyline australis,* which is safe outside only in southern Florida and California. Gray sea kale or lamb's ears can add mellow, grounding bass notes to these color symphonies.

Interweave a spiky plant with a dramatic vine. Use *Yucca filamentosa* or the bronze form of *Cordyline australis* and twine in another plant: a white clematis, or the delightful crimson starglory *(Mina lobata)*, which has dramatic, three-lobed leaves, and interesting orange-and-yellow flowers borne in racemes.

Plant the unstoppable pale pink *Clematis montana rubens,* to clamber around other plants, hang by wires, snake through porch posts, or ascend a pine tree or antique Bourbon rose.

Spiky plants are invaluable, the exclamation marks in any garden. They look particularly good near round-leaved varieties such as *Ligularia* ''Desdemona.'' Among them is the fine orange-to-yellow colored *Eremurus* ''Shelford Hybrids'' that grow several feet high.

The variegated yellow-and green leaves, and its graceful fall, make the Chinese grass, *Hakonechloa macra* ''Aureola'' a favorite. Combine it with a long-blooming blue catmint (which some think as good as a dozen blue delphinium) and in the foreground place a drift of yellow-eyed white viola or delicate yellow *Cosmos* ''Moonbeam.''

A tall variegated white-and-green-striped grass combines vividly with white *Echinacea*

purpurea "White Swan," and rusty-red *Helenium* "Moerheim Beauty."

Walls of vines, such as English ivy or Virginia creeper, turn brilliant red in fall. Put them at the edge of a porch. Or make a summer wall of vegetables—Malabar spinach *(Basella alba),* cucumbers, or curvaceous-necked *Zuccheta,* the climbing summer squash. Let a clematis or morning glory sprawl up the same wire structure, to provide flowers through the summer, though Malabar spinach is handsome without them, with its red stems, petioles, and flowers.

The large, ornamental variety of rhubarb, *Rheum palmatum,* with its red fingers of blossoms running up the tall stems, makes a fine show when planted near a clump of birches or aspen.

A structural form to delight the eye is the Egyptian onion, *Allium cepa viviparum.* It multiplies through the bulbils that form in the flower cluster at the top of the plant, giving it a dramatic silhouette, especially when placed near a drift of English lavender and white, daisylike chamomile.

Deep red chicory, including the centuries-old *Cichorium intybus* "Treviso Red," gives a beautiful, lush color accent to a garden, and has the additional advantage of be-

ing edible. In late season the leaves are cut off and the roots produce a second, smaller head with magenta coloring and white veining. Newer varieties such as ''Giulio'' and ''Medusa'' form into heads without the trouble of cutting back the first leaves.

Chapter Twenty-eight

SHE WAS IN HER own yard, passing the bamboo garden outside the family room, when she felt the stalk through her heavy workboot. It had emerged from the rich, leafy mulch of the forest floor, recently bolstered with rain. She stopped and crouched down and felt a strong, invincible baby bamboo emerging from the ground.

A thrill of fear ran through her. This was just what Bill had warned her about, a year or more ago. One rainy day, perfect for transplanting, she had dug up and dragged these clumps from the far reaches of the yard to this site near the house. Bill had predicted that the bamboo would escape the little circular plastic barriers she installed around them.

From her squatting position, she looked up at the beguiling effect the bamboo created. The plants were set on a small hill against a partial stone wall that was a graceful platform for cascading jasmine. But the garden was not more than fifteen feet from their recreation room door and it was becoming just what Bill said it would become—a threat to the very foundations of the house.

She put a hand up to her damp brow. Didn't she have enough to contend with? Not nature going against her, too! As she straightened up, she felt her limbs trembling with fatigue; she was too tired to even think about the invasion of the bamboo.

She slowly crunched her way to the recreation room door, standing wide open. She realized dusk had fallen and it was time to do as Detective Morton and her daughter Martha had warned: Lock up. She stood in the gloom of the empty family room and felt an acute sense of being watched. Roger's warning had left her on edge. Quickly she went to the windows and twisted the wand that closed the Levolor blinds. Then she flooded the room with light by turning on the lamp to its full wattage.

Looking around, she realized with a sharp thud of her heart that someone could have sneaked in here: The house had to be searched before she locked up. With a false bravado, she strode through the rooms, turning on lights, throwing open closet doors. Finally satisfied that she was alone, she secured the locks and closed the curtains, fussing vainly with the gap in the ones that fronted the patio. As she approached the kitchen, she heard the somehow comforting beep of the answering machine.

Geraghty's phone call had come in just moments ago. She wasn't surprised, since she'd known the detective wanted to talk to her just by observing him when he and Morton departed the neighborhood this afternoon. And he might even have heard from someone of her investigations—after all, she appeared to have stirred the pot if people were inquiring at the *Post*.

"Mrs. Eldridge, I need to see you again." Geraghty's tone was abrupt, completely devoid of warmth. *"It would have been one thing if you had a little evidence of one kind or another that you picked up around your own house, but it's quite another thing to obstruct justice by slipping under the police tape at the Mougeys' and taking God knows what out of the scene of a crime."*

She could hear the growing anger in his voice. *"You were seen by neighborhood kids, whose* parents *called up and told me. Described you to a T. You know how kids are—they see everything, they know everybody. I mean, you have one yourself, that Janie, who along with her friend Chris are better detectives than you are."*

This hurt. Why did he think she considered herself a good detective? And why was he slamming her? Because he knew she was withholding something.

"So you get back to me pronto, *Mrs. Eldridge."* There was a sharp click and no good-bye.

With fingers made awkward by exhaustion, she fumbled through the Rolodex cards until she found the facetious card Janie had made for her; it said "FAIRFAX FUZZ." Holding the well-worn card, she tapped in the number and took a few deep breaths to compose herself. With her free hand, she opened the refrigerator and got out the container of milk and poured herself a glass. Then, she took the plastic chocolate syrup container out of the turnabout cabinet and slowly squirted chocolate into the milk.

''Detective Geraghty has been called out on an emergency,'' said the police dispatcher. ''Do you want me to take a message, or shall I give you his voice mail?''

She hesitated. Here was a chance to buy more time. ''His voice mail, please.'' Maybe before Geraghty returned her call, the proverbial light bulb would go on in her head and she would suddenly know who the murderer was.

''Detective Geraghty, I, uh, apologize for going over to the Mougeys', but I needed to feed the fish: I'm babysitting them for the family, you know.'' Lying was coming so easily to her these days that it frightened her. ''Actually, I've had an amazing day, and I'll be glad to tell you all about it.'' She sighed, hoping he would hear it and recognize how fatigued she was. ''I'd rather come in early tomorrow morning than tonight, because Bill arrives late tonight. But of course that's up to you.''

Then she collected her book and her milk and went to the couch, spreading a washable cotton throw to protect it from the grime she might have collected from tramping through the woods. She was too tired to bathe right now; she just wanted to curl up, read a few pages, and take a nap for an hour or two.

Knowing she would turn everything over to police tomorrow should have made it easy for her to relax, but there was some unfinished business still nagging at her consciousness. What Roger said hadn't been conducive to her inner peace. But in addition to that, there was something bugging her.

She had forgotten to do something. What was it?

Her mind was so exhausted that it would hardly function. Too exhausted even for reading. She swigged down the milk, then put her tousled head back on the pillows and immediately drifted off to sleep.

• • •

It was not a light sleep, and when the noise awoke her, she saw by her watch it was almost ten, and realized she had been unconscious for nearly two hours.

It was just a brief sound, emanating from somewhere out in the hall.

She had searched the house: She could hardly be locked in the house with an intruder.

Then she heard another sound, and her body went cold.

It was incredible: She had done so much, stumbled across the crucial evidence that the killer had wanted, and then done the right thing by promising to turn the evidence over to Geraghty in the morning. She put herself in this danger because she was too anxious to solve the case of Jay's death on her own, for fear others would muff it.

She continued to listen, but there was no further noise; she began to relax again. Those were just little house sounds. They could be laid to any number of things: a plant in the guest room, dropping one of its leaves; or a book, perhaps, falling off a ledge in one of the bedrooms.

Then, there was a squeak right behind her and she leaped up from the couch, but not soon enough. Someone pulled her arms back painfully and pinioned them beneath an arm that seemed as strong as steel. Then came the familiar noise of tape being ripped from a roll, though she didn't know how the person did it one-handed, and realized it was with great difficulty, and by holding one end in his teeth.

For it was a man, a big man, she could tell, frantically wrapping her hands tight. She could hear him breathing heavily from the effort. Once her hands were secured, he let out a big breath, and out of the corner of her eye she could see him readjusting something—his face mask.

Then he pushed her before him over to a small antique table and pulled out a sturdy, straight-backed Detroit chair with a cane seat that her grandmother had given her. Without speaking, he shoved her into it and stood in front of her. He was tall and muscular, wearing an oversized black pocketed jacket, as if to make himself appear even larger, and jogging pants. Over his face he wore a Frankenstein mask. "Sit still," he hissed, and he bound her to the chair with more gray duct tape.

"Who are you, and where on earth did you come from?"

He continued his harsh whisper. "I hid in your smelly little closet, if you must know. And I want what you have of McCormick's."

"But I don't *have*—"

"Don't lie," he rasped. "We know you have to have it. Tell *me* about your amazing day, just like you were going to tell that cop."

She shook her head. The neighborhood Christopher Robins may have seen her in the Mougeys' yard, but this man couldn't know that. And no one had seen Melissa hand over her father's backup disk. "You overheard me—well, you've made a mistake. I didn't have much to tell the police. Maybe they know something, but I don't."

The man paused and looked uncertainly about. She realized he was considering whether he should continue searching, or work on her.

Her hopes sank when she saw that she was his first choice. Had he only spent more time searching the house, Bill and Janie and Chris might have arrived to save her. She sat very still while he approached her, and even though she thought she was ready, it was a surprise when his rubber-gloved hand struck out like a snake and gave her three sharp cracks against the face, knocking it to and fro as if it were on springs. It was with such force that it wrenched her neck and left her head wobbling.

After finessing a number of dangerous situations, she had finally gotten herself in a position from which there was no escape. The man had enormous strength, all focused on her. Who knew what he would do next? Her head felt as big as a cantaloupe, throbbing from the blow.

A small curl of hope remained inside her. It came from the fact that he had whispered so she couldn't recognize his voice: This implied that he intended to leave her alive, even if seriously injured.

It was surreal, as Louise looked from the spooky mask, down to the alert boxing stance of the man. He was dancing back and forth in place on his toes as if he were facing an opponent instead of a helpless woman tied in a chair.

She steadied her head and gave him the most hateful look she had ever given anyone in her life. It said, "If I ever get the chance, I'll return the favor." After all, it was too late to whimper, far too late to try to talk her way out of this mess.

Apparently, he didn't like her unspoken insolence. She could tell by the way he was approaching that he was going to hit her again. This time, she thought of the resources at hand: her grandmother's chair, with its flexible bend from years of use. Her body, healthy and rested. They weren't much against a two-hundred-pound male. And yet . . .

When he was about two feet away, she shoved the wobbly chair back with a strong movement of her hips, then rocked it forward again. With her right leg, she struck out at his private parts with her steel-enforced garden boot.

The man screamed and retreated, falling back on the couch and clutching his groin.

Gasping and sweaty from the effort, Louise smiled weakly, experiencing the mastery of it. Then, with a sinking heart, she realized she had made matters worse. The attack on his male parts would only madden him further.

She deep-breathed to try to restore her calm and ready herself for the next attack. The man, still grasping his privates, sat up a little.

"You bitch. You're going to get it now. It doesn't pay to piss me off like that."

"What do you expect," she hissed back, "that I'm going to sit here and let you kill me?"

And yet she was afraid to provoke him too much, as he sat there cursing softly and trying to overcome the pain. He was bestial enough without further baiting.

After a few minutes, he rose slowly from the couch and lurched over and retrieved the roll of duct tape. "You won't do that again," he said, and she noticed he was forgetting to whisper, and it sent new fear into her heart. Now, she would be bound like a mummy. He would knock her about all he wanted, with no threat of reprisal.

Her body felt extremely heavy, as if it were made of lead. Only one other time in her life had she had this feeling, the feeling that she was going to die. It was on a storm-ridden night with lightning bolts surrounding their plane. She and Bill and the girls had been traveling from the continent to London. The plane bucketed violently up and down until even the flight attendants were frightened out of their wits. Bill had held her and the girls' hands and said, "The odds are that we'll get through this all right." Tonight, the odds seemed much worse.

Chapter Twenty-nine

THIS TIME, WHEN HE approached her, he came from the side, so as not to get in the way of her mulelike kick. With an iron grip he held her legs down and began winding the tape about them and the two front stanchions of the chair. With every turn of the tape, her hopes faded further.

The macabre masked head bobbed close to her as he knelt beside the chair. "Now, my clever Mrs. Eldridge, save yourself by telling me what I want to know." The voice was familiar: She had heard it this very day.

''You've already searched the house,'' she argued. ''You've had hours to go through our things, and you know you haven't found anything.''

''Shit!'' he cried in disgust. ''You're not dumb enough to leave it in plain sight, and if you're not going to cooperate, then you obviously want more of this.'' His big hand came up in the air.

And then she heard the sounds at the front door. So did her attacker, and she became terrified with the thought that it was Bill and Janie. She screamed a warning: ''Stay away!'' He reached in his pocket and whipped out a gun.

''No!'' she yelled. ''A gun!''

He was leveling it at the darkened end of the living room, when the figure rushed forth from another quarter with the long-handled cultivator. But it wasn't Bill. It was a small but solid avenging angel who had dodged down the hall and outflanked the man by emerging from the shadows of the kitchen. Tessie Strahan struck with the cultivator just as the gun went off, knocking the bullet's trajectory askew. The sharp tines of the cultivator drew blood; the masked man howled. The gun careened across the room. Barbara McNeil came from the direction of the living room with a triangular-shaped hoe and delivered a vicious blow that dug into the man's muscular shoulder, and the howl turned into a scream. Meanwhile, Donna Moore used her heavy iron shovel to whack his legs, and he tripped and fell heavily to the floor.

Tessie's neat bun of dark hair came undone and streamed around her shoulders, giving her a witchlike aura. With the imposing Barbara and muscular Donna, they made a terrifying trio standing over the prostrate man. And all armed with her garden tools. Gil Whitson hovered behind with an English pitchfork.

''Don't you dare move, or you're a dead man,'' growled Tessie.

''Looks like Frankenstein has a few extra gouges beyond the normal,'' noted Donna, in a detached sort of way.

''Let him bleed a little, I say,'' commented Barbara.

Louise cried out to them, ''Don't trust him—bind him with duct tape!'' She cocked her head to indicate where it lay on the floor near her chair.

Tessie picked it up, looked at Louise's swollen face with its cuts and the clear mark of a hand. She said, ''Oh, Louise, honey, what has he *done* to you?''

''No,'' cried Louise, ''don't bother about me. You must bind him up quickly: He's strong as an ox.''

Even from where she sat across the room, she could see the bulky man inching up, trying to sit. But Barbara stood there, five feet ten at least and probably one hundred seventy-five pounds, and as befitted a warrior queen, holding the wickedly sharp hoe poised over his head now, ready to strike. ''Stay, you sonofabitch,'' barked Barbara, ''and hurry, Tessie—get his hands first.''

Louise noticed, as Tessie worked frantically to secure first his hands in front of him, and then his feet, that Gil Whitson added a formidable but misunderstood presence. He stayed mainly in back of the women, and Louise guessed he was frightened silly. But his face had become very red and his cat's eyes looked wild. He presented a frightening looking enemy, holding the wicked pitchfork with its three narrow, sharp tines. The masked man probably was terrified that, if he decided to rise up and try to overcome the three women, the lone man, Gil, would administer the coup de grâce with that traditional farm implement.

The intruder was now undergoing a more mummifying experience than Louise. ''Do you have enough tape to tie him to the leg of the piano?'' Louise asked. The antique Knabe weighed about half a ton.

''I think so,'' Tessie said, and once this was done, they came over and took care of Louise. Tessie cut the duct tape from her arms and her legs, all the while muttering imprecations about the man who had done this. ''And we saw it happening through the crack in the drapes. That's when we grabbed those tools and ran in to get you.''

''Thanks. What would I have done if you hadn't come?'' She rubbed her legs to try to restore the circulation.

Barbara laughed. ''You're lucky we're the sort who never leaves town without saying good-bye to our friends.''

She resisted her friends' attempts to dress the bleeding cuts on her face and went over to look at the prone man. ''First thing we have to do is find out who this guy is, because he can't be Frankenstein.'' She bent down beside the attacker, ready to rip off the mask.

Barbara intervened. ''Let me do it, Louise,'' and with one of her sidearms, a linoleum tool with a curved blade, she sliced down the middle of the plastic face, as the man inside it made an agonized groan, and divested him of his mask as neatly as she might divest a perennial plant of its plastic pot.

Lying there, tied like a boned roast, was Ted French. Louise let out a little cry. ''We meet again, Mr. French.'' As if showing off a prize, she stretched a hand toward him and said, ''Folks, this is Mr. Ted French, a member of Congressman Lloyd Goodrich's presidential campaign staff.''

''*No* kidding,'' exclaimed Gil Whitson.

French looked up at Louise, his blue eyes blazing. ''You—bitch.''

''Have it your way,'' she said calmly, ''but maybe it would be better for you if you didn't piss me off.'' She leaned over and methodically went through his jacket pockets, finding his cell phone. She turned to her plant society buddies, now all gathered around. "This is what I was looking for."

She leaned back over French, having a great desire to give him a good slap, or maybe a head clubbing with his own phone. But she refrained, not wanting to take on the face of the enemy. She whispered to him. "So first you send a thug out here to my house to spy on Jay McCormick."

"Yeah, we did," muttered French. "He didn't hurt anybody—*you* nearly broke his leg with your damned trash cart!"

"And then you killed my friend Jay."

In the background, Donna gasped.

Tessie said, "A murderer: I knew it."

"The *hell* I did," contended French. "I don't know how he died. I just came here to do someone a favor: to get his disks. He was a fuckin' spy! We gave him a job, and he skulked around after hours and he fuckin' *spied* on us. He had no right to whatever story he got. He got it through false pretenses, and we'll damn well sue."

"If you didn't kill him, who did—Rawlings?"

French's expression became instantly guarded. "Hell, how do I know?" he snarled.

"Tell me more about Jay McCormick," Louise said, sitting back on her haunches. She looked up at Gil. "Listen carefully, now, to this story."

"He called himself *John* McCormick. He infiltrated our campaign. Wrote Goodrich some damned good speeches. You already know that, since you called campaign headquarters and weaseled the information out of some dumb phone volunteer."

"Yes? Go on."

Five people hovered around him, and his eyes moved nervously from one to another. It was as tough as any vigilante mob he might meet. "No way. I'm not saying more until I get an attorney."

"That's all right, Ted. We have enough." Louise handed Gil French's cell phone. He crouched down beside her. "Why don't you press the redial button and we'll see what comes out of the woodwork. Somehow, I don't believe he's the principal player in all this."

"What will I say?"

Louise pondered. "Make it a half whisper so it won't be easy to tell you aren't really Ted French. Tell whoever answers that everything is safe and under control, that you've got the disks, and you need them here. And then ring off, before the person can ask more questions."

"Okay." He looked at the prone man, struggling now against his bonds, and said, "What if he mouths off?"

"Simple solution," barked Tessie. She looked like a long-haired avenger as she ripped off a couple more strips of duct tape and slapped them enthusiastically across French's mouth.

"And stop wiggling," commanded Barbara, standing primly now beside French and holding her hoe much like Little Bo Peep held her staff, "or I'll happily give you a little poke."

Gil pressed the redial button. The call was answered quickly, and his eyes widened in surprise. For a few moments he seemed paralyzed. Louise caught her breath; she saw the whole plan dissolving before her eyes. How could she have suspected for an instant this man injured Jay McCormick? Why, he didn't even have enough nerve to make a phony phone call.

Then, with a little nervous shake of his head and body,

like a dog shaking off water after a bath, Gil rose to action. He spoke the brief message in a hoarse whisper, and a fair imitation of French's voice. French's eyes blazed up at him.

Gil turned off the phone and gave Louise a brilliant smile. "They even answered me. Said, 'Okay, be there in less than three minutes.'"

French groaned, a long, hopeless lament. Louise glanced at him coldly.

"How did the person sound?" she asked.

"Like me: nervous and whispery," replied Gil.

Tessie looked at Louise in disbelief. "Three *minutes*? Listen, folks, we have a problem: How many more people do we have to subdue tonight? How do we know this guy doesn't have three other guys with him?"

Louise jumped to her feet. "You're right, Tessie. We shouldn't have done that. Now we have to act fast. We need the police, and while I'm calling, Gil, move your van from in front of the house. Park it far into the Mougeys' driveway so whoever's coming can't see it. And hurry: You don't want them to get here and see you."

Giving her a terrified glance, he ran out the door. Suddenly, Gil was having to do all the gutsy things, and she was pretty sure he was not used to that role.

She was connected almost immediately with Detective Geraghty, who apparently was working late. Quickly she told him the bare facts about her friends capturing an intruder, and about redialing the man's phone and reaching an accomplice.

"Had to do it yourself, huh?"

"I hadn't intended to."

"Since you made that call, there's no time to debate this, Mrs. Eldridge. I want you to do exactly as I say. And don't you and your friends try to be heroes, understand?"

"I understand."

Moments later, he rang off and she spoke to Tessie, Barbara, and Donna. "The police want us to turn off some lights and leave just enough on so whoever comes isn't suspicious." She looked at them, standing there with their garden weapons. "And they want all of us to 'safeguard' ourselves by going into a bedroom and letting *them* capture the guy."

Gil burst back in the front door, his eyes wide with fright. "Should I leave the door unlocked, or should I lock it?"

"Leave it unlocked, Geraghty says. Let's go. He wants us out of the way." She smiled. "But we'll still get a good view."

She led them to the guest room; all of them brought their garden implements in case something went wrong. She slid the window open so they could hear, and the soft sound of the cicadas floated in and reminded them there was a peaceful night world out there. Then, she took Bill's binoculars from the closet shelf and proffered them to the others. "Does someone want to use these?"

Barbara took up the offer, training the glasses on Louise's driveway. Not more than a minute later, she cried, "Here comes a car into the cul-de-sac, but, God, Louise, I haven't seen any police."

"Well, then, we'd better be ready to defend ourselves," Louise said. Donna patted her back and reassured her. "They'll be here. You said they're just a couple of miles away."

The car without lights pulled into the driveway, far enough so that it was under the canopy of trees and outside of the immediate sight of passersby.

Louise had a moment of panic: If the police were delayed, they would have to defend themselves again with primitive tools against what would undoubtedly be guns in the hands of their opponents.

"Why don't they get out of the car?" asked Barbara.

"Shhh," scolded Tessie, "they might hear us."

For almost two agonizing minutes, nothing happened. Louise's neck ached from her encounter with French. She wished she had accepted her friends' ministrations—at least a couple of aspirins and a glass of water. Tessie took the opportunity to twist her hair back into its tight little bun and secure it with hairpins. Gil paced nervously in a tight little circle.

Tension in the guest room grew, until finally the car door opened and out stepped a single figure. Barbara gave a second-by-second report. "Only one so far. Walking into the woods, away from us. Probably wants to avoid the light on the path. He's nearly out of sight." She dropped the glasses from her eyes.

Then, a glare of searchlights clicked on and probed the yard. They quickly converged on the figure, now close to the house. A deep voice shouted through a megaphone: "Police! Stop right where you are!" Louise thought she saw a flash of red. She and her friends rushed from the bedroom to the entrance of the living room, not wanting to go farther until the police gave permission.

A cadre of officers brought a half-stumbling, handcuffed Lannie Gordon into the house. Geraghty followed close on their heels.

"My God," murmured Louise. "I should have known it. So many motives."

"Is she the murderer?" asked Tessie.

In a low voice, Louise answered, "I think so."

Lannie looked like a wild woman, her red hair in disarray,

her face smeared with dirt, as two officers held her on either side. Although she wore a smart taupe jogging outfit and Mephisto tennis shoes, she probably never had felt so far from the comforts of her private country club.

What brought the woman to a stumbling stop was the sight of Ted French, lying on the floor, tethered to the piano like a calf at a rodeo. She spat it out: *"Idiot!"* Then she straightened. Turning to Detective Geraghty, in a shaky voice she said, "I am Lannie Gordon and I am an attorney. You have made a terrible mistake, and you need to release me right now. Otherwise, there's going to be no end of trouble for the Fairfax police."

"I'm sorry, Ms. Gordon," said Geraghty, "we're taking you in for questioning." Then, Lannie saw Louise. The woman gave her a long look, as if she were pleading with a friend who had shown her sympathy in the past. It seemed as if they were the only two in this crowded house.

"Louise," she moaned. Louise's heart wrenched, and impulsively she took a step toward her. Then the red-haired woman sagged and began sobbing uncontrollably.

Louise slowly approached. The woman was torn apart by whatever she had done: betrayed her husband to a killer, or murdered him herself, it didn't much matter.

Geraghty stepped in front of her. "No, Mrs. Eldridge, please: I don't want you talking to a suspect," and with a pointed finger he indicated she should go back across the room.

Then the big detective turned to Lannie Gordon, reading her her rights as the patrolmen escorted her outside. Once the woman was gone, he returned to the living room and beckoned Louise over with a nod. He looked down at her curiously. "I thought you didn't know Ms. Gordon."

"I didn't, until yesterday."

"So, that was just a rush of sympathy, is that what you're saying?"

She looked into Geraghty's eyes. "I don't know," she said bluntly. "Do you believe she killed Jay?"

"Her showing up here is pretty incriminating."

"I think she did it, maybe accidentally, but I'd guess in anger. I've got Jay's computer disk, and when you read his story, you'll find out she has a motive: She has serious problems with the law."

"There you got an edge on me, Mrs. Eldridge," he said dryly. "You've found the disk, huh, and read the story?"

The guilt came rushing back again: She could have told Geraghty all this much sooner. She took a deep breath. "I'll turn it right over to you. But I think Lannie did everything for the sake of her career and her daughter. It must have driven her crazy to think one story could ruin her whole life and send her to jail. Now she's sunk so low—she'll lose everything, including her daughter."

"We don't know yet whether she killed Jay McCormick," Geraghty corrected brusquely, "but we can hold her for questioning. And based on what's gone on here, we're going to search her Great Falls house. Meanwhile, let's talk about *him.*" He turned his attention to Ted French on the floor.

French was shaking his head, as if to plead for someone to take the tape off his mouth. Geraghty stooped down and with surprising gentleness did so. He asked Louise, "Do you know this man?"

"He's Ted French. He works in the Goodrich presidential campaign." She laughed bitterly. "I saw him only today in the Capitol, eating lunch with Congressman Goodrich."

"Looks like he's wounded. Know if he's hurt bad?"

''He has a couple of gashes, that's for sure.'' Her heart was not full of sympathy for Ted French.

''He broke into your house.''

''And he was armed. So I guess you call that breaking and entering with the intent to do great bodily harm.'' She said that for the man's benefit; French gave her a walleyed look in response. ''His gun is lying right over there.'' She pointed to the black weapon that had flipped under a nearby chair. ''We all tried not to disturb the crime scene.''

The tape was off now, and French cried, ''I want my lawyer.''

Geraghty shook his head. ''Just a minute, buddy.'' He turned again to Louise. ''He tied you up, and I see he roughed you up pretty bad, too.''

She merely nodded, all the time staring at French and remembering how brutal he had been.

''And those people in there,'' Geraghty said, nodding to her P.P.S. friends, now herded into the nearby dining room by a patrolman, ''were they all witnesses?''

Louise looked over at her friends.

''Yes,'' said Tessie, stepping forward in her familiar role as spokesperson. She summarized everything in rapid-fire fashion. ''We got here and came around back for reasons I won't go into now. We could see through a crack where Louise's drapes didn't quite meet. We were *horrified:* We saw him slapping Louise. So we grabbed some garden tools from the nearby shed and raced around as fast as we could to the front door.''

''How did you get in?'' asked the detective.

Barbara spoke up: ''Louise has a key in a fake rock.''

Geraghty nodded. ''Oh, you knew that? Heck, the whole world probably knows that. Well, you did her a darn good turn.''

"I always said we like to help a body," declared Tessie.

He took Louise's elbow and helped her back to her feet. "I'm glad you're all right; you have good friends there. Better get your face washed first; there's some abrasions there. We'll take care of this man French, and then we need statements from you and the others. So, tell your friends to stick around, okay?"

Louise smiled. "Sticking around is no problem with them."

Geraghty bent his white head down toward her. He said, "And I think you have some evidence for me."

There Is No End of Uses for Garden Tools

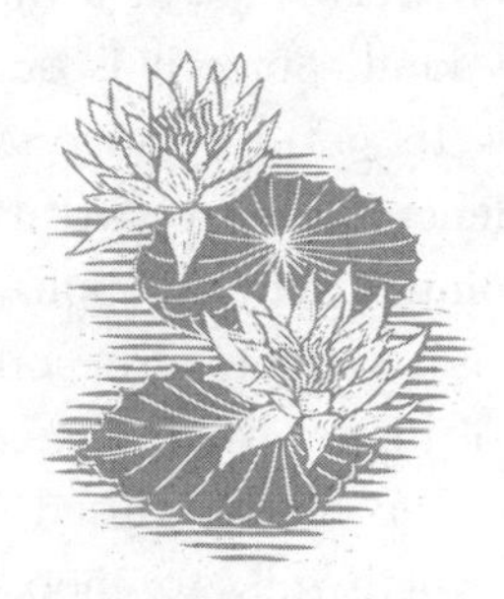

WE ARE STILL SHARPENING arrowheads, so to speak. The use of tools has been traced back to the earliest ancestors of man, who have been busy perfecting them ever since. Amateur gardeners love tools, and can be found in the tool sections of stores in record numbers every garden season, mulling over their choices. Gardeners can go cheap or expensive, but these days, many are choosing to go light. They are buying light shovels, light mowers, light cultivators, light grass trimmers, light ladders. It makes sense, since about half of adult Americans complain of a bad back, and many gardeners are women with less upper-body strength than their male counterparts.

Take the lightweight rototiller, for instance, which can till the soil in a path as narrow as six

inches and cuts ten inches deep: It weighs about 20 pounds, instead of 150 to 300 pounds. Of course, the larger tiller is still the favorite of many people, who feel it takes deeper bites and handles better.

Or consider the fine, lightweight English shovel, which weighs about a third less than the ordinary kind. Since it is our most used tool, it pays to get a good one, and most serious gardeners have to have at least a couple: with pointed end, and square end.

Quality, not weight, also comes up with the subject of loppers and pruners. They are probably the second-most-used tools; some believe it is worthwhile to choose the top of the line, fashioned of Finnish or Swedish steel, while others do just fine with what they buy at the neighborhood hardware store. Anvil-type pruners seem to work better than the scissors type, which are apt to get dull faster.

How many of us have run around the yard on a hot summer day, sweating and wrestling with a gasoline-powered string grass trimmer as if it were a resisting lover, cropping grass edges and sometimes girdling young trees in our wild, abandoned desire to have a neat yard? Polluters that they are, their use shouldn't be encouraged. If they are used, buy a compact one that weighs less and by the same token emits fewer fumes into the environment. It will safeguard your back as well as your tender tree trunks.

Hoes are a favorite tool of the gardener.

The stirrup hoe and shuffle hoe both work on the concept of slicing right through the soil and weeds—as well as unsuspecting plants, if you make a misstep. If you're in the market for a lawn mower, buy one with a mulching attachment, for we know now that we can save on fertilizer by leaving grass clippings on the lawn as natural nutrients.

Buying a wood chipper takes some thoughtful consideration, rather like deciding whether or not to buy a blue-chip stock: Wood chippers are expensive. Once you are familiar with the rate at which your trees sluff off limbs, you can decide whether you need one. (Remember, if you have a natural yard, fallen limbs make great homes for little animals, so leave the bigger branches on the ground.) Wood chippers seem cumbersome, but those who own them swear by them. They are low-maintenance when used correctly, but then, isn't everything?

There is absolutely nothing like the old-fashioned wheelbarrow to make us feel like lowly beasts of burden. Wheelbarrows are classics, but do we really need those cumbersome beasts with inflated wheels and wooden handles? Another choice is the lightweight cart with bicycle wheels. It is easier on the back, because the wheels are nearly centered under the load. But beware: Large-volume carts can buckle under too much weight, which is why many people swear by the old-fashioned brontosaurus type.

Incidentally, some people, when discuss-

ing lightweight tools, preface them with the adjective "lady's": lady's shovel, lady's wheelbarrow, lady's tiller. And yet there are many men weary of bodily injury who like these products just as well.

Pliers with wire cutters for trellis work, hammers, a file to use on a regular basis so the tools don't get dull, and a fiberglass ladder are other valuable additions to the toolshed. Wooden and aluminum ladders are less hardy than the newer, more expensive fiberglass variety.

And then there is the indispensable hand trowel, with which we dig small holes and plant smaller plants. There are even tools for the growing number of people with carpal tunnel syndrome and arthritis. "Fist-grip" hand tools keep the wrist straight in use, and trigger-grip varieties are becoming a common sight in garden shops. Another idea to make garden work easier is to attach foam rubber pipe insulation to the handle of your hand cultivator or trowel. This will make the tools easier to hold, and cushion the impact of digging.

The first tools that a beginning gardener should buy are a hand file and an electric grinding wheel for sharpening the other tools. A few strokes of the file will keep many tools sharp, avoiding a bigger job later. And *clean* your tools. Use a soapy scouring pad to shine up tools after you've rinsed off the dirt, then always rub them with oil to protect them from rust. Don't forget: Cleanliness ranks right up there with Godliness and sharpness.

Chapter Thirty

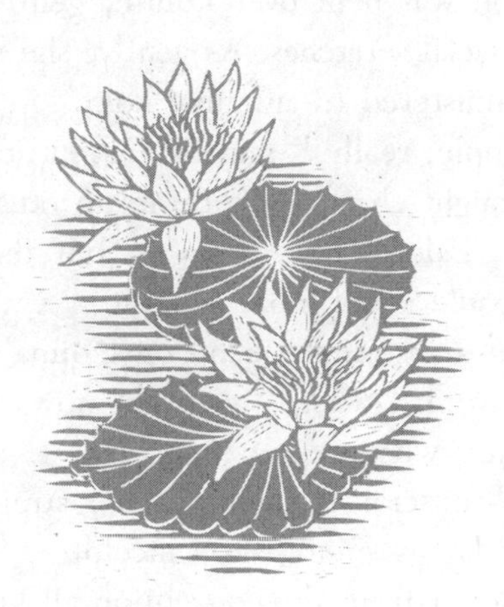

"WHAT I CAN'T UNDERSTAND is how you knew something was wrong." Louise was slumped luxuriously onto plump cushions her friends had arranged against her back, and feeling that euphoria experienced by survivors of near-death and mayhem. She was sipping a small glass of dry sherry Tessie had pressed on her.

"We nearly rang the bell."

"What stopped you? If you had, French would have laid low until you went on your way again."

They were sitting in the recreation room. Tessie had slid by the police in the living room to get ice, water, and a box of cheese crackers, in order to set up a little bar there. The police were still busy in the adjoining room, releasing Ted French from his duct-tape mummy wrappings.

Gil Whitson was bent over Louise, gently dabbing antiseptic on her facial scratches. As gently, she was sure, as he would have ministered to an ailing koi.

''It was simple, really,'' said Donna, sitting quietly composed in a straight chair. ''We came up on the porch, and really, Louise, I don't like to say it, but the light on that porch really could stand more wattage . . .''

Barbara put a restraining hand on Donna's arm. ''Don't tell the poor woman what to do right now. Hasn't she had enough? Tell her what we *saw*.''

Donna self-consciously smoothed her straight blond hair, which already lay as smooth as Lancelot's. ''We saw those perennials you got from the convention all kicked around.''

''A real mess,'' chimed in Gil, as he selected a bandage from the box. ''Plants toppled over, fallen out of their pots. Not something we thought *you'd* do.''

Barbara said, ''We knew you were such a gardener, and such a neatnik besides, that you would *never* treat plants like that. So we realized someone came in your house unexpectedly. First, we thought it could be your hubby''—she smiled broadly, and gave her curly, graying hair a little shake—''and we didn't want to interrupt any big romantic homecoming.''

Tessie continued the story. ''So we just decided to take a *little* peek through that crack you always have in your curtains. That put us into action. Gil, bless his heart, ran to the toolshed and quick as lightning pulled out some weapons for us.''

Louise looked at him fondly. His yellow, catlike eyes were concentrating on sticking the adhesive onto her cheek.

"Oh," he remonstrated, "it wasn't that much."

They heard a commotion in the other rooms. Gil lurched back, as Louise sprang up and ran to the living room. It was Bill and Janie, with Chris behind them, his hands full of luggage.

Her husband was appalled when he saw her, holding her at arm's length so he could see her bandaged face. "Who did this to you?" he demanded in a shaking voice. "That man on the floor?"

"Ma!" cried Janie, and came over and gently hugged her. The girl looked different, older. "And to think I was gone when you needed me. Who *is* that weirdo?" And her curiosity took her over to where French was being unwrapped.

"Just hold me a minute," Louise said to Bill, and fell silently into her husband's arms, resting her uninjured cheek against his chest for a long moment. Then, she said, "I'm all right, really I am. Where should I start? So much has happened since you left."

"At least give me the highlights," insisted Bill, as he gently brushed her hair away from the injured cheek.

"It all started when Jay was killed two days ago, and someone stole his computer."

"My God, how did he die?"

"I found him, at the bottom of the Mougeys' fishpond, with his head bashed in . . . ."

"Aw, Louise, you poor thing." He gently stroked her hair. "Do they know . . . who killed him?"

"We think it's his ex-wife, Lannie."

"Louise, you should have *called* me."

"I thought you'd know soon enough. I found some evidence in our toolshed. That explains all Jay's nocturnal wanderings. And I also happened to find his computer disks—found one, rather, and had the second one given to me by his daughter, Melissa. And by the way, Bill, we have to take Melissa under our wing; she'll need us."

He shook his head in disbelief and looked down at her with his probing blue eyes. "How could you get involved so fast in a thing like this?"

"It was just by chance. I ran into Lannie yesterday, and I guess she became suspicious that I might have the disks. And then, of course, I had lunch with Tom Paschen in the Capitol—"

"Is he still bugging you to put on that program?"

She smiled. "Tom's like a dog with a bone. At that lunch, I got a lead on what Jay was doing here in town. I called Congressman Goodrich's headquarters to check it out. Bill, they definitely are in on this, because that man over there is one of them—it's Ted French."

"What?" cried Bill, and jerked his head around to look at the man on the other end of the room, who was now handcuffed and preparing to get up with the aid of a patrolman. "*Sonofabitch*—French!"

She held him a little tighter, not wanting him to go. "Bill, he isn't the brains behind this. Somewhere along the line Lannie Gordon decided I must have the evidence. She got French to help her. He sneaked in here tonight and tried to strong-arm the information out of me. Then my plant friends came along and rescued me."

"That bastard dared to lay a hand on you," growled Bill, staring at her cheek. "Look at those bruises, and what the hell's under that bandage? We'll see about that. I'm talkin' to Geraghty." He pulled himself away from Louise and stalked over to the detective, who took one look at Bill and quickly stationed himself in front of the prisoner.

Janie was huddled, talking to Chris. Now she came over to her mother. ''Gee, Ma, maybe I shouldn't have done it.''

''Done what?''

Her dark-lashed blue eyes were filled with guilt. ''I didn't know it was going to be so squirrelly around here, or I wouldn't have invited them.''

''Invited *them*?''

Janie nodded vigorously, and Louise noticed for the first time that the front of her long blond hair was braided into cornrows. Louise reached out and touched them, and though liking the cornrows, missed the soft, smooth feel of her daughter's hair.

''I could cancel,'' continued Janie. ''They're not here yet.''

''Cancel who?''

''My buddies,'' she said. ''I invited a few of them to come and stay for a long weekend. I didn't think you'd mind.''

Before Louise could stop herself, she said, ''What's a few more houseguests? It'll be fun. You'll have to double up, though; we have another girl coming to stay.''

Her daughter turned to the elated Chris, gave him a high five, and exclaimed, ''Right *on*!'' and they turned to go off together, but Janie suddenly whirled and returned and gave her mother another hug. ''Thanks, Ma.''

Louise watched the young people skirt around the police and go out somewhere, and she hoped not to Chris's house, empty of parents. More houseguests, and *young* ones, who liked grunge and rock and heaven knew what other kind of music. But how could she scorn houseguests? Where would she be right now had it not been for her guests, who felt compelled to stop in to say good-bye?

Geraghty apparently was giving Bill more details. She

took the opportunity to go and find Gil Whitson. Leaning over his chair, she murmured, ''You were great tonight, Gil.''

He basked in the praise. She said, ''I want to ask you another enormous favor.''

''Anything, Louise,'' he said.

''Mary Mougey's koi: I'm just a little worried about them. They're not as frisky as they were a week ago, you know, before they ate those fast-food snacks, and before Jay . . . ended up in the pond.''

''Hmm,'' said Gil, frowning, ''and you want me to go over and take a look.''

''Would you?''

''I'd be happy to; it could be the filtration system needs looking at. And on the way, I'll neaten up those perennial plants scattered all over on the front porch. I'll stick them back in their pots so they'll be all right until you have a chance to get them in the ground.'' He reached up and took her hand. ''Louise, I've always felt guilty about McCormick.''

''Why? Just because you had a fight with him?''

He looked up at her with his catlike eyes. ''It was a real fight. I popped him one, Louise, more or less in the nose. But I didn't kill him, because he was laughing his head off when I left, honest. I was just too scared to say anything after I heard he was dead: I was afraid maybe he had a delayed reaction and fell into the pool.''

She squeezed his hand. ''Jay died from wounds to the back of his head. And he probably deserved a pop in the nose. Poor man. He just didn't deserve to die.''

When her husband came back to her side, she told him more about Jay's story of the Goodrich campaign's dirty tricks and Lannie Gordon's role in huge illegal campaign contributions. "I'm sure, from the way she acts, that she was the one who killed Jay, though they may not ever prove it. She had more than one motive."

"You mean, she lost major custody rights to Melissa," said Bill. "You'd think a mature person could handle that."

"Maybe she could have. But this story of Jay's would have totally ruined her, Bill—wait until you read it. Lannie tipped the Goodrich campaign people to the neighborhood where Jay was living, I'm sure of that—because they sent a big thug to our house the day before Jay got killed."

"My God, Louise—" cried Bill.

"It's all right—I chased him off." She would tell him details about that later, if ever. "Ted French insists that *he* didn't kill anyone, just came here to try and get back the information that leaked out."

Then she remembered something Melissa had said about how her mother started locking her bedroom against her daughter. "I have a feeling that when the police search Lannie's house, they'll find Jay's computer stashed away among Lannie's fancy clothes."

"Louise," said her husband, "you've saved the President's chances for reelection, do you realize that? Tom Paschen's going to be one happy man."

"I think he will be." She looked over at Geraghty. "But right now I have to go get some things for the police. Want to come with me?"

"My dear, I wouldn't think of leaving you on your own."

They went out to the toolshed and Louise took out her favorite English shovel. She grinned at Bill. "This one was considered too lightweight for my plant friends to use as one of their weapons, you'll notice, but it's perfect for me." They went to the patio garden. "I feel a little like Whittaker

Chambers,'' she said, as she stepped carefully among the plants.

''*He* hid his secret documents inside a pumpkin,'' said Bill. ''Where are yours?''

''Oh, scattered about.'' With the shovel, she made one sharp thrust at the base of a pink nicotiana plant. Neatly, the robust annual popped out of the earth like the fat lid of a pot, only soggier. Underneath was a big, muddy plastic bag. She raised it up jubilantly. It contained the folder with the memos. ''That's the first one, the memos. Actually, they don't prove anything.''

She carefully replaced the plant in the damp earth, then moved deeper into the garden and scooped up a wet clump of purple coneflowers. Resting underneath was a small double plastic bag, which she pulled out and offered to her husband. ''A little dirty, but this is it: Jay's story. And now one more.'' On the far edge of the garden was a meadow rue. She prodded it up and reached underneath to extract another plastic package containing a disk.

''Just insurance, huh, burying this stuff in separate graves?''

''Yes, in case someone tried to torture it out of me, I thought separate hiding places would be good. I would hardly give up all three.''

Geraghty had apparently noticed their absence. He trailed out to the patio after them. With a huge smile lighting her face, Louise clambered out of her garden and handed him the packages. ''Here, Detective Geraghty. And don't say I never did anything for you.''

The detective turned to Bill. He raised an eyebrow and inclined his head toward Louise.

''Sure, if it's okay with her,'' said Bill.

Geraghty gave her a big hug.

• • •

''Our first guest tonight is Charles Hurd II, who helped uncover one of the biggest scandals in the history of presidential campaigns. The search for this story led to the tragic murder of his colleague, Jay McCormick.'' Channel Five newsman Jack Lederle was beginning his lead story on the evening news, his smooth face masking the frustration he felt at not getting two key parts of the story.

''We regret we were unable to have with us tonight Albert Kirkland, editor of the *Sacramento Union,* the paper that broke this dramatic story. We hope to be able to talk to Mr. Kirkland tomorrow night.''

First, the newsman recapped the sensational charges about presidential candidate Lloyd Goodrich's campaign that immediately deflated his high poll numbers. How the Justice Department was preparing charges against top members of his staff, if not the congressman himself. How Jay McCormick's former wife, Lannie Gordon, a tobacco industry spokesperson also implicated in the scandal, faced both murder charges for killing McCormick, and charges for illegally funneling hundreds of thousands of dollars from a charitable, tax-deductible foundation into the Goodrich campaign. How she was also implicated, along with Goodrich aide Ted French, in the assault with intent to do great bodily harm to WTBA-TV's garden show host, Louise Eldridge.

Lederle didn't go into further detail as to how Eldridge figured in the affair, for, much to his annoyance—and even with the woman on their *own* Channel Five staff!—that tale was too tangled to be cleared up before air time.

''Now, Mr. Hurd,'' and Lederle turned his shoulders to gaze at the young man seated across from him. Hurd, in the newsman's opinion, was a bit of a PONSI, with his blond, blown-dried hair, Brooks Brothers summer suit, and self-important manner. Truly, a Person Of No Significant Influence. Though Hurd couldn't have been more than twenty-five, his expression was prematurely grave, as if he thought God had endowed him with an enormous intellect, and the world should pay attention.

"This story has a strange genesis," said Lederle. "Tell us how it developed. *Your* name, for instance, is there as contributor to this story, underneath the late Mr. McCormick's byline. Mr. McCormick came from California months ago, *expressly* to infiltrate the Goodrich campaign, did he not? And when did you meet him? What was your role—leg man? Researcher?"

"Oh, more than that. But let's be clear on this: I give Jay McCormick full credit for the idea. He saw these men in action out in California during the fall Senatorial campaign . . ."

"Now, of which men do you speak? The ones mentioned in yesterday's *Sacramento Union* story?"

"Yes. Franklin Rawlings, Willie Upchurch, Ted French—that whole crew of political operatives. When he learned they would orchestrate Goodrich's political campaign, he left a ten-year speechwriting career and jumped back into investigative journalism"—his gaze dropped modestly to the interview table—"which of course I've been engaged in exclusively for several years at the *Arlington Herald*."

"So he came here to Washington . . ." coaxed Lederle, trying to get the young reporter back on track.

"Yes. That's when we teamed up. I did the leg work, traveling to many states—thirteen, in fact, including California—to turn up the facts of the case. I dictated my stuff back to Jay on a daily basis."

"But wait, Mr. Hurd, surely Mr. McCormick *also* was

turning up the facts of the case. We're talking about a *political plant* here, aren't we? Wasn't Jay McCormick clever enough to infiltrate Goodrich's campaign, without even breaking any laws?'' The news anchor gave a polite chuckle. ''These days, that's really accomplishing something.''

''Well, yes,'' said Hurd, wiggling uncomfortably in his chair. ''And Jay turned up some good stuff—which, after consulting with me, we were able to follow up on. Lannie Gordon's setting up of a 501 (C) (3) charitable non-profit foundation, for instance, that funneled huge amounts of money to Congressman Goodrich.''

''I understood Mr. McCormick is the one who picked *that* information up straight out of the downtown Goodrich campaign headquarters.''

Hurd put up a hand. ''Mr. Lederle, you have to understand how this worked. None of this was handed to us on a silver platter; there was no convenient leak like 'Deep Throat,' as there was in Watergate. We had to scramble for every fact—to work very covertly and very hard. I did the follow-up of every one of his leads. And then when he got *made* . . .''

Lederle raised a worldly-wise eyebrow. ''That's an odd way to put it isn't it? He wasn't a criminal, now, was he?''

''No, but he was recognized, and from then on, I essentially had to take over the story . . .''

Lederle's eyes widened in disbelief. ''But Mr. McCormick's editor told me that Jay McCormick was the only one who had his finger on the whole story to the day of his death in that fishpond . . .''

Hurd, though a print guy, had mastered the politician's art of interrupting and giving answers to questions Lederle had not asked. ''The disks were temporarily lost, that's true, but they were *returned* to the *Sacramento Union*. And then before publication, Al Kirkland asked me out there, and I was the one who was able to fill in and provide all those little extra details they needed. I guess you could just say it was a question of being in the right place at the right time.''

Lederle watched Charles Hurd smile at the camera, and knew just what he was up to: not too wide a smile because that would be smirking; just wide enough to show that besides being a damned good reporter, he was also a nice human being.

The news anchor thought, *The little prick: he probably would have killed McCormick for the story himself, if someone hadn't beaten him to it.*